Love Ain't No Joy Ride

Love Ain't No Joy Ride

A SHADYBROOK SERIES NOVEL

BOOK THREE

BY

CONNIE KUYKENDALL

Printed in the United States of America

First Printing, 2022

ISBN: 13 978-0-9970272-8-0 paperback
ISBN: 978-0-9970272-9-7 ebook

Those who keep waiting for the LORD will renew their strength.
Then they'll soar on wings like eagles

Isaiah 40:31, ISV

CHAPTER ONE

Catch Me if You Can

"Did I win?"

The voice came so softly, Tanner thought he'd imagined it. But when she moaned, his eyes lifted heavenward. Frankie was back! His lips cracked into a smile, which he expeditiously suppressed. If Frankie noticed, she'd wonder why he was acting nice. She'd snap out of her hazy dreams of a checkered flag and realize her dismal reality.

Tanner pushed off the doorframe holding him up and, in two strides, stood at Frankie's bedside. He clicked the call button and noted the strengthening heart rate on the monitor. When he caught his reflection in a mirror on the wall, he wiped at the hot red streaks on his face, inflaming them. Tanner had changed his singed clothing and scrubbed the oil and dirt from his skin and nails, but the full dark beard didn't cover the reminders of that night and of the things he should have done differently to protect her.

"You couldn't claim the victory this time, slo-mo. Took your time waking up from surgery too." The dryness in

Tanner's throat forced out a voice that was more grumble than he'd intended. "Are you in pain?"

Frankie blinked repeatedly before focusing those electric blue eyes on him. *Here it comes.* He nearly smiled again as he waited for a snappy comeback about how infuriating he was. Maybe she would fire off another mystifying car metaphor only she could understand: *You're one to talk about slo-mo. I've seen the way you drive, Granny. I'd get more torque from a pony on a pogo stick.*

But the words that came out of Frankie's normally smart mouth punched him in the chest.

"I'll never race again, will I?"

The blank expanse of the hospital room erased her voice and face of all emotion, energy, and hope. Separating from any appearance of feelings or humanity was Tanner's specialty, not hers. Never hers. Frankie was sunshine personified.

"One thing at a time," he said, unwilling to break eye contact and risk her eyes closing forever. "For a while there, I thought you'd never *breathe* again."

Before last night, he'd have sworn Frankie Newman was unbeatable, untouchable, and unbreakable. His protection services were as useless as the brake lights on her race car. But here she lay, tangled under a heap of stiff white sheets. Fluorescent lights bleached the pink from her cheeks and the shine from her long, strawberry blonde hair.

Finally, Tanner looked away, swinging a tray across Frankie's bed, pouring a cup of water, and setting it in front of her. He could have knocked back that whole pitcher himself, but it would have been impolite.

"Answer me, Tanner Ashton." Her voice cracked as if it

was trying to rev up some power. She winced and hugged her broken ribs. "You're stalling."

That would be an affirmative. Sweat trickled down his back. He hit the call button again. A doctor or at least dear old Daddy should be the one to break the news. Her best friend, Selah, had answered Tanner's call but was delayed on a flight to Virginia from Los Angeles. Selah's momma, Margo Morgan, had come and stayed during Frankie's tests and surgery, until Tanner couldn't take her clucking and fussing any longer. Frankie needed to recover in peace.

"I'm just your bodyguard, Frankie, not a doctor."

"Please." She grabbed his hand before he could head for the nurse's station and haul in reinforcements. Frankie's hand was as icy as the Antarctic hospital air, but surprisingly soft and strong. "This is my *life* we're talking about."

Tanner racked his brain and couldn't find one word that would make her life better or help win the fight that lay ahead. He could, however, take action. Slipping a free hand under his jacket, he tested the security of his weapon. Tanner would find the man who shattered Frankie and stole her joy, if it was the last thing he did.

A Week Ago

If it's the last thing I do, I will escape from you. Ooh, wouldn't that make awesome song lyrics? Humming the words, Frankie peeked around the corner of the main house. So far so good. She slipped on her titanium headphones and cranked up the 80's classic "Break My Stride." Perfect! Pulling her ponytail through a Wonder Woman ballcap, she snuck another peek.

No sign of him. Silently, she clapped her hands. Squee! Her plan was working. She could make it past the gatehouse unseen if Lefty, the Speedway's best spotter and mechanic, distracted Tanner long enough with stories of Shadybrook's good ol' days.

Frankie tugged her sagging leggings, adjusted her shades, and took a breath before sprinting down the three-mile dirt road that connected the speedway to Main Street and crossed the border of West Virginia into Virginia. Her heart was already racing from her great escape, but it chugged a little faster as she climbed the hill leading to the rim of the dirt track—*her* track. As she ascended, she smiled down at the barn where her steel babies slept until the next race. Saturday night couldn't come fast enough.

When Frankie cleared the Speedway's gatehouse and her feet hit asphalt, she laughed at the sky and pumped her fist. "I win. Again."

Mary had finally shaken her little lamb. The captive had been liberated. How she had missed her freedom!

The peace and quiet along Shadybrook's Main Street were glorious. Her BFF Selah had always resented the sleepy little town, but Frankie made her own excitement. Frankie inhaled deeply, rewarded with the scent of butter-drenched maple-bacon pancakes and cheese biscuits wafting out of Good Company, the diner owned by Selah's family. Actually, all Frankie could smell was cooking grease, but food tasted better when you visualized it first.

Selah's momma Margo stepped out the front doors and shook a rolling pin at her.

Love you, too, Momma, and I'll be by to terrorize you as soon as I've worked up an appetite.

Frankie circled the restaurant and headed towards the koi ponds at Chinese Willie's. Willie, in his signature fatigues, stood at the front window of the tiny restaurant, shaking a carving knife at her. Weird dude. Tasty chicken lo mein though. She threw up her hand and kept running. Back on the main road, she passed Selah's aunt Ruby walking her pot-bellied rescue pig.

"Hey, Aunt Ruby! Hey, Porkchop!" Frankie hollered as Ruby shook a walking stick in the air.

Maybe I should run for mayor. This town adores me—all the wacky, kind-hearted, camouflage-wearing country folk who had helped raise her when her own momma wasn't around to do it.

As Frankie turned the corner onto Somerset Drive and ran past Momma's house, she peeled off the drenched ballcap. A warm breeze lifted her hair like a parachute behind her. Inhaling again, she caught the not-so-faint odor of manure. That part of country life she could do without, but it was home.

When TobyMac's "Unstoppable" filled her ears, Frankie got so caught up in the moment she didn't see the man behind her until he tapped her arm. She gasped and clasped her chest, stopping cold as his breath seared her neck.

"Sorry, Wonder Woman, you'll have to try harder to shake me."

"Tanner," was all Frankie managed to spit out before she got her breath under control. She'd lecture him about giving her a heart attack, but he'd lecture her that he could have been the bogeyman, she should pay more attention when running with headphones, she needed him to guard her, and blah, blah, blah. Same ol', same ol'.

Frankie was, however, slightly impressed by his athletic ability.

"No way you caught up to me. I had a four-mile head start, and you are so obviously out of breath."

When Tanner shot her a side glance, Frankie laughed and picked up her pace. She should have gone easy on him for a bit, but where was the fun in that?

"You had to drive around to find me, didn't you? Ain't tall, slim guys supposed to be natural runners? It's in the human anatomy manual somewhere."

He could trademark that look—somewhere between an eyeroll and a glare. Even Tanner's dark beard looked grumpy. It was like running under the shadow of a massive storm cloud.

Tanner grunted, peeling off a black leather jacket—the same shade as his eyes—and tying it around the waist of his black jeans. The movement revealed a black t-shirt that stretched across six or eight of the long, lean abdominal muscles in that anatomy manual. She stared at his body for longer than was safe given the potholes on Main Street. Maybe she'd underestimated his fitness level. Was the man free-basing protein powder or what?

Frankie swallowed, but her mouth had gone dry. "I'm thirsty and hungry. Let's head to Good Company for mancakes. I mean pancakes. Pancakes."

Nope. Nuh-uh. Cut that out. *I am immune to muscles. Six-packs have no effect on me.* But Frankie would have to be dead not to notice Tanner's bad boy bodyguard appeal and the fact he pulled out chairs, opened doors for her, and ran on the outside of the street to protect her from passing cars. None of which meant she *like* liked him. He didn't *like* like her either and never would. He'd made a point of explaining that any courtesies he extended towards her were part of the job.

So, that was that. They shared a mutual irritation society.

"You don't seem to comprehend the severity of the danger you put yourself in by continuing to run away from me." Tanner's rich baritone penetrated her thoughts like a needle dropping on a vinyl record. "So, turn around and head for the barn, because that's where you'll stay for the rest of the day."

"You're not the boss of me."

Frankie hated how juvenile she sounded and how much she enjoyed Tanner's attention.

"Technically I am."

Frankie shook her head, rolling her eyes. In the process, she noticed Tanner was huffing more heavily now, so she dug deep and turned the pace up another notch as she headed for the diner.

"I possess both muscles *and* speed. So, why again do I need a bodyguard?" She was exhausted but determined to make him work for it. "I am a grown woman in my thirties. Better yet, I am a queen, not some damsel crying in a tower, waiting for the dark prince. The man who encouraged girls to aspire to be princesses with all the poof and pink and pretty never considered that we are perfectly capable of saving ourselves."

Frankie sideglanced Tanner and nearly ran face-first into a stop sign. "Did you crack a smile? You did. The one time you laugh and you're laughing at me."

"Just picturing a Disney princess in Daisy Duke denim shorts, black leather knee-high boots, and motor oil." He squinted at her a moment before looking away quickly and sucking back air. "Let's g-get the queen back to her castle."

"You can't guard both me and Daddy at the same time, so you might as well run or limp, as it were, back home to him." Frankie sputtered.

Tanner wasn't paying attention, because he was busy scanning the bushes and chicken coops along the mean streets of Shadybrook for some imaginary threat conjured up by her overprotective father. That was just fine because Frankie was busy calculating whether grits, corned beef, and hash browns would adequately supplement chocolate pancakes. And right on time, there was Good Company a quarter mile away. She was going to set a personal record in sprints today!

"I'll head home with you, boss," Frankie gave Tanner one last glance, "as soon as you do one tiny thing for me."

His head snapped around, no doubt suspicious of the sugar in her tone. "Do tell."

Frankie put it in gear, shot toward the diner door, and hollered, "Catch me if you can!"

CHAPTER TWO

Drop a Gear and Disappear

By the time Tanner caught up to her, he'd developed a side stitch and shin splints and Frankie had already ordered their meal and agreed to appear on Margo Morgan's reality cooking show, *Momma's Family*. He heaved into the booth, rubbing a napkin over his face and the back of his neck so he wouldn't have to see Frankie's smirk. He couldn't block out her snicker.

When breakfast arrived, Frankie plowed through it like she plowed through traffic, while Tanner slowly savored an oversized stack of maple bacon pancakes.

She snatched one off his plate before he could finish. "Our reality show would be called 'The Tortoise and Hare.'"

Tanner grunted, scanning the exit doors and the diner patrons seated along the central chrome counter. The counter separated the front booths from the kitchen. The enormous windows stretching the length of the restaurant provided abundant natural light to the TV crew set up in the back corner but offered Frankie little protection from attack.

"I don't like this." Tanner mustered his best steely-eyed glare.

Frankie was safer back at the speedway and her barn where she could tinker and get lost in her cars for hours, and he could use cameras and tighter security to monitor her. When would she get it through her thick skull that the danger was real and being splashed on TV was not in her best interests?

"*You* don't like anything." She shot back, motioning for Momma and patting her belly. Surely, Frankie wasn't asking for more to eat.

"Someone threatened your life and your father's life, but here you are putting yourself front-and-center on television."

"The so-called bad guys already know where I am, so they're going to threaten me whether I hide from them or not. Murderers don't watch cooking shows. Well, maybe that cannibal guy." Frankie tittered, high on maple syrup. "It's not likely the boogeyman will care about my bit part, so to speak."

Tanner didn't blink. It would only have encouraged her blasé attitude toward personal safety.

"Besides, you'll be right here to protect me, my knight with a shining 9-millimeter. What could go wrong?"

"Let me count the ways."

Momma set a supersized cinnamon bun at Frankie's plate and drew back her hand quickly like a zookeeper feeding the tigers. Tanner watched in awe as Frankie inhaled it. His own stomach was "full to bursting" as she would say.

When Frankie started moaning and licking her fingers,

Tanner was drawn in once more as her tongue flicked over the frosting on her upper lip.

"What?" She twisted her mouth as he twisted in his seat.

He'd never simultaneously enjoyed a job and wanted it over so badly in his life.

Tanner frowned. "I'm late for a meeting with your father. We need to park you at home so I can protect him."

Frankie's blue eyes fluttered. "I'll try to hurry then. Please keep Daddy safe. He's not a young man anymore, although he thinks he's invincible."

Finally, he'd gotten through to her.

"Let me get some fried food in my belly and help Momma with the show first and I'll be ready to roll."

Tanner sighed. "You've already had bacon, eggs, and hashbrowns with your man-cakes."

Frankie flashed a wicked grin. "The inferno inside me burns infinite calories."

Something hot flickered inside him.

Momma's shadow descended over the table again. "My inferno is going to burn your backside if you don't get over yonder so we can start the show. Time is money."

"I'm too old for paddling. And it's illegal." Frankie downed her orange juice and popped out of their booth.

"Someone spared the rod and spoiled you, child." Momma swatted her lightly with a spatula and brushed back Frankie's damp hair.

Frankie nodded absently, eyeing the last piece of bacon on Tanner's plate.

"Now listen here. You have *one* job." Momma waved the spatula in front of Frankie's glazed eyes. "While I'm preparing the fish, you wait for the hush puppies to turn golden brown. Then, scoop 'em and plate 'em up."

"Scoop and serve, got it." Frankie swiped Tanner's bacon, tossed it in her mouth, and offered the empty plate to Momma so quickly he got whiplash.

Momma huffed as she jerked the plate away and plunked it on a nearby tray. "I don't need a repeat of the episode where clodhopper Selah blew my cheese fritters sky high to heaven, understood?"

"Are you capable of saying one kind word about your daughter, Margo?" Frankie clapped back.

It was no wonder Selah, Tanner's poor sister-in-law, who possessed a master's degree, a prestigious job, and more brain cells than he and his brother combined had moved 3,000 miles away from this town.

The irony of *Momma's Family* was that Momma had no family around. Frankie, the woman Momma had practically raised, spent most of her time at the track racing cars and Russ, her husband, spent most of his time betting on race cars. Perhaps Momma's crankiness was a front for loneliness.

Momma's mouth pressed into a thin line. "Thank you for your parenting advice, Francine, but I wouldn't be a good momma if I didn't educate Selah on her limitations. Her cornbread just ain't done in the middle."

Tanner struggled to form some semblance of a straight face. Frankie shot him a look that said Momma was the only living person who could use her given name and he better not try it. He would most definitely try it when it became useful.

"Now put on this here cover-up." Momma wrapped Frankie in an oversized Good Company apron and cinched the strings in the back so tight Frankie gasped. "Oh and keep an eye out for the creature that's been tearing up my garbage and sneaking in the back door to steal food."

"Creature?" Frankie scoffed. "Could you narrow it down? Lots of creatures around this town."

"Always bringing home a new creature to care for, sweet Tanner. It's a regular Wild Kingdom around here." He heard his own mother's voice clearly even though the night he'd adopted that bunny had to have been twenty-five years ago. Tanner was far from sweet now. How would she feel if she knew the real reason he'd come to Shadybrook?

The show's director clapped, scattering the memories and quieting Momma's chatter. He instructed her and Frankie about the length of the segments and hitting their marks.

Momma patted her auburn beehive. "Prepare yourself, boys. This is what perfection looks like."

After another half hour of adjusting lights and cameras, the director counted down, "We're rolling in five, four, three, two—"

"Hey y'all. I'm Margo Morgan and I ain't your momma, but I'm gonna show you how to cook up Southern favorites that'll make her proud. This here's my assistant, Francine Newman."

"Frankie Newman." She corrected, waving with more energy than anyone should have after a five-mile run at the crack of dawn.

Momma swirled her spatula like a fairy wand over the food. "Today, we're fixin' to fry catfish and hush puppies. Any fish will do for this recipe, including white fish, red snapper, and that fancy tilapia. But really, why would you want to eat anything other than catfish?"

Frankie snorted when Momma pronounced it "tie-lah-pie-yay."

"First, I'll mix up cornmeal, salt, garlic, and onion powder, while Francine drops a few of the pre-made fish and puppies into the oil."

Momma beat the ingredients into submission with a spoon. Frankie happily dropped dough balls into the sizzling oil, watching them like cars on the last lap at Talledega.

"Those hush puppies will definitely stop the dogs from growling in your belly," Momma said. "If you're expecting the gluten-free, dairy-free, or fat-free version of this recipe, change the channel to Paula Deen. She done sold out to them health nuts."

"We're all lard here," Frankie added, although *Alice in Wonderland's*, "We're all mad here," accurately described Shadybrook as well.

Momma and Frankie grinned like Cheshire cats and patted their bellies and love handles, not that Frankie had any visible love handles. Not that he was looking or would ever look.

Tanner indulged a grin at their antics. That last line was ratings gold and most likely the show's new tagline.

Momma continued her spiel. "Now, don't set that fryer higher than 375 degrees or you'll burn up your oil. If you want hot, add red pepper sauce. That'll make 'em stand up and flap their fins."

Took Tanner a few times to realize that the "all" they were discussing was cooking "oil."

Momma laid out more strips of fish and doughballs and extrapolated on the origins of the hush puppy, called red horse bread in South Carolina, wampus in Florida, and red devil in Georgia.

Frankie being quiet should have been his first clue that she, like the wampus, was stirring up trouble. While the camera was trained on Momma, Frankie began stuffing her face with hush puppies. Frankie would set out a freshly-fried batch on a plate, pop a few more in the fryer, and clean the plate. He'd seen at least seven go down into her bottomless pit already. Tanner had to take an antacid just watching.

A hush puppy rolled out of Frankie's hand and onto the floor. Frankie dove for it, kicking open a door behind them. She bounced up into position and smiled sheepishly at the camera.

"Lands sakes, Francine! Where are my hush puppies?" Momma took a dishrag and wiped crumbs off Frankie's chin and cheek. "This ain't *I Love Lucy*."

Around a mouthful of bread, Frankie mumbled, "Mmph. Umm. There's more cooking in f-fryer. So goo. So goo."

Momma grunted as she batted Frankie's hand away and removed the last of the doughballs from the "all." "This will be the scene at your home, folks. Your family won't be able to keep their hands off these puppies. Let's get some catfish into the fryer too."

The duo dragged more strips through the cornmeal batter. Movement in the doorway behind Frankie caught Tanner's eye. He drew his gun quickly, but it was too late. An airborne projectile had already struck Frankie in the head.

CHAPTER THREE

Kiss My Tread Marks

"The creature!" Momma screamed, grabbed a spatula, and smacked at Frankie's face. "Shoot it, whatever it is."

Frankie gasped for air as something white, warm, and vibrating clung to her nose. When she tried to pull it off, it sunk its claws in deeper. Judging from the smell of it, her tombstone would read, "Death by sewer rat."

"I can't shoot her in the face, Margo. Just relax, Frankie." Tanner's voice was even and commanding, a contrast to the skitter in Frankie's chest. He rarely spoke, so hearing his deep, sexy voice would have been a treat if the creature wasn't eating her alive.

"Do something!" she cried, but the beast's gut smooshed against Frankie's mouth and muffled any sound.

Tanner ordered, "Stop fighting it and drop the fish."

Oh! Of course, it wanted the catfish. She released the food. The creature used Frankie's face as a springboard to jump onto the counter and devour the remaining fish.

Sated, the thing plopped down and began to lick the black spots on its white paws.

Frankie sucked in air and stumbled back.

Momma threw her arms around Frankie for one motherly moment and squeezed. "Are you okay, child? Of course y'are. I raised you tough."

"Let's get you cleaned up." Momma bumbled around in a wall cabinet for a minute before emerging with a First Aid kit. She wiped blood from Frankie's cheeks, lips, and neck and bandaged her.

The crew stood by, unphased and still filming, not making a move to help. Guess they'd seen it all. She'd have to watch the playback to piece together what in the world had happened while she was eating those heavenly fried delicacies.

Tanner holstered his weapon and edged carefully toward the counter. Staring down the cameraman, he said, "I do not consent to any use of my image, got it?"

The cameraman flashed a thumbs up as he stepped back quickly, pointing the lens away. Tanner scooped up the flying rat with a dish towel.

"Eww. Don't touch it!" Frankie hollered, squinching her nose.

Something that ugly had to be infected with rabies or scurvy or bubonic plague, not that anything could get under Tanner's skin. He seemed impenetrable. Frankie sighed. Oh well, there were other fish in the sea. On second thought, she'd avoid fish altogether for a while.

The creature snuggled into the crook of Tanner's arm and began to vibrate. Frankie wondered how many women had curled up in his arms. She clenched her fists. Don't go there.

He said, "We have confirmation that it's a cat."

And then Tanner actually smiled. Not at her witty repartee. Not at the killer tank top she was wearing. Not at her dazzling eyes. Tanner grinned down at a cat that looked like someone had turned Mr. Potato Head inside out. Unbelievable.

"Well, get it out my kitchen. It done ruined my fish fry and like to near killed my helper." Momma shook her perfect hair as she patted Frankie's bandaged face, inflaming the pain. "I ain't heard this much commotion since Wayne Newton's tour bus broke down outside the church during the senior ladies' prayer breakfast."

Frankie gave a silent scream as Tanner cradled and spoke softly to the bald badger, which had fallen asleep. Was it wrong to want to trade positions with that thing?

After he took the cat outside, Margo touched up her makeup and signed off the show.

"That's the way real cooking is, y'all. Gotta expect the unexpected. Sometimes you fry up catfish and net a real cat. Always stay hopeful but be prepared for cat-astrophes."

When the camera cut to Frankie, she rolled her eyes and walked off set. The producers perked up then, shouting for her to come back. They wanted a post-show confessional about how it felt to be mauled by a feral feline on camera.

Frankie had had enough showbiz for today. After she made a quick call to Lefty to pick them up, she found Tanner on the sidewalk cradling his demon child.

"Some bodyguard you are."

Tanner chuckled.

Again, this cat was making him do all sort of things she didn't think possible, laughter for instance.

"You got me there. I wasn't expecting a sneak attack quite like this one." Tanner walked toward her with the cat, but she held up her hands. "Let's head next door to Ruby's pet store and ask if somebody's missing a purebred Sphinx."

"I figured it crawled up from Middle Earth." Frankie did her best impression of Gollum, which Tanner did not laugh or smile at.

The cat, however, awakened and growled.

"Kitty heard you."

Frankie growled back. "Hey, I fed you fish and you tore my face off. Don't bite the hand that feeds you."

Tanner stroked the cat's head, whispering, "Don't listen to her, Kojak."

"What?"

"Kojak. You know. Bald cop, sucked on a Tootsie Pop? 70's TV icon? I thought you were a TV fan."

Frankie had watched an episode online, but she mainly stuck to *Wonder Woman* and Selah's soap opera, *The Winds of Change.*

"Let me get this straight. You were assigned to protect me, but you've named and apparently fallen for the monster who tried to assassinate me? Worst bodyguard ever."

Who was this man and what had he done with her stone-cold protector?

"Who loves ya baby?" Tanner winked.

Frankie stopped in her tracks.

"Classic tagline from the show. You're so out of touch."

Why was God punishing her with this man? When Frankie went for her rabies shot, maybe they could vaccinate her against Tanner as well. "If the car ever gets here, you and Cujo cat are riding in the back."

~

Tanner flicked catsup from his jacket and loosened his holster, which was considerably tighter after breakfast at Good Company. How had he gone from, "I'm taking you straight home, Frankie," to "I'll just have coffee while you eat" to "One order of hashbrowns, eggs, maple bacon pancakes, and cheddar jalapeño griddle cakes?"

And then, the ordeal with the catfish and Kojak, which Frankie kept calling "cataclysmic." His cheeks ached from an excessive amount of smiling and eating.

Mercy. This girl.

Tanner'd protected actors who gave less drama than Frankie Newman. The speedway queen was tucked away safely in the barn, preparing her car for Saturday night. The largest dirt track race that Podunk had ever seen was Tanner's security nightmare, so naturally Frankie would land smack in the center of it.

Speaking of security, Daddy Newman's meeting was taking too long. Frankie's father had been vague on what business he was transacting with their visitor from Washington, D.C. Wallace P. Owens, like Kenny Newman, came off like a good ole boy but had ice in his eyes and ties to the cartel in Juarez. He was more than just a high roller being courted to finance Newman's fledgling casino.

Whatever the real action going down inside the organization, Tanner wanted in. That meant he had to work to win Newman's trust. Keeping his daughter out of harm's way was a good start. A surprise attack like the one this morning, feline or foe, could never happen again.

He leaned his ear to the door, straightening quickly when it opened. Newman turned the dial on an old-fashioned wall safe and followed his visitor to the coatrack by the door. When Newman slapped him on the back, Owens shrunk under the force, then smiled nervously at his host.

"Remember, Wally, I eat spinach and my enemies for breakfast," Newman smirked as he nodded at Tanner.

Mom always said to take a man at his word and proceed with caution. Tanner swallowed against a sudden rush of the despair that had been nipping at his heels for the past few years. It hit at random moments. It grabbed him by the throat when he lay in bed staring at the ceiling, willing himself not to dream about the night his mother and father were ripped away, or when his thoughts drifted to the woman who'd left a hole in his chest, or when Frankie's easy laughter reminded him happiness existed in this world but it taunted him just outside his reach.

"That'll be all son," Newman said. "I'm going to take our guest on a tour of the facility and sample the state's best moonshine."

Newman slipped on a white Stetson and jacket over a holstered weapon. *Watch your back, Wally.*

Ignoring Newman's directive, Tanner fell in line behind them as they moved down the hall. Newman unlocked an unmarked door using a key that hung around his neck. Every exit and entrance operated on a pin pad, except this one. Two security cameras beamed down on them. The swish of the door swept in air that was too humid for the climate-controlled betting stations.

Even if Tanner could get his hands on the building's blueprints, they might not tell the whole story. Parts of the complex were modern, while some had been standing since before the Civil War.

Newman leveled his gaze on Tanner, his voice firmer this time. "I've got this handled. Go take care of my little girl."

Dismissed, Tanner stepped back and watched the duo disappear into the dark passageway. It was past time to call in reinforcements of his own. Tanner hit speed dial on his phone.

"¿Quién habla, por favor?" said the very formal voice of a man who knew exactly who was calling.

"I'm collecting on that favor you owe me," Tanner said, leaning back against the wall so he could study the cameras and door frame. "How soon can you take some leave and join me in Shadybrook?"

"No entiendo." The man rattled off more Spanish for a full minute.

Tanner snorted. "That didn't work the day you started an international incident and it won't get you out of this now."

The voice erupted into raucous laughter. "Mario at your service, chief."

"That's more like it." Tanner smiled, picturing the 20-something hacker who had acquired the moniker because of his thick curled mustache and hair and penchant for hats and vintage video games.

"Took you long enough to call. I was worrying about you, out in the boonies with no license to kill and nothing to lose."

Frankie's electric blue eyes flashed in Tanner's mind. Soon, she would lose everything.

"Newman asked me to shake up the security team. I need someone I trust on the inside. Mostly I need your fancy equipment."

"I bet you're still going old school with those thumb drives." Mario guffawed when Tanner didn't respond. "The dinosaur finally admits he needs the youngster's help. I'll be there ASAP."

Tanner breathed a sigh as he hung up. This was going to work. He stared down the cameras and turned to leave, for now. When others saw a locked door, Tanner saw a challenge.

The locked passageway would have to wait until he checked on Daddy's little girl. Tanner had a feeling Frankie Newman would be the biggest challenge he'd face.

CHAPTER FOUR

"I'm not speeding, I'm qualifying."

—Unknown

She bore the face of an angel, but she trained like the devil. Tanner held his breath as Frankie executed a pull-up from the rafters of the barn. Her sun-kissed skin glistened as sweat dripped from her straining triceps. Why hadn't she put down a crash mat for safety? The same reason she hit the accelerator, not the brakes like a sensible driver, when approaching a sharp curve in the rain.

The pristine three-story barn could compete with a NASCAR garage, complete with space for six vehicles, a bed, a bathroom, and a desk where Frankie did a little accounting work for Daddy. Very little from what Tanner could see. She spent most of her days eating, running, repairing cars, eating, trying Tanner's patience with stunts like this, and, of course, eating.

Frankie paused a moment mid-pull, grunted, and swung herself up again. She never stopped moving. If someone opened her chest, they'd likely find the Energizer Bunny.

If someone opened your chest, would they find anything but darkness? Nope. Tanner sighed, wiping his hands on his jeans and quietly climbing up beside her. He hung for a moment, gathering strength. First, running. Now this. Why did a driver need to work out anyway if she was just going to sit behind a wheel?

Frankie gasped as one of her arms dropped. "Hey! What you are doing up here?"

Panting, she struggled to grab the bar again. Tanner reached over and pulled her arm up.

"Thanks," she muttered, shaking her head and spraying him with sweat.

She started another pull-up. He joined her in a competition of endurance and stupidity. Finally, he surrendered and climbed down before gravity did it for him.

"I will leave the barnyard Olympics to the professionals," Tanner said.

She grinned, did one more pull-up—probably for effect—before hurtling down like a monkey after a banana.

He held out his hand to "help" her dismount, but she shrugged it off and said, "You wish."

Frankie rolled her shoulders and bobbed and weaved, sending a one-two punch in his direction. "I didn't peg you for a quitter."

"Too much of a gentleman not to let the lady win."

"Gentleman," she scoffed.

When she pulled off her ballcap, her hair drifted to her shoulders, leaving a few tendrils stuck to her cheeks. Grabbing two towels from a metal cabinet, Frankie slung one around her neck and hurled the other at his head. Tanner caught it, muscles screaming.

"Stop sneaking up on me. If I didn't know better, I'd say you were trying to kill me." Her blue eyes pierced his soul.

"Maybe you'll get it through that perky head of yours that you need to be more cognizant of your surroundings. Someone could snatch you anywhere when you aren't paying attention."

"These *surroundings* are my home." Frankie slid the towel from her neck and swept it in the air around the room. "Are you telling me I shouldn't feel safe here? Should I be aware of something or *someone* who is a threat to me inside my home?"

Her glare held a pointed intensity. Did she know more about him than she let on?

"Just be more careful when you're alone." He sunk into the rolling desk chair facing her computer.

"Careful is not in my vocab. Neither is safe. That's *your* job."

Being careful had kept him alive for this long. But was it a life worth living?

Frankie pulled two bananas and two waters from an immaculate fridge. When he reached for a water, she said, "Oh, did you want one too?"

Tanner chuckled as she tossed a bottle his way. He caught it, uncapped it, and took a swig that said, "I'm only slightly thirsty." If only he could chug it after that workout, but he had an ego to protect. What was left of his ego, that is. She'd shredded most of it like Kojak had shredded his paper towels and toilet paper and napkins.

Frankie pointed the bananas in his direction. "Pew, pew, pew. Think fast, Frank Farmer."

He frowned down the smile that flared at the mention of

Kevin Costner's character in the classic film, *The Bodyguard.* Frankie aimed the banana at Tanner's face when she threw it, but he caught it first. High school football coming in handy.

Frankie rolled her eyes at his feat and popped the hood on the red, white, and blue late-model Chevrolet she was prepping for Saturday night's race. He pulled out his phone, scrolling through security footage. Newman had returned from his walk-through alone and was locked away in his office again. Tanner'd check on Wally later. The scene here was more entertaining.

She tapped her index and middle fingers twice on the Wonder Woman figure stretched across the hood and doors, one of her many rituals involving the cars.

"So, what'd you do with Silly Putty?" Frankie asked.

"With what?" Tanner thought for a moment before remembering his long, bald cat imprinting itself on Frankie's face. "Dropped Kojak off at the vet for shots, spay, and nail trim. Put out some calls to the animal shelter and surrounding pet stores to locate an owner."

"I'm sure there's a line to reclaim it." Frankie shook her head.

"You can barely see the scratches on your face now. Plus, thanks to Kojak, you're up-to-date on your vaccinations for the next ten years."

"I'll be sure to send it a thank-you note."

While Frankie worked, Tanner surreptitiously snooped her desk. His pulse quickened as he eyed her laptop, which was open and running. When she ducked her head under the hood, he slipped a tiny USB device off his keys and into the laptop's port. It would operate undetected in the background to copy her drive and leave behind spyware surveilling her online activity. Sometimes, he did his best work in plain sight.

While he waited, Tanner propped his feet up on her desk and studied the framed photos it displayed. The first was a laughing Frankie playfully punching her daddy. Frankie always radiated joy, even when she hurled sarcasm and eye rolls Tanner's way. Kenny Newman smiled obligingly, his eyes one degree warmer than a dead man's. Tanner already had this photograph memorized, including the silver necklace around Frankie's neck, which dangled a checkered flag and a pink "Speedway Princess" charm.

Another picture showed Tanner and Frankie watching, hands covering their mouths, as Cane spun new bride Selah during a hilariously awful dance at their wedding reception.

The minutes ticked by as Tanner stared at the photo, caught up in the memory of that day. He, in a tux, and Frankie, in a black wig and a frilly white gown, had disguised themselves as decoys to allow his twin and Selah to escape the paparazzi in Los Angeles.

His brother was a goner. Tanner couldn't say he'd ever forgive Cane for their parents' death, but he also couldn't deny that the sweet and stunning Selah had changed Cane for the better.

Tanner's throat tightened. What would it feel like to be as deliriously happy as Cane and Selah? What would it feel like to be happy at all?

Tanner turned the frame over and laid it flat on the desk. He'd taken a bullet in the name of love once. No more.

"So, what are you doing here?" Frankie asked.

"Working. You might try it sometime."

"I *am* working." She craned her neck around the hood

to glare, then returned to the engine. "Not that it's any of your business."

"How about the Speedway books?"

"Balancing our budget doesn't take long, especially when you're a genius. It's computerized, pretty straight forward. Daddy doesn't have that much for me to do, especially after tax season."

There was nothing straight forward about this operation or her involvement in it.

Frankie looked over her shoulder again. "What are you angling for and why am I explaining myself to you?"

"We're just making polite conversation."

"*You* don't make conversation, unless you're ordering me around or gathering information. You're definitely not polite. Tell me what you want and get your dirty clodhoppers off my desk while you're at it."

When Tanner moved his feet, he kicked the external mouse. The screensaver scattered, revealing a webpage full of men's faces. He picked up the laptop with one hand, slipping the USB from its port with the other.

"What is this?" He groaned as he saw an inbox full of messages on MissMatch.com. "I know that you would not sink to online dating. That is a very bad idea."

Now, he had an even bigger problem on his hands.

"Put that down!" Frankie lifted up suddenly and bumped her head on the hood. "It's private."

He relented, setting the laptop on the desk, but clicked through a few direct messages. "Are you aware that sexual assaults increased by twenty-five percent with the rise of dating apps? There are 18,000 registered sex offenders in this state. Wonder how many are on this site?"

Probably seventy-five percent of the 355 men who'd winked or messaged her.

She stomped over and slammed the laptop cover closed. "How would you know such specific statistics? What about the 19,000 couples who met online and got married? What about that, Big Brother?"

"Why take the risk? Why do you feel the need to offer yourself up like a sacrifice?"

"Why do *you* feel the need to constantly meddle in my business?" Frankie stood across the desk from Tanner, hands on hips, looking more like Wonder Woman than the figure on her race car.

"Because I'm paid to make it my business." Would she never understand his job?

"I want to be loved, Tanner. Is that so awful? No man in this town will look me in the eye. I had one date ten years ago and he never contacted me again." She heaved a breath before stepping back from him. "And *you* have made it clear that you will never be attracted to me."

The moment hung heavy between them. Tanner nodded curtly, looking her square in the eyes to make it *crystal* clear. Selah had teased him about falling for Frankie, even inventing a girlie name of "Tankie" for their pairing. It was inane. And it was never going to happen.

"You don't really want me. You're just tired of being single."

"What am I supposed to do?" She pleaded.

A convent came to mind.

"And don't suggest a convent." Her eyebrow quirked.

Tanner wasn't sure whether to be annoyed, impressed, or concerned that she could read his mind. He'd think a little quieter next time. If only Frankie'd think more and talk less, it would make his job so much easier.

"You don't want to date some stranger online."

"You're right, I don't, but I have prayed and prayed and prayed about it. I am not typically a pray-er. I'm not a Bible reader. That's all Saint Selah, believing for moved mountains and parted seas and such. I'm just a normal…

"Normal," Tanner snorted.

Another glare. "A normal, ordinary woman living a simple life who has only asked God for a total of one thing in her life—love. I don't bother Him with fame or fortune. I've never asked him to help me win a race, although I do pray for the safety of all drivers. I merely want to be cherished by someone who sees the real me."

The hardness in his heart shifted. Could this be the genuine Frankie? Just a sweet girl wanting to live an honest life? He slipped the USB drive into his leather jacket's side pocket. Tanner would find out soon enough.

Frankie jabbed her finger at the laptop. "I about gave up on my dreams until I saw these dating sites and realized they were my answer. Cane literally fell at Selah's feet, but some of us have to work for everything we get. Selah's Bible says that God helps those who help themselves."

"That is a proverb from *Poor Richard's Almanac*, not the Word of God."

Frankie came around to Tanner's side of the desk, opened the laptop, and stood way too close for comfort. "Go ahead and look. You'll see there are some nice, regular guys who have contacted me."

Tanner thought he might lose his lunch as he read the screen name for one of Frankie's matches. "Clearly,

SexOnaStick from Disharmony.com is not a match made in heaven."

"Aww, that's Darrell, a sweetie. He's cross-eyed on account of he fell out of a deer stand as a child."

Tanner clenched his eyes shut a moment to prevent Darrell's image from settling there. Some things you couldn't unsee. "Did he also get run over by a reindeer coming home from our house Christmas Eve? That looks like a hoofprint on his head."

"It's a tattoo."

"No way am I letting you date Charles Manson."

"How about this one?" She reached around him and opened up an equally disturbing photo on a second dating site.

"BobbyTaco from OkayStupid.com?"

"What's wrong with Bobby? He loves his momma and goes to church."

"His favorite pastime," Tanner read the profile aloud, "is massage. Favorite book: *Shades of Grey*. Although one questions whether he can read at all."

"I like massages," she shrugged. "I like books."

"Frankie," he said firmly, "you are too old to be this naïve. You know what BobbyTaco is after."

Her face bespoke an innocence that again rattled the cage around his black heart and reinforced Tanner's belief that she was way over her head on these websites.

"Maybe I'll try out for *The Bachelorette*."

"If you keep going the way you have been with these guys, you'll end up on a Lifetime movie of the week."

"Whatever," Frankie muttered as he pulled up

PlentyofFreaks.com. "Fisherman is a doctor with lots of acceptable hobbies."

Tanner couldn't control the seizure in his jaw as he read the message: **Sup, sexy. I want to get to know u deeper, ya feel me?**

Frankie's cheeks colored as she reached around him and slammed the laptop shut again. "Stay out of my life."

Her perfume—wildflowers and motor oil—drifted over him. He inhaled deeply, stopping when he opened his eyes and met her wide ones.

Clearing his throat, Tanner said, "Not while you are in danger."

"Don't worry your pretty little head, Tanner. Nobody stays interested in me for long, whether it be a potential date or murderer. I can't figure it out. Do you think I intimidate men?"

She stalked across the floor in thigh-high leather boots smeared with grease and dirt. When she tossed a wrench onto a workbench, the sound echoed off the rafters she'd just been hanging on.

"Nah." His mouth twitched. If men weren't a little intimidated by Frankie Newman, he'd question their honesty and common sense.

She cut such a figure bending over the car, Tanner averted his eyes. Her shorts got shorter every day.

"Is there something I'm doing to turn men off? I have all my teeth, an education, and a job. I take showers and brush my hair. I'm kind to people and animals, well, except that rodent of yours who threw the first punch. I'm not always kind to Momma, but I mean, it's Momma and she gets on everybody's nerves. Other than that, I'm phenomenal on paper."

Frankie flipped her long locks and performed a little Beyoncé dance.

"You put all the single ladies to shame." He was not liking the direction this conversation was headed.

She stomped her foot. "I'm serious, Tanner. Do I put off some vibe with men?"

For all her bluster and hostility towards him, Frankie had the most entertaining personality he'd ever encountered.

"Am I unattractive? Be honest." Insecurity burned her cheeks and put a sag into her normally straight shoulders.

His gun wasn't as loaded as that question. Tanner let go of the mouse he'd been gripping and shook out his fingers, which had turned white and tingly. If he had to babysit her much longer, he was going to have to learn to meditate to deal with the pressure.

"Stop that garbage." His exhale came out like a whistle. "It isn't you and you know it. You are Frankie Newman. You hold the record for the most points won by any male or female in your division for the last sixteen years, which means you've been a champion driver since you were a teenager. You've got a patent pending for a steel safety doohickey I can't pronounce that could revolutionize every race, local or NASCAR, in this country."

Her eyes widened. "How did you—"

"Because I, too, am good at what I do. I know who my client is and what she needs."

Tanner reopened the laptop and half-expected the word "liar" to flash on the screen. He was holding back the very information Frankie needed to help her stop questioning her self-worth.

The real reason men never came around was that Daddy had signed a death warrant for anybody who messed with his "kitten." Every man within a twenty-mile radius of Kenny Newman's shadow knew it.

The looming threat to her safety from Newman's enemies and to Tanner's safety from Newman necessitated that Tanner keep that little secret, among others. Exigent circumstances. Scaring off the local weaklings she didn't want anyway benefitted her in the long run as well. The right man wouldn't worry about Daddy's threats but would move heaven and earth to make Frankie his.

These out-of-town online suitors posed a problem, however. They had no clue about Kenny Newman and his power to squash them.

"Tell me." Her plaintive voice stopped him cold in his rationalizing.

Frankie swallowed. "Tell me what I need, Tanner."

You need me. The whisper wafted through his mind like the scent of pie baking at Good Company.

He tapped his ear with the palm of his hand to shake the thought loose. Of course, she needed him. That's what he'd been hired for.

"You need to hold off on communicating with any idiots on your laptop for a while."

"Why?" Her sagging shoulders began to rise to her ears again.

"For your safety. Trust me for once. Thirty days is all I ask."

Tanner's mission would be over by then.

"Once we neutralize the threat against you, you're free to make a heart connection with," he paused to look down at the screen, "'Your#1MuscleMan.' Really? Have some self-respect, dude."

He rubbed the bridge of his nose as Frankie watched, tapping her foot and clenching her fists. He'd have to come up with a Plan B here, because she was not going to last two weeks without diving into the dating pool. If he had Mario hack in and delete her profiles, she'd know it. Maybe if Tanner tweaked her settings, suitors would lose interest. Would she realize it if he changed her profile picture to something less likely to attract degenerates—one of *The Golden Girls*, perhaps?

"I can't just ghost him. It's not polite."

"And the crude things he said to you were polite?"

She dipped her head, then turned her attention back to the car. "Ghosting is not kind. I know you have a hard time with the whole concept of what we humanoids call 'feelings,' but I don't enjoy hurting people."

"His disgusting, disrespectful mouth is hurting you. In less than five minutes of 'meeting' you online, he asked about your bra size, waxing, and position preferences. C'mon." Tanner had half a mind to hunt him down and teach him a lesson in respect.

She leaned back against the car, her place of safety. "Isn't that a guy thing? Ninety percent of the ones who message me ask those questions. Women have to put up with the locker room talk to find love, right? The sexual revolution and all that?"

He couldn't believe what he was hearing. Her misty eyes and sad, half-smile betrayed what she was really feeling.

Frankie'd been raised with little motherly influence and clearly Kenny hadn't shown her how a gentleman treats a lady.

"These men set the women's movement back a hundred years and it pains me that they've made you doubt yourself."

This was above Tanner's paygrade. He was no therapist. In fact, any therapist of his would need his own therapist.

Frankie slid down the car door and sat on the floor beside it, leaning her head against Wonder Woman's lasso of truth. "I hoped that online dating would be like a vending machine: you choose the qualities you want, put your money in, and voila! Mr. Right comes down the chute like a tall cool can of Mountain Dew."

She laughed a little at that one.

He shouldn't engage, shouldn't provoke her to soul search, but Tanner had to make Frankie see that the cans coming down the chute would explode in her face. "What qualities would you choose?"

Frankie closed her eyes a moment before reopening them and looking off into the distance.

"A man who… ignites the deepest part of me that only comes alive when I hear an engine rumble to life." She wrapped her arms around herself. "I want to love on someone until he says uncle. I want to snuggle and dance and hear him shout to the world that I'm the best thing that's ever happened to him. He must understand my need to race. Am I asking for too much?"

She looked up suddenly, her blue eyes catching his. She was a prickly pear—hard-headed and tough outside, but tender inside.

"Well?"

"You don't need my approval for the things *you* want. You definitely don't need Goober666 from Batesville's opinion either. If he doesn't rev that engine and bring you closer to what lights you up, why are you keeping him around?"

She nodded. Maybe he was getting somewhere.

"What lights *you* up, Tanner?"

"Nothing," he said too quickly. Not even this mission to unearth the truth and give Kenny Newman what was coming to him. It was an obsession, not a fire.

"Sad." Frankie cocked her head, still following his eyes. "I'm sure there's someone else out there for you. Don't they have dating sites for cyborgs?"

Don't pity me. His life was fine and would be finer when they were done here. He looked away, scrolling through her messages and changing the subject back to her.

"No sadder than SexonDaBeach1950 here on PlentyofFreaks. Since you're so gung-ho on not ghosting these creeps, how about you take out the trash or I will?"

"I have an idea to do just that," Frankie smiled, pushed herself up, and strutted over. "If I don't like the guy, I'll act crazy. Then, he can block me or whatever and keep his dignity. It won't hurt him, but it gives him power too. Ha! I am wise beyond my years."

"And ever so humble."

Frankie leaned in too close again and typed a reply to her suitor: **We make dinner for hour later? Could you send $$? Finally appointment with immigration lawyer. Maybe I get green card if cards play right.**

She added a fingers-crossed emoji.

When Frankie refreshed the screen, the man's profile

had vanished. "He officially blocked me in under a minute. Satisfied?"

"Tremendously." Tanner blinked, unmoving. "Deleting the profiles on your laptop will lower the risk of bringing in outside threats."

These men would give Tanner a fresh batch of nightmares tonight. Not that he ever slept more than a few hours.

"Fine." Frankie frowned at him, then turned back to typing.

"Good."

"Great. Is there anything else you'd like to control in my life?"

"I'm sure I can come up with something if I put my mind to it." Tanner rubbed his chin.

She slapped him on the back hard before abandoning the laptop and returning to the Chevy. She hadn't turned off the computer, so she trusted him.

Tanner sat back to watch her hustle. There were very few areas of life where Frankie wasn't in control. He'd finally nailed down her weaknesses: a desire for fairy-tale romance, cars, and—

"Hey Tanner, what's for dinner?"

Hunger.

CHAPTER FIVE

I'll See You in My Rear View

The hunger was so intense Frankie could empathize with the Nature Channel wolves howling for a mate. She had analyzed this perfectly healthy carburetor three times just to keep from reaching for the long fingers gripping her computer mouse, staring into eyes the color of black coffee, or stroking the mysterious scar that stretched across Tanner's neck and into his beard.

She peeped at him again over her shoulder and he was watching. No use in reading anything into it. Tanner studied everything as if there was going to be a test on it. How could it be that Frankie's true #1MuscleMan was sitting right in front of her and was looking at her like a wolf looks at a green bean?

What did he really want with her and when would she be free of him? Never, if her heart had any say. Her brain said "no," but her body said "go." The more he worked that jaw and laid out infuriating demands to "protect" her, the more he fanned her fire. Frankie knew a smokin' hot guy when she saw one, but she'd never felt one down to her toes every time he walked in.

But Tanner wasn't *the one.* It was just a coincidence that he was Cane Ashton's twin and that a relationship with Tanner would make her and Selah Ashton sisters officially. It wasn't going to happen.

Frankie blinked back tears, leaning against the car for support. *You are too strong for this. Loneliness has no power over you.* Wonder Woman's alter ego, Diana Prince, needed no man, not even scrumptious Steve Trevor. Eyes on the prize. The only thing that mattered was winning the race, meeting her youngest fans, and raising money for charity.

Alright, enough of this pity party. It was past time to get on Tanner's nerves again. Frankie threw a wrench into the toolbox beside the desk. Tanner never flinched. If you peeled back his skin, he'd be all iron and steel like the Terminator.

"Would you at least tell me who is after me, so that I can prepare or be on the lookout?"

"You and your father have received credible threats from his business associates."

"Could you be more vague?" She reflexively rolled her eyes. Doggone it. She'd tipped him off that he was getting to her. "Daddy runs a racetrack in a rural community of 9,000 people. Who would want to hurt him? Also, who guards him when you're not around?"

"Your father insists that I stay with you." Tanner's eyes darkened, like swirling black holes enveloping other black holes. "I'm bringing in a new head of security who will keep a closer eye on him. Your father is capable of protecting himself."

"So am I." She scraped the car with her fingernails, chipping the paint. Frankie patted the car, cooing softly, "Sorry baby."

"Apology accepted. *You* need me." He tapped on the laptop, then stood up to pace and inspect every corner of the barn with laser eyes.

More than you know, you arrogant jerk. She swallowed against the lump in her throat. "Go back to wherever you and that rat climbed out of so that I can think clearly again and prep for the race."

Tanner shrugged. "I want you off the track as soon as it's over. No pre-race meet-and-greets. Get in, get out. The crowd makes you vulnerable."

"Mingling with the kids is the best part of the gig, Tanner. You'd be a tyrant to deprive them of the money raised from admission and concessions."

"In. Out. Done." He flipped a light switch on and off and on.

On second thought, maybe she wasn't as infatuated by him as she thought. She'd live life on her terms, not as his prisoner. Just because Tanner tied a leash around her neck didn't mean she couldn't bite, growl, and howl at the moon. Frankie Newman wasn't rolling over.

"How cold are you to deny a child? To suck the joy out of this day and punish the innocent because some faceless wackadoodle has a beef with my father? Isn't that like letting the terrorists win? I thought you were a better man."

Tanner's jaw jumped like a monster truck over a mud bog. It was the only tell he had. The wheels in his head were turning, even if his face gave away nothing. His twin had that same jaw tick. Another wave of loneliness swept through her. If only Cane and Selah were here.

Frankie continued to needle him. "You *were* a kid once, right? You didn't just mutate into existence on a distant planet?"

The corners of his eyes crinkled. Somehow, he had moved in front of her, dangerously close as she backed up against the car.

After a few moments of intense frowning, Tanner sighed. "Fifteen minutes with the kids before the race. I meet the parents first."

"Great! That's settled." She clapped her hands.

"You think you've got me all figured out, Wonder Woman." He leaned closer, trying to look menacing but managing to look sexier and give her a whiff of a cologne as smooth as Momma's deep-dish dark chocolate brownie pie.

"I d-do. You were created in Dr. Frankenstein's lab," she croaked. "And what I don't know about you, we'll talk about on the way."

"On the way where? It's too late to go out."

"Well, Daddy," Frankie dropped her voice an octave and blinked slowly. There went the jaw again. If she couldn't get Tanner's attention, she'd have fun tormenting him. "We have to eat dinner. I know just the place—small and cozy. If you say no, I'll just sneak out at 2 a.m. and interrupt your beauty sleep, so you might as well say yes for the sake of your sanity."

Tanner had obviously checked his sanity at the door—a splintered, bloodstained, enter-if-you-dare kind of door. This door fronted Marbles Saloon on Old Cowpasture Road. It was small, but not his idea of cozy.

A skeleton wearing a sheriff's badge and a bullet in his head hung from a light pole.

"That's a homey touch." He cringed, rubbing his thumb along the skeleton to test whether it was legit fake. This called for a Lysol bath if he ever made it home again.

He checked the parking lot, interior, and exits and confirmed that the location was as secure as a roadside dive could be. Pushing the door open, Tanner gritted his teeth as it screamed with rust. Frankie shoved him forward into the bar and shot around him. It was line-dancing night. Wonderful.

No bodyguard in his right mind would think this a good idea, allowing your client to shuffle in and out of smoke and shadows, encircled by strange men. But whatever Frankie wanted, she got. If he didn't give her room to play, Daddy would hear about it and Tanner would be out of the organization.

Big 'n Rich's "Save a Horse" stampeded over his eardrums, forcing him to read her lips, as she jumped up and down and squealed, "I love this song!"

She grabbed his hand, tugging toward the dance floor. When he didn't move, she rolled her eyes, jerked her hand away, and skipped off. A line of six or seven boot-scootin' men and women opened up when Frankie approached.

Not even Danielle had been able to convince him to dance. Guilt knifed Tanner's gut. No matter how dirty Frankie's hands were, she would not end up like Danielle. He'd make sure of it.

Clearly, Frankie was an expert at everything athletic—strutting and rocking and pivoting with precision. She dug and twisted her heels in girly cowboy boots and shorts that showed off entirely too much leg. Excessive shimmying and booty shaking was going on out there. Tanner would speak to her about that.

Not that she would listen.

When she touched the tip of her hat and grinned at him under a whirlwind of blonde hair, it took his breath away. The man next to her noticed, too. He was so busy eyeing her up that he startled and tripped when his girlfriend punched his arm.

Tanner settled onto a bar stool next to the dance floor and ordered two water bottles and two buckets of wings and onion rings. Just a hunch that Frankie would eat them.

All part of his modified strategy for taming Frankie Newman and getting a foothold in the organization. The tighter he made her leash, the more she yanked it. So, let her think she was getting her way. *Play nice, Tanner*, Mom would say. *You kill more flies with honey*. But nice was exhausting. People were tiring. Socializing was excruciating.

He squinted to find her in a haze of smoke, sweat, cologne, and barbecue sauce. This was going to be a long night.

The local country boys watching Frankie kept their distance. Probably knew who she was and didn't want to end up floating face-down in Chinese Willie's koi pond. Tanner had heard Newman threaten to do worse to another driver who spent too much time with her. Lefty steered clear of the family business and was the only true ally she had now that Selah was gone.

The businessman at three o'clock might be a threat. He'd had a lock on Frankie since she bounced through the door. Her magnetic energy and radiant smile lit up hope in this miserable dump. As much as Tanner'd rather be anywhere else and he'd love for this job to be over, she exerted a pull that would be hard to walk away from.

The suit set down his Corona beside a black velvet Elvis shrine and moved toward Frankie who was dancing the "Cha-Cha Slide". Tanner slid off his stool and into the man's path.

"I beg your pardon." He swatted at Tanner as if he were a gnat. "I've got a date with that fine piece of—"

If Tanner shot him for disrespecting a lady, would anybody miss the guy back home?

"For your own protection, that one's off limits."

The suit finally dragged his eyes away to glance at Tanner. Tanner stepped closer, widening his stance.

"Just looking. She belong to you?"

"Owning" Frankie would be like trying to hold a thunderstorm with his bare hands.

"She belongs to the state in a matter of sorts. I'm her parole officer and she's just out of prison for killing her third husband in 'self-defense'." Tanner threw in some air quotes.

"She might be worth the risk."

"I don't know. We've yet to locate the bodies of her first two husbands."

The suit slunk away. Tanner shook his head. He couldn't decide whether the moisture dripping down his face was an allergy to the suit's cologne or tears of boredom. They were leaving in five minutes if he had to throw Frankie over his shoulder.

The ruckus quieted as Dan + Shay's "Nothin' Like You" drifted out of the crackling speakers. Frankie was still swaying as couples danced around her. The sweet upbeat rhythm and lyrics suited her. Her long fingers stretched out gracefully to write stories in the air. Her hair splayed across her cheeks, which pinked when she looked up and met his eyes.

Frankie stepped into a beam of light, her eyes shining with stubborn pride. Suddenly, Tanner wanted nothing more than to take away the loneliness it masked. No woman that stunning should have to dance alone.

Whoa ho ho. No. Whatever you're thinking, cease and desist post-haste.

But then, she smiled.

He was her protector, bound to keep her from humiliation. He was doing his job, a public service really.

Bad idea. Abort.

He reminded himself of every rule in his training:

Be friendly, not familiar.

Do not interfere with your client's life, unless required.

Remain invisible.

Always retain control and calm in high pressure situations.

But Tanner couldn't stop himself from stepping forward and pulling her into his arms. Something shifted in his chest as her hand brushed against it. Her hair, softer than he expected, drifted across his cheek.

Another bodyguard would shoot out his kneecap if he could see Tanner compromised like this. He'd worry about that later.

It was Frankie who pulled away first, pushing his hands from her waist and stepping back. "Quit!"

He blinked off the fog. "Am I hurting you?"

"Yes," she hissed. "Stop pitying me. Stop being so nice and then not liking me. It doesn't suit you. Stop being so handsome and then hating and resenting me for having to protect me, a job I didn't hire you for."

A crowd was gathering around them and the suit was laughing as the jukebox teed up Jerry Reed's "I Got the Shaft."

"I don't hate you." But he hated the coldness in her eyes, reminiscent of her father.

He started to explain, but Frankie was already pushing her way through the crowd towards the door.

Tanner sprinted to catch up, finding her revving the engine of the Speedway's Hummer. He used to think he was in pretty good shape before he met her. He barely jumped in the seat before she peeled out.

He could feel her glare in the dark. "I drive from here on out. We start briefing for the race at 0900."

"Don't you have something to say to me other than a direct order?" She huffed. "I'm not hearing an explanation or an apology."

Tell her what really happened. Tell her it bothered you to see her dancing alone, hurt and rejected by every man in town, so you stepped in and somehow crossed a line and hurt her too. "You were in a vulnerable position by yourself on the dance floor with visible threats encroaching."

"For the millionth time, I can handle myself. No one will ever touch me because, apparently, I repel the male species."

"A woman like you should not have been in a place like that in the first place."

A growl erupted from her throat as the car lurched forward. "And what kind of woman am I exactly?"

An extraordinary woman.

He was saved from responding because he lost all ability to speak when Frankie took the next curve like a racehorse on a downhill slalom course. Tanner gripped the doorframe as tires squealed and she ground to a halt at the entrance to the guest house where he'd been staying.

"We need to talk." Frankie jumped out, slammed the door, and stomped toward the house, tripping the porch light.

Frankie's hands were on her hips, her hair tousled from dancing, her mascara gone rogue.

Mercy. This girl.

CHAPTER SIX

If Dust Ain't Flyin', You Ain't Tryin'

TANNER GOT NO mercy from Frankie and never any peace. She ran up the steps two at a time, jiggling the doorknob to his room, and tapping her foot. He sighed as she beat down another boundary between them. How could he regain control of this situation? Did he want to?

He soaked up the silence for a few minutes, then finally rolled out, still dizzy from Frankie's driving. He took his time mounting the stairs and unlocking the door. "I cannot protect you if you're constantly ten steps ahead of me."

"Then keep up, old man." She slid past him into the house.

The smile froze on his face when she screamed and staggered toward the sofa.

"I'm hit! I'm hit!" she cried, thrashing wildly and clutching the back of her head.

Drawing his weapon, he scanned the room. No intruders. No signs of a break-in.

When he located the source of the attack atop Frankie's head, he chuckled. "Kojak! Bad kitty! Is that any way to treat a guest?"

"Not that flying rodent again!" Frankie stopped struggling as Tanner disentangled claws and paws from the silky blonde hair he'd had his own hands tangled in only a short time before. The closer he was to her, the thinner the air in the room.

"Could you hurry this along?" she said softly, their faces inches apart.

He cleared his throat and restarted his task and his brain. When he'd extracted feline from Frankie, he cradled the cat in one arm and stepped away from Frankie, the real wildcat.

"You okay, buddy?"

"I'm fine, thank you," Frankie gave a crooked smile, then frowned. "Oh, you're talking to *it*. What is that thing's problem with me?"

"She senses that you are uncomfortable around her."

"Nah. I hate its guts." She laughed when Tanner cupped his hand protectively over Kojak's pointy ears to protect her from the trash talk. "But the way you treat it reveals a teensy-weensy Grinch-sized heart that beats inside you."

He'd certainly felt Frankie's heart quicken as they danced. He brushed off the thought. She was still the enemy, at least until he could take a closer look at what her hard drive revealed. How embroiled was Frankie in her father's shady dealings?

Frankie shook out her hair and inspected her arms and

collarbone, presumably for new scratches. "I hadn't paid attention before, but it makes sense that it's a female, panting after you and marking you as her territory."

"Don't you mean purring after me?" Tanner held the cat's cheek playfully against his. Kojak was all mush.

"Go away. I liked you better when you just glared and didn't speak."

"It is *my* room you barged into. Also, it was you who wanted to talk to me." *Please let it be about anything except women and hearts and feelings.*

Frankie ignored Tanner, casing the room, picking up his framed photos of Grandma, his parents, and Selah and Cane, and setting them back perfectly in place. He'd locked up everything that would arouse suspicion. She paused her snooping for a moment and cocked her head at the *International Journal of Medical Sciences* and the *Pharmaceutical Research* journal on the nightstand.

That was the extent of his decorating. He wasn't staying long enough to put down roots. Shadybrook was a pit stop.

"Okay then, let's talk security for the race," he said.

Bristling, Frankie picked up a file of old newspaper clippings from his desk. Tanner removed it from her hands and laid it down again.

"Everyone who enters will be wanded. There are security cameras, but stay alert and tell me if you see or hear anything that seems out of place. A ten-minute meet-and-greet, then straight off the track when you finish the race."

"When I win the race, you mean." She gave the room another once-over and headed to the door. "I'm not short-changing the kids because some coward threatened me."

"It's not up for debate"

She whirled around, fire in her eyes. "Stay out of my way."

൳

If only Frankie had stayed out of her own way and given up online dating.

Whatever possessed God to make so many weirdos? Sure, it would be challenging to make billions of men unique, but did they all have to be freaks? In one hour, Frankie had swiped left on 300 guys who sported beards down to their knees and tattoos of Satan and tarantulas creeping up their necks, snapped their profile photos standing in front of dirty toilets, posed naked and covered personal parts with emojis, or wanted her to join them and their wives for some swinging fun.

Some demanded to show her how good pain could feel when she was chained to the walls in their basements. Others proclaimed to live in gated communities, which translated to prison.

Three hundred of them! On one website! And from the looks of what she was scrolling through now, there were 3,000 more in the queue.

She blocked the latest prospect who messaged, **Let's meet 4 drinks. Your shape turns me on. What's your size, babydoll?**

Frankie shuddered. Every single one of them talking about sex right off the starting line. Even those who answered "extremely important" to the question about how God fit into their lives would, in the next breath, state that they were looking for hookups, expected to sleep with someone after three dates, and needed to have sex before marriage.

Did people talk like that when they met in real life? If one should meet her in, say, the grocery checkout line, and not online, would he ask for her bra size within a few minutes of conversation? Good grief, five minutes into dinner, would he be asking, "Pass the salt and your panties?" Maybe they didn't want to date offline. Maybe they just enjoyed texting or calling a live woman at the other end of the sexy talk and photos. Maybe Frankie served as free personalized porn.

Is that what men thought about all day? Yeah, probably.

Tanner was right. Thank goodness he hadn't seen these "men" or he would have banned her from dating for life, not just thirty days. She agreed to the laptop but never promised she'd delete the apps on her phone. If only she had.

With every profile and message, Frankie sunk a little deeper. Romance was a lie concocted by the books she read and the soaps she watched. Gentlemen and chivalry were dead. Maybe they'd never existed. Her stomach roiled. It was all too much.

A guy named Kyle or LovePotion#9 slid into her DMs on Instagram and appeared sincere in his appeals, but how could she trust a random stranger? There had to be a better way to fall in love and get married.

Wedded bliss seemed like a pipe dream on account of every married couple she knew was miserable. According to the ladies of Shadybrook, even the "decent" men weren't worth it. She'd sat in the diner listening to Margo Morgan complain about her gambling husband's inability to clean, cook, or perform any job except spend money and watch TV.

"Love ain't no joy ride, Francine."

"Consider yourself lucky to be single. Ain't a one worth keeping. That's why I'm a free agent." Selah's Aunt Ruby had jumped in to add her two cents. "There's no equal division of labor, as you young folk call it. Their mommas ruin 'em, and they expect their women to spoil 'em the same way. They take and take and then point to the Bible and preach, 'The man is the master, and the woman must submit.'"

Four other women in the restaurant had raised their sweet teas and said "Amen" to that.

Frankie's thumb hovered over the face of a guy with a contorted mouth and vacant eyes who asked her for an arranged marriage. Instead of swiping left and viewing more profiles, she clicked on the settings and deleted her account. All of the accounts she could think of—Christian, secular, even the NASCAR lover app—gone. If only Frankie had a bonfire. Maybe it would erase the sick feeling that had replaced her hope. Spinsterhood was looking good.

She faced the full-length mirror in the barn and stood Wonder Woman strong, laughing when the light hit her teeth just so and demanded a "Ching!" sound effect. *You can do anything. You are happily independent. You are magnificent on your own.*

Frankie picked up a wrench and twirled it like a baton. Her palms itched to caress the steering wheel. Once she took home the trophy, she would conquer the world. Tanner Ashton better stand back or eat her dust.

CHAPTER SEVEN

"Wide open until you see God, then brake."

–Unknown

"MISS FRANKIE, CAN you sign my wheels?"

"I can and I will." Frankie squatted so she could look into the wide blue eyes of a ten-year-old girl sitting in a manual wheelchair.

Seemed like she should have an electric chair to zip around in, but the kid had made the push chair her own. She'd pimped out the contraption in a Mountain Dew green like Dale Earnhardt Junior's Impala at Talladega. A felt shark covered her below-the-knee amputation.

Frankie teased, "You should have tricked this out in Wonder Woman red and blue, like my car, instead of wasting it on the boys."

"Ha!" The girl rolled her eyes at Frankie and tossed her ruddy corkscrew coils over her shoulder. She ran her fingers along the spoiler of a 1970 Chevelle late model, which was on display with a few other vintage beauties beside the bleachers.

A woman with matching eyes and hair stood behind the child. "Angel is your biggest fan. She loves racing and fell in love with you and your car."

"Wanna know why I'm in this chair?" Angel dragged her gaze away from the Chevelle and said somberly, "I accelerated too quickly when I exited the corner on the last lap."

When Frankie's eyebrows shot up, Angel erupted laughter that was louder and baudier than any little girl she'd ever met. This kid was the best! Angel's mom laughed a bit too, although her hunched shoulders and pinched expression said that whatever had really happened and whatever her baby faced was way more difficult than taking the checkered flag on the Speedway. Angel joking about her situation proved that hope and miracles existed.

Even "McBroody" the bodyguard, whose eyes never stopped roaming their surroundings, betrayed a hint of a smile and seemed lighter in Angel's presence. He didn't have kids, as far as she knew, but something about him said he would spoil a child the same as he spoiled that dumb cat. Why had he shut himself off to a family, to love of any kind? Had he been jilted? Was he still broken from his parents' tragic deaths? He'd certainly put a kibosh on her love life.

Frankie squeezed Angel's hand lightly and leaned in. Instinctively, she knew the girl's feet would never move a gas pedal or bust out a victory dance, but she was dancing on the inside. "Sometimes you have to feather the throttle or make adjustments. Ease up a little and release control to stay in control. Got it?"

"I think so." The girl's mouth twisted in concentration as she nodded.

"You're smart, Angel." Frankie looked up at the girl's

mother. "You'll find the sweet spot. Just don't stop moving forward. Don't give up."

Angel gave her a mighty fist bump. The mom beamed down on her with such love, Frankie felt like she was receiving light from a real angel. Her mom should be here. What would she say if she could see Frankie now? Would she tell her racing was too dangerous? Would she cheer her on from the bleachers? Would she be a hugger? A crier? A sign waver?

She would be loving, Frankie knew that. She couldn't remember her face, her walk, or her smile, but Tanya Newman loved her, because Frankie longed to spread love and make others happy. That had to come from somewhere. Not that Daddy didn't love her, but he reserved compassion for her and had no tolerance for such "weakness" in others.

Frankie turned away quickly, wiping at the tears in her eyes and plowing into Tanner's chest. He steadied her, grabbing her shoulders and searching her eyes.

"Sometimes your past sneaks up on you, doesn't it?"

"How did you know?" Frankie couldn't even piece together what she was feeling on this July 4th, the anniversary of her mother's death.

Her mother was all around her and yet painfully absent.

"I just know." His usually commanding voice was soft as he gave her one last meaningful glance and then dropped his hands. "Now, let's get this race over with ASAP."

He was all business again after a brief flash of humanity, like a comet not to be seen again for a thousand years.

"Always scintillating conversation, McBroody." She waved at Angel and stomped off, Tanner on her heels.

On the way to the car, she breathed in the track—her little slice of heaven. It wasn't NASCAR or GT, but you were dead inside if your stomach didn't rumble at the scent of corn dogs and fried everything, if your shoulders didn't relax at the sight of fans laughing and cheering and forgetting their troubles for a few hours, if your eyes didn't tear up at hoist of the American flag and the drop of the green flag, or if you didn't feel like a kid again as the cars whizzed by and a hot blast of wind ruffled your hair.

Catching sight of her wheels and the 860-horsepower engine inside the open hood, she smacked Tanner on the arm, hitting solid muscle. "There she is! Beautiful."

Tanner nodded, his eyes on her face. A thrill ran up her spine.

"Hands bothering you?" he asked.

Frankie stopped mid-scratch of her palms. "Pre-race itch. Happens every time."

"Frankie," he said as serious as if he was reading her rights. "Eyes open. Don't let your guard down. If anything seems off, get out of there."

"Don't worry. Danger can't catch me."

Tanner sighed jaggedly as he rubbed the bridge of his nose.

A grin spread across her face. This was the life. Tanner's Eeyore cloud of gloom and doom couldn't darken her sunshine. She'd been over that car inside, outside, upside, and down and it was ready for the winner's circle. No way would she disappoint Angel today.

After she dropped the hood, she zipped the fire-retardant suit that was her bunny slippers and fuzzy bathrobe. Frankie slid behind the wheel and checked vitals.

She touched the photo of her mother that she'd tucked inside her Conquer helmet. The helmet slipped down perfectly over her head, but the inside of her noggin was a different story. Frankie couldn't shake the sadness of knowing she'd claim another victory her mother wouldn't witness.

Frankie didn't need Lefty's help to harness her up and strap on the safety net, but her senior mechanic had looked out for her for as long as she'd been alive and his presence calmed her.

"Watch yer back, kid," he said, rapping on the roof and stepping aside.

"Let everyone else watch my back," she corrected.

"There's only one Frankie Newman."

"Doggone right!" Frankie gave Lefty a thumbs up.

The voice of the announcer, the chatter of the crowd, the blare of horns faded. The first note of the symphony was a quick prayer before she turned the key and the engine rolled like timpani. The drumbeat crescendoed as she hit the gas and the trumpets sounded.

Race day, baby!

It didn't take long to find her sweet spot as the car sailed from gear to gear, corner to corner, with the precision she knew it had. Frankie was winning. Duh. Was there ever any doubt?

The track, the turns, the finish line, the flag had already played out in her mind thousands of times. In her dreams, the car never ran out of gas, the crowd never stopped cheering, the race never ended, and the corn dogs never contained calories. She didn't have a perfect handle on how to interact with God yet, but He had to be a stand-up Dude if He was giving her this life before she even made it to heaven.

A wobble brought Frankie back to earth. That was new. The car pitched, forcing her off the gas. Gauges normal. No smoke, but the air seemed hazy and it was only lap four. She popped it back to second to take the turn and punched it on the straight.

She groaned when Red Rover from Alleghany got a wheel ahead of her. Yes, that was his given name and he'd be barking like a mad dog if he won and could hold it over Frankie Newman.

Shoot, there it went again, sending a chill through her body. She was too loose. What was she missing?

Get out of there. Tanner's pre-race warning rattled her rafters.

She had a half lap before she could pit. Red Rover made a slingshot around her taking the lead. She was completely fogged over and shaking.

Frankie gasped at the sudden screech of metal cutting metal. Sparks flickered in her eyes. She tried to steer away from it, but she headed for the sawmill. Frankie could only brace as pain crushed her chest and back. To protect herself, she let go the wheel. Hopefully, Jesus still had hold of it.

CHAPTER EIGHT

"A smooth race never made a skilled racer."

–Unknown

THIS COULDN'T BE happening again. Tanner hadn't protected his parents. Now Frankie would die, too, because he couldn't protect her.

Tanner's hands clung to his head as his feet lurched forward. He was moving but he felt nothing—no air circling in and out of his lungs, no heartbeat, no heat against his skin.

Ain't tall, slim guys supposed to be runners? It's in the human anatomy manual somewhere. He could hear her teasing him about his speed, her voice deepening with her accent. She'd be proud today as he beat everyone across the track to the carcass of her vehicle.

Liquid seeped from the twisted metal. No time for protective gear. The shouts around him intensified as he reached inside the car.

Sickness lurched in his gut at the thought of that little girl watching her idol die in front of her. The kid was the sweetest he'd ever seen and the way she looked up at

Frankie... He choked back the lump in his throat. No. He refused to allow another person to be torn from his life, on his watch.

"Frankie, it's Tanner. Fight. Don't let go." Heat seared his arms as he leaned forward to check her pulse under the cracked helmet.

When he unhooked the Kevlar strap from her pale, bloody face, the strap fell off in his hand. Frankie stirred.

Thank God, she was still breathing! He took a breath himself and choked on smoke.

Before he could calculate his next move, Lefty, his race crew, and the rescue personnel surrounded the car. Tanner struggled as Lefty pulled him back and water sprayed down on them.

"Muscle and a hard head won't get Frankie out of that mess, kid," Lefty shouted, putting him in a headlock.

When Tanner stopped fighting, the mechanic released him.

"What went wrong?" he shouted, but Lefty was already limping off to join the crew extinguishing the fire.

Tanner clutched the chinstrap, pacing and kicking the dirt while someone else saved the woman he was supposed to shield from harm. Firefighters and EMTs put their specialized equipment to work in cutting off the roof of the car and lifting Frankie's seat from the floorboard.

Tanner heaved a sigh as they finally eased her limp body out of the wreckage. Frankie was alive. The woman on her car's logo was sliced in half from the waist down.

Wake up, Wonder Woman, and demand your victory!

"What happened out there, Tanner?"

Tanner turned away from Frankie a moment as a man

in his sixties with a Mark Twain mustache and longish woolen hair lumbered over.

Russ Morgan looked positively stricken. Selah's father had been a second dad to Frankie. He'd probably bet on her during the race.

"Did you see anything unusual from where you were standing?"

Russ scratched his head. "No. Frankie has never lost control, even when she was a wee powder puff."

Over Russ's shoulder, Tanner spotted volunteers herding crowds. He needed to gather evidence before it walked away. The perpetrator was likely nearby, surveying his handiwork.

While Russ chattered, Tanner punched in the number of the head of his security team. "Nobody leaves this complex without confirming their identity, videotaping them, and confiscating footage from phones."

When Mario started in about the constitutional implications, Tanner shot back, "I don't care about the Fourth Amendment. I want this guy dead, so don't talk to me about search and seizure and due process right now."

"I dropped everything for you in less than 24 hours. I'm on your side, Tanner."

Tanner squeezed his eyes shut a moment as he clutched the chinstrap against his chest. "I know, man. I'll update you when we get Frankie to the hospital."

A shout came from behind him. "Are they taking her to the hospital or the morgue?"

When Tanner spun around, Kenny Newman met him with a fist to the jaw.

One of his loan sharks and Deputy Sheriff Cody

Buchanan flanked him, but Kenny needed no assistance. He threw a punch as hard as the iron in his eyes.

"Kenny! Don't make a tough situation worse," Russ hollered.

As an EMT rushed over, Newman slipped his hand into his pocket and stood unmoving, chillingly quiet, staring down at Tanner. Tanner didn't move or speak either, just kept his eyes on Frankie's father and his hand on his weapon.

If there hadn't been witnesses, Newman would have tried to finish him off. Tanner knew it from personal experience.

"She's alive." No other explanation, no excuse would have been tolerated.

"I paid you to protect my little girl."

And I haven't spent a dime of your dirty money, old man.

Tanner said, "I shouldn't have to remind you of the lengths to which I have gone and will go to protect you and your family."

A chink of tension loosened in Newman's face. Hopefully, he was remembering the day that Tanner saved his life and they first realized that the vague threats against him and his family were real. Tanner had smelled bitter almond in a drink delivered to the old man's office and thwarted an attempted poisoning by cyanide. It had been his first invitation into Newman's confidences, but he'd have to fight to regain that trust.

The EMT looked from Newman to Tanner. "Best behave yourself, Kenny. Your daughter needs her Daddy by her bedside, not in prison."

Newman smiled tightly, "Mind your own business, Pete. When is that chopper getting here?"

"She's coming in now," Pete answered. "Let me take care of those burns, son."

Tanner ignored the EMT's outstretched hand, picked himself up off the ground, and got toe-to-toe with Newman. "Instead of wasting precious time, you can lock down the complex and limit access to the car. We need to collect all video and photographic evidence on our end and from the crowd."

Newman's eyes could vaporize Tanner.

As the breeze began to swirl with the beating blades of the medivac, Tanner pounded his fist in his hand, which sent a flame of pain so fierce it made his teeth chatter. "The longer you stand there interrogating me, the longer she is alone and unprotected in that helicopter and the hospital."

"Go with her. If she dies…"

"Not gonna happen." Tanner sidestepped Newman, shoved his goons aside, and pushed at the blasting wind as he made his way to the helicopter. "I'll pull her back from the edge if I have to."

CHAPTER NINE

"If you're not on my team, stay out of my way."

–Frankie Newman

FRANKIE MOANED AS the lights flickered again. Fireworks! That was it. They'd detonated the Fourth of July fireworks too soon. That flash of light and heat had been too close. Was anyone hurt? Frankie's ears were squealing like bad brakes.

There was so much shouting. What a wild victory lane party! They were passing around the moonshine already. She tried to join the voices but could only cough. The scent of brake fluid and gas filled her nose with every breath she sipped, setting off alarm bells she couldn't answer.

Fight. Don't let go. The voice floated around her.

Hands lifted her. She was in someone's arms! That was nice for a change. Maybe her man had finally come for her. Frankie could rest now and sleep forever.

When somebody finally turned the lights on again, Frankie was determined to stay awake and celebrate. But, boy oh boy, was she tired. She drifted off again and woke with a gasp, sending pain, like a million shards of glass, through her chest.

"Did I win?"

Hearing no answer, she took stock of the stiff mattress beneath her and the monitors flanking. Everything seemed to be shifting and spinning. When she finally got her equilibrium, the light dawned. It was cold, sterile, and quiet, so she must be in the hospital. The car crash. The helicopter ride. The surgery. She must have gone down in a blaze of glory. There was no other way.

"Not this time, slo-mo. You took your sweet time waking up, too."

Tanner. Only he could get away with calling her slow, because they both knew the truth about her skills.

She gazed up into dark eyes the endearing shade of black-out curtains. Today, they were different. They looked… kind.

She must be dying.

"Are you in pain?" he asked softly.

Define pain. Every time she inhaled, her lungs seized. When she tried to push herself up, her arms, head, and neck felt as if she'd been tumbling in the dryer on high heat.

As for the rest of her, she felt… nothing.

A cry caught at the back of her throat as she clutched the sheets stupidly covering limbs that weren't working. Maybe the medication seeping through the needle in her arm had sucked her energy. Maybe they'd tied her down to the bed. Maybe her body was in temporary shock. And maybe Tanner was secretly the Easter Bunny.

His jaw was set as hard as the truth that he wasn't telling her. She knew drivers paralyzed in crashes. Their lives had literally turned upside down with the tiniest of overcorrections on the track. They'd become shells of their former selves, devastated, not from the loss of movement, but from the loss of their passion. When racing was over, life was over.

Summoning all her strength, she placed her hands on her thighs. *Let's go, legs. Look alive!*

The only thing moving was the hot rush of tears threatening to spill.

Please, God, not in front of him.

"I'll never race again, will I?"

Tanner studied her face a moment before placing a hand on top of hers where it rested on her leg.

Frankie flashed back to the night his hands had wrapped around her waist at Marbles. In that brief moment, she'd let the music and the heat and his breath on her neck deceive her into believing he might have feelings for her after all.

Would she ever dance again like that? Walk down the grocery aisle, stand in the shower, sprint down Main Street waving at her squirrely neighbors? So many little things she'd taken for granted.

"'Never' is not a word I associate with the unflappable and fearless Frankie Newman." The corner of his mouth lifted. The unexpected praise stopped her tears in their tracks.

So did the entrance of a man in a lab coat who must have slipped in while they were talking.

"I'll answer that question with a hearty 'no.'" he said, shuffling toward her monitors and IV bag. "Racing and other dangerous pursuits are out of the question. It's what got you into this situation in the first place."

Tanner was on his feet in superhuman time, towering

over a doctor she might have thought was handsome if he wasn't explaining that life as she knew it was over.

"You're not her surgeon," Tanner growled.

Swoon. Maybe if she concentrated on his finer points, Frankie could block out the horrible picture of her future that her fears were painting in her mind.

"Down, boy," the doctor chuckled.

Tanner lifted the man's lanyard. "Dr. Pepper?"

Frankie snorted.

"Yes, William D. Pepper, the third. My office hours are 10, 2, and 4." Dr. Pepper stared back. "If you'll kindly unhand me, we can get this show on the road before I send in my colleague, Dr. Paine."

Frankie's hand went to her mouth. Tanner sucked his lips to his teeth before dropping the lanyard, patting it with force against the man's chest, and begrudging him a few inches of space to work. Her bodyguard was a sharp contrast to their surroundings, with his black jeans, black beard, black t-shirt, thick and wild black hair, and a jagged scar on his neck.

"Perhaps your bodyguard would like to step back into the Matrix while we chat."

"Tanner stays." Frankie grabbed his hand, then dropped it when he whirled around, eyebrows raised.

Tanner took her hand again and squeezed. "Someone tried to murder her, so you'll understand that she can't be alone under any circumstances. I've already spoken to hospital security."

"Well then, Miss Newman, let's get to it." Dr. Pepper continued, checking the monitors and typing on his iPad. "You've suffered a serious trauma. Your surgery to fuse the vertebrae and stabilize the spinal cord went well, as did the therapeutic hypothermia, but I'll need a more thorough neurological workup now that you're awake."

Tanner stood by her side, arms crossed during the tedious examination. Frankie hoped he remembered the details and instructions the doctor was doling out. Her eyes started to droop even as her fears mounted.

"How long are you going to yak and prod before you tell me when I can walk again?"

The doctor swung a hanging computer monitor toward her, revealing X-ray images. "You suffered spinal cord compression, which severely impacted your lower middle back, causing paralysis."

Paralysis. The word jolted her eyes open. So, there it was in black-and-white. No sugarcoating by Dr. Pepper. He just stood there on two working legs with blank eyes and a bored half-smile while his pen traced a path of destruction on the image of her back.

"You'll require intensive physical ther—"

"How soon will I walk again?"

"Your images are unsettling. My best guess is that the paralysis is permanent."

"Your best guess, huh?" Tanner scoffed as he laid a hand on Frankie's lifeless leg. "With all due respect DP, you don't know the iron will of Frankie Newman."

She surely was high on morphine? Did Tanner actually say another incredible thing about her? She studied his face, dark and tight, as he stared down the doctor.

The doctor nodded curtly. "She appears to be a young, vital woman with a strong support system. That's powerful. But, based on the evidence before me and clinical studies, most patients with this particular injury will not regain complete use of the lower extremities. Partial mobility is possible, but the tenuous positioning of the vertebral impingement on her spinal cord makes getting behind the wheel of a race car monumentally dangerous. Another accident could lead to permanent paralysis or death."

"I don't have accidents. This was sabotage."

"You obviously have a hard head, Miss Newman, because a weaker person would not have survived your injuries. Put that head to good use and focus on your recovery. Forget racing."

"Get out!" Frankie tried to yell but her voice came out weak and shaky.

The doctor frowned down at her. "Excuse me?"

Frankie winced as she squared her shoulders. "You're fired."

Doctor downer looked uneasy. "Your father flew me in specifically for your case, because I am the best in the state. I am—"

"First of all, I don't care if you're Doctor Who, because the best doctor in the state wouldn't be so calloused as to give up without a fight." She ticked off her arguments on her fingers, every movement setting off another jolt of pain. "Second, my father doesn't call the shots."

"I'll alert him that you've decided to reject sound medical advice, but I don't give refunds. Good luck." He made a notation on the tablet and left.

Tanner followed, inspected the hallway, and shut the door behind them.

"Good job taking out the trash." He jerked his thumb over his shoulder. "What's the plan now?"

Oh, you know, sitting in a dark corner in a wheelchair, sobbing, throwing back Mountain Dew, and lining up Netflix series for the next fifteen years. The usual post-paralysis party.

"You leave me alone to sleep and find who did this to me." She leaned back against the pillow. "Go, Tanner, I'm fine."

All at once, she wanted to throw up, scream, cry, and jump out of her skin from the pain. Wooziness took her head on a tilt-a-whirl as she glanced down at the buttons on the bed and then up at her bags, desperate for relief. Would Tanner ever leave so she could figure out how to use the pain pump?

Be strong. Take courage. The first mile is the hardest. People in the Middle Ages survived being stretched on a rack, you can survive this.

Breathing and praying through it weren't working. Her affirmations were dead in the water. Her fears, however, picked up speed as they spiraled. She wasn't strong. She was a failure at racing, at dating, at life. She sucked in a breath as a sharp jolt of pain hit the back of her head and neck. Why was this happening to her? She was mostly a good person who would never hurt anyone. But someone had succeeded in hurting her. Would they come back to finish her off? Would this pain last forever? She needed her mother or Selah or Daddy—anybody.

Tanner reached across her and pulled a cord from under the covers. Wordlessly, he took her hand, wrapped it around a little device, and pushed the button. Soon, warmth coursed through her veins. The look he gave her said he was wise to her plan to hide her suffering and soldier on without his help.

As the ache eased, Frankie wanted to thank him for the medicine and for being there when no one else was, but the urge to cry was so powerful, she didn't dare. Minutes ticked by before the catch in her throat subsided.

She mustered enough energy to lift her chin. "I'm not going to stay paralyzed. I will beat the odds. I'm registered for the Shadybrook Shake-a-Leg 5K in October, so I have to walk again. Recovery will not take years of my life, you know."

"I know." Tanner's eyes hadn't left hers since he'd pushed her pain pump.

For once, his poker face was comforting. He didn't look at her with pity or worry. He wasn't unfeeling or accusatory, as the doctor had been, or reactive and dramatic. He was just Tanner. He gave her room to sort out her emotions without having to feel guilt over his.

"You're moving to a more secure facility tonight. Not only can they protect you, but they're doing groundbreaking work with nerve growth and stimulation in paralysis. After that, we'll get you set up at home with rehab."

"That actually sounds… positive. Like we agree on something."

He'd already researched it! Maybe he did care. Nope. *You're just loopy from the meds. He's protecting you, doing his job, earning his money. Keep your eyes on the goal.*

"Take me to the car first."

"As soon as you're released."

"I'm the only one who touches it." She protested.

"It's already been impounded. Rest tonight and we'll

brainstorm tomorrow about what really happened on that track. Give you a little distraction."

Tanner squeezed her leg. A man was finally touching Frankie's leg and she couldn't feel it. Her eyes fell closed. She wasn't going to be that girl, the one who cried *Why me?* and shook her fist at God. The one everybody felt sorry for. *Frankie's handicapped now, bless her heart.* She was Wonder Woman, a fighter, not a victim.

But right now, she'd give anything if she could bury her face in his chest, feel his arms around her, and let somebody else be the strong one for once.

CHAPTER TEN

As THE SUN rose outside her room at the intensive rehab facility, Tanner was there to open the blinds. "Need anything?"

"Don't you ever sleep?" Frankie couldn't sleep either for the pain and having to depend on someone to turn her every few hours. "At least go home and plug your batteries in the charger."

Tanner's eyes were smiling as he squeezed Frankie's shoulder with one hand and pulled up a chair with the other.

"What she needs is her best friend. Move it, buster!"

That Southern drawl made Frankie's heart burst open. Sunshine in the form of long, black curls and vanilla sugar swept through the door and into Frankie's arms.

"Selah!"

Tanner cleared his throat, venturing a little smile as he jerked his hand from Frankie's shoulder.

Frankie longed for someone to wrap her up in love and she'd gotten it above and beyond.

"Shoot, I'm sorry. I didn't hurt you, did I? I tried to get here days ago." Selah released her hug and slid into the chair beside Frankie's bed. "Look at those painful bruises and burns on her pretty face! Who is responsible for this atrocity, dear sweet brother-in-law?"

The pinch of Selah's brow and mouth was anything but sweet. Selah had found her voice and quite a bit of confidence after winning a job as writer on their favorite soap, *The Winds of Change*, and marrying its dreamy star, Cane Ashton. Cane wasn't as infuriatingly sexy as his twin, but a close second. Selah had become less obsessed about her "big girl curves" as she called them and more in love with life and her husband.

A pain struck Frankie in the center of her breastbone. Nothing a doctor could fix.

"Good to see you too, little sis." Tanner came around to his sister-in-law's chair and ruffled her hair. "The initial police investigation determined driver error to be the cause of the accident."

"What?" Frankie and Selah cried simultaneously.

"That's ridiculous," Selah said. "Frankie is the best. She doesn't make errors. Who was the investigating officer?"

"Cody Buchanan."

Selah and Frankie exchanged glances.

Selah said, "Spawn of the devil, bless his heart. Cody hates me, my family, and my friends. If brains were dynamite, he wouldn't have enough to blow his nose."

This feistier version of Selah was the best medicine!

"Don't shoot the messenger." Tanner raised his palms. "I trust that guy like I trust Frankie or that dog in your purse to guard my sandwich."

"Ha! That was actually funny," Frankie smiled up at him. "Because I could eat a sandwich lickety-split right now."

Frankie slapped her leg, the smile dropping from her face when she couldn't feel the weight of her hand on her skin.

She shook off the doldrums again. "Hold up. There's a dog in your bag, Selah? Ooh ooh. Did you smuggle in Faith? Lemme see!"

She stretched out her arms and Selah gently set a tiny, wiggling, three-legged Brussels griffon onto her belly. Faith not-so-gently launched herself at Frankie's face, licking every bruise and burn and snuggling in at her neck.

Despite her best efforts, a tear slid down Frankie's cheek. The outpouring of love was pushing at the dam. She quickly rubbed her face against Faith's wiry brown fur. "I mi-missed you guys."

Selah stroked her fingers over Frankie's face where the tear had been. "Life isn't as full without you either. Please don't scare me like this again."

Frankie leaned into her palm. "Where's your Shirtless Wonder?"

Tanner snorted at the nickname Selah had given her hot husband. Frankie had lost count of all the nicknames she'd given Tanner under her breath.

"Cane is keeping that shirt on for the camera these days, or else." Selah reddened. "He had a severe reaction to the new infusion therapy for his MS, so I couldn't leave."

"Oh no! Of course not." Frankie's heart sank again. Cane had been doing so well in his multiple sclerosis treatment and then, bam, this setback. Life had turned on its head for everyone. "How is he?"

"Cane's back on set today in Los Angeles against my wishes," Selah said. "He'll be here next week. As soon as you're ready, he's contacted a football trainer friend to do your at-home physical therapy. He's known him since he played in the NFL."

Maybe Frankie could relax a little now. She had her BFF by her side. She could go home after she finished this intense rehab to a skilled physical therapist. She'd focus one hour at a time.

Selah turned her attention to Cane's twin. "Who did this to Frankie?"

"Once we study the footage and Frankie can piece together what happened, we'll get some answers. Until then, I'm not leaving her alone, even here, when she's exceedingly vulnerable."

Frankie swallowed. Great. She was not only lonely, paralyzed, teary, needy, and weak, but also vulnerable. "Stop with that, McBroody. Go take care of business. I am just fine."

Tanner naturally ignored her.

"This will make you feel even better." Selah plopped insulated bags on a tray table and pulled it across Frankie's lap.

Frankie's eyes nearly fell out of her head when she opened the bags to find an In-N-Out Double-Double Burger and strawberry-stuffed donuts from the Donut Man on Route 66 in California.

Frankie inhaled deeply and sighed. "I love you so much. You're my very best friend."

Tanner said, "Are you talking to Selah or the food?"

"It's a toss-up." Frankie went to work on the fried feast like a beaver on a Redwood.

She moaned at the sweet and savory goodness. Catching a wee grin on Tanner's lips gave her almost as much pleasure as the chow.

"I'll be here until you start your home therapy," Selah

said. "I made sure Cane picked a cute therapist. So, wear makeup and tight leggings, okay? Not that you need either one to be stunning, right Tanner?"

Tanner didn't answer, but his eyes had turned as inky black as the writing on the wall: Tanner felt nothing for her. She would have lost her appetite, but the food was too good.

Selah swiftly turned her interrogation of her brother-in-law back to the subject at hand. "So, you believe it was sabotage too? Any suspects?"

"Kenny Newman has more than a few enemies attempting to take over his territory."

Selah shared a look with Tanner before taking a nibble from a donut and slipping a bite to Faith.

"His *territory*?" Frankie released the burger a moment. "Daddy owns a small casino and a racetrack. He's a business owner on the outskirts of nowhere. What's so cloak and dagger about the sports betting industry?"

Tanner and Selah watched her quietly.

"What's with the look? There's danger in every successful business, but this is outrageous."

She didn't bother with the particulars of what Daddy did. She kept the books in the black and the cars in the running. Just because Selah's father was a gambling addict who lived at the speedway and had dragged his family into financial ruin didn't mean Frankie's father was crooked for running the place.

"My priority is not the business but determining who rigged that car to fail," Tanner said. "Time is of the essence and no one at the track saw anything out of the ordinary, so you'll need to inspect the car and talk to the veteran crew loyal to Newman. Is that incentive to walk out of here?"

Frankie choked on a donut. "Let me get this straight, you're asking for my help?"

"Wasn't asking."

"Ahh, demanding. Makes more sense." She waggled a finger at him. "Admit it though. You *need* me, and it kills you."

Tanner's jaw twitched. "While you ladies catch up, I'm heading out for a meeting with two new, uh, employees. Stay put. Anyone who enters or exits goes through the guard."

"*Now* he leaves," Frankie huffed, shaking a French fry at the closing door. "Instead of admitting that I am valuable to him, he walks away and gives me an order like I'm a child."

"So… Tanner's been by your side since the accident?" Selah kept her voice light.

"If you're digging, you'll find no treasure in that shallow hole." Frankie shrugged. "He's just my bodyguard, unless Daddy fires him over my wreck."

"Tanner is a curious specimen." Selah's eyes narrowed. "For someone who pretends not to care about you, it's interesting how quickly he went from making meatloaf at the diner to maneuvering into Mr. Newman's good graces and yours. Your family needs someone with bodyguard skills and, magically, Tanner appears, ready to serve."

When Frankie's stomach clenched, she pushed her food away. Tanner had rolled into town and steamrolled her life in less than a year, but he still felt like a stranger. His twin had become like a brother to her. "Does Tanner ever talk to you or Cane about his past?"

Selah shook her head. "His Grandma Iris knows, I think, but she'd never betray her darling boy's secrets. People don't close themselves off like Tanner has unless they've been deeply hurt."

"Is Tanner still in that much pain over an accident that happened all those years ago?"

"Trauma and grief don't disappear with time. They take on different forms and we change too for better or worse." Selah's kind eyes met hers.

Had grief changed Tanner for better or for worse? Frankie flashed back to a childhood jump rope game she used to play—Angel/Devil. Kids would stand in a circle with one person swinging the rope. When the rope stopped, you were whatever word, angel or devil, was being spoken. Was Tanner an angel or a devil?

How has it changed you? Frankie startled as the strange question floated through her mind. Losing a mother she couldn't remember hadn't changed her and, as for the wreck, she was just fine, thank you. No faceless coward would leave a permanent black mark on her life.

"Tanner still resents Cane, but I suspect there's something deeper going on," Selah said. "Ask him. See how he reacts. If someone outsmarted you in order to wreck your car and kill you, then you can't trust anyone, including Tanner and your father."

The warning, spoken by a woman who believed the best in everyone, sent chill bumps down Frankie's arms.

"I love my brother-in-law, but I got your back," Selah cringed. "Poor choice of words. What I mean is, we'll stand together against your enemies. Ugh. I'm saying all the wrong things, I'm sorry, but you scared the living daylights out of me. I've missed you and missed out on so much of your life, but I'm here now to help."

As Selah started to panic, Frankie smiled reassuringly. "Don't worry, Selah. There's no sense tiptoeing around or boo-hooing about the mangled state of my legs."

Selah grasped Frankie's free hand. "You can stop now."

"Stop what? Really, I'm not embarrassed by my condition. I am gonna ride that wheelchair like I stole it. 'Cause that's how I roll." Frankie looked up from her food into Selah's violet eyes, brimming with tears. She'd expected her friend to laugh and roll with her.

"You can stop fighting." Selah sighed. "All that warrior strength, positivity, and humor that make you the incredible person you are. Just let Wonder Woman and her stiff upper lip rest a minute."

But if Frankie let go, she'd start feeling. Ain't nobody got time for that!

Frankie held up her hands. "What does worrying and bawling solve? Aww no. Quit trying to make me blubber too."

Selah's tears fell hard as she wrapped Frankie and Faith in a warm, vanilla sugar-scented embrace. Frankie didn't return the hug for a moment, but Selah kept squeezing, impervious to Frankie's force field.

"I just need to race again."

"You will. I have no doubt." Selah gripped her even closer. "I'm scared, but I believe in you, Frankie, and the healing, miracle-working power of God coursing through your body."

Frankie stiffened. Her heavenly Father seemed about as far away as her earthly one did right now. Maybe Daddy was back home moving heaven and earth to find her saboteur. Maybe the hospital reminded him of her mom, so he'd stayed away. Maybe she wasn't as special to either father as she thought she was.

"Rest, you need rest." Selah continued to hug her, rocking now.

Frankie had no use for rest or fuzzy platitudes and touchy-feely dreams of miracles. Hard work would see her through to victory lane. The sooner she started therapy, the better.

Frankie tightened her fists behind Selah's back and grumbled, "What I *need*, Selah, is for you to help me get out of here. I need to figure out what happened on that track. I need a doctor who'll have me on my feet and release me. I need to get on Tanner's nerves as much as possible, so he'll move on to a real damsel in distress and set me free."

The pounding in her head and the volume of her voice accelerated as she blurted, "What I really need is for you and Tanner and the doctors to stop telling me what I need and let me get to work fixing this!"

When Selah pulled back and her dark curls fell away from her stricken face, Frankie instantly regretted her outburst. A realization hit just as suddenly. Selah was the one who needed rest. She'd endured a cross-country flight, her husband's relapsing-remitting multiple sclerosis, and whatever else she wasn't saying, but she'd left all that to bring Frankie her favorites—burgers, donuts, Faith, hugs, and the promise of a hot physical therapist. Frankie had repaid her with a personal attack.

Oh, Frankie had fixed things alright. She was fixin' to trash their nearly twenty-year friendship and the respect of the wide-eyed little girl in the doorway.

CHAPTER ELEVEN

"Setbacks are just caution flags on the drive to victory lane."

–Frankie Newman

TANNER HAD SEEN enough hospitals to last a lifetime, but he couldn't avoid another visit. He hauled Kojak's crate into the Shadybrook Animal Hospital and waved at the blonde receptionist who was on the phone. Kojak let out a heinous howl at the woman.

"This is your first official assignment, partner, don't mess it up," Tanner put the furball on notice as he chose a seat outside the receptionist's line of sight. He set the crate and an envelope on the chair beside him.

Russ Morgan peeked around the door, shuffled in, and threw a few bags of dog food in a donation bin. He stuffed his hands in his pockets, took them out again, looked back at the door, and finally locked eyes with Tanner. Russ had to get his nerves under control before they set Tanner's plan in motion.

"Mr. Ashton, what a surprise. Is that rascal sick?"

"One last checkup and round of shots." Tanner jerked his chin. "Take a load off."

"Glad to see its days of hustling for catfish at Good Company are over." Russ chose the spot beside Kojak. "Should Frankie be left alone by herself? Momma's mad as a hornet that you kicked her out of the hospital."

It was a question Tanner had asked himself fifty times already. "I've got guards round the clock and Selah's with her at the rehab center."

"Selah's home?" Russ' mouth lifted in a smile, then sank just as quickly. "Guess she'd want to visit her friends before her old man."

Tanner felt a familiar tug for his old man. Maybe Russ would figure things out before it was too late. Helping Tanner was a step in the right direction, although Russ probably hoped that nailing Newman would cancel his debts.

Tanner picked up the large envelope from the chair and set it on top of Kojak's cage. "You remember what we discussed. Turn on the phone and lay it on the table between you. The roving bug will do the rest. I've got some hidden cameras as well."

Russ opened the envelope, slipped the phone into the pocket of his overalls, and stared hard at the smaller envelope of money.

"Keep your money or give Momma an extra-large tip when you're in Good Company." Russ' voice dropped to a growl. "You don't have to pay me to bring down Kenny Newman. If he's a threat to my wife and daughters, it's over."

"Understood." Tanner nodded, grateful that Russ considered Frankie one of his own.

"Just don't implicate me when you finally get your revenge."

"It won't touch you." Tanner said. "You gave me a job in the diner when I first hit town, and I won't forget it."

Russ' bloodshot eyes followed the envelope of cash as Tanner stuffed it in his jacket pocket.

Tanner couldn't leave since Kojak had an appointment, but something prodded him to repay Russ in another way. "You know, Mr. Morgan, regardless of what happens to Newman, there will always be another debt collector or loan shark knocking at your door. Don't you get tired of your gambling losses hanging over your head? Your daughter moved across the country to get away from her life here. Your wife seems miserable."

"Are you anglin' to be one of them fancy life coaches?" Russ wrung his hands and then plunked them on his knees. "After I hit it big, we'll be sitting pretty. Won't have to answer to nobody."

"Right." When Kojak growled, Tanner looked up. An elderly couple was bringing in a collie on a leash. It sniffed at the cat and turned tail toward the other side of the room. "So, gambling it is then."

"You ain't my son-in-law, so you don't give me advice." Selah's father sat back, legs spread, arms crossed at the chest.

"Your son-in-law has cleaned up his act for that girl of yours and is the happiest I've ever seen him." Tanner surprised himself by defending his brother. "I never wanted a family after our parents died, but Selah is like my little sister. Tells it like it is, but with love, you know?"

Russ grunted, scowling down at the crate when Kojak

poked a paw through the top. If Russ wasn't listening to Tanner's advice, he'd have left by now.

"You can see that Selah's heart's been broken, because she tries to fix everybody else's—her mother's, Frankie's, even mine. Seems to me like a father might not want to be the one who continues to break that heart."

Russ leaned forward, avoiding Tanner's eyes and stroking Kojak's paw with his index finger. The tattered dress shirt under his overalls strained against the pressure of his gut. His face was drawn as he swiped an arthritic hand across his eyes.

This might have been Tanner's finest Barbara Walters make-em-cry moment if the door hinge hadn't cracked.

A vet tech waved at Tanner and made a kissy face at the cat. "We're ready for you, Kojak."

"Looks more like a cue ball to me," Russ muttered, his mind ever on the game.

Russ would do right when the time was right. It had taken Cane 17 years to turn himself around and the jury was still out on that one.

"Time to get your act together, Mr. Morgan." Tanner jumped to attention. "I'll text that phone when everything is in place. I expect an Oscar-winning performance."

"Says the hoodlum dressed like a cat burglar and holding a bald Franken-cat."

Tanner snorted, glanced down at his black jeans and t-shirt, and slung his black leather jacket over his shoulder. Frankie had given him a hard time about the look as well.

The cat blinked up at him and rubbed her face against the crate.

At least somebody appreciated him.

~

"Angel!"

The kid she'd met in the infield zoomed out from her mother's grasp and into Frankie's room. The new security guard shut the door behind them.

Selah wiped her eyes before pasting on a smile and turning away from Frankie to welcome their visitors.

Angel rolled up to Frankie's bedside. "Why were you yelling and why aren't you walking yet?"

"I ask myself that same question." She was happy to see Selah and the kid, but she kind of hoped the physical therapist would drop by early and they could get started today. "This is my best friend. Selah, this is Angel, race car driver in training, and her mother.

"I'm Janet," Angel's mother nodded at Selah and Frankie. "I am so sorry for barging in. She has been begging to come see you after that awful wreck. Tanner called to let us know you were okay. I hope you don't mind."

Always thinking of everybody else, that Tanner.

"Best surprise I could have asked for." Frankie leaned over and gave Angel a fist bump. "I'm sorry you had to witness me crash. I planned on winning the race for you."

"Super scary, but I knew you'd be okay. I told Mom I had to come check on my roll model," the girl tittered, causing Frankie to crack up. "First rule of wheelchair club: laugh."

The kid had the kind of positive energy Frankie craved. Not the "take-it-slow, be vulnerable, rest yourself" vibe she was hearing from everyone else.

Angel's eyes roamed the room and Frankie's bed and landed on the bag of donuts.

Selah noticed too and handed the bag to Angel, "Help yourself, but it comes with a dog."

Faith bounced off of Selah's lap and onto Angel's.

"Mo-om! A three-legged dog! We need a dog." Angel kissed all over Faith and got it right back.

"Maybe," Janet rolled her eyes. "Only one donut, please, ma'am."

Angel and Frankie returned the eye roll.

Selah stood and patted Janet's arm. "Why don't we check out the facility while the girls catch up? They need a break from mothering."

When Selah's voice caught, Frankie couldn't take it anymore. "Selah, wait. I always need you. I'm sorry."

"No, *I'm* sorry. You almost died, Frankie, it's okay."

The hurt that lingered in Selah's tired eyes said she wasn't okay.

"Being paralyzed isn't a free pass to act like a jerk," Angel said, munching on a donut.

That cut straight to the heart.

"Angel!" Janet gasped.

"Don't punish her for speaking truth," Frankie said, motioning for Angel to pull her chair closer. "Angel obviously has this disability thing figured out and I am—"

"Differently abled," Angel interjected.

"Differently abled," Frankie repeated. The words felt foreign on her tongue. "See. I have much to learn, sensei."

Selah sighed. "We all do."

"Just be cool." Angel swallowed the last bite of donut, let Faith lick her fingers, and clapped her hands together. "If one way doesn't work, find a better way."

"That's all well and good in theory, but what if I…"

Frankie couldn't voice the possibility that she'd never race again.

"What if you learn to fly?" Angel took Faith soaring through the air and back to her lap again. "You aren't wheelchair bound. It's not a cage. Make it your magic carpet."

Frankie recoiled at the well-meaning platitude from a little girl who claimed to understand her obsession with the track. Angel was staring at her now, eyebrows lifted, waiting for her to embrace the magic. Surely, she didn't expect Frankie to abandon her dreams, living her "best life" in that chair. She'd accept nothing less than running and racing competitively again, fully abled. There was no other way, was there?

CHAPTER TWELVE

Everywhere Your Eyes Go, the Car Will Follow

"If you would slow down, I'll show you some tricks to using the slider to transfer yourself."

When Frankie's new therapist raised his voice to her, Tanner ended the voicemail he was leaving Kenny Newman and spun around.

"I will never slow down, Mark." Frankie waved off the slick, rectangular contraption he was holding out. "Catch up. Are you even a real therapist? I'm strong enough to move myself."

Tanner should know Frankie had it under control. Frankie successfully pushed herself up out of the wheelchair and onto a chair with a loud grunt.

Dear Daddy should be here to see this. He never responded to Tanner's texts that Frankie was starting a PT session. Newman had put his money and connections to work in getting her into a state-of-the-art rehab facility, building this gym in an old conference room at the Speedway's main building, and securing her a spot in an upcoming clinical trial for electronic stimulation of her limbs. Guess Daddy thought he'd done his duty and was too busy to give her what she really needed—a warm welcome home.

"I read that, loud and clear," Mark chucked her on the chin before stepping back and checking her alignment. "Your level of fitness is impressive, but you need to pace yourself."

"You noticed my muscles, did you?" Frankie waggled her brows.

Mark shook his head but squeezed her bicep. Tanner restrained himself. Entirely too much physical contact between these two.

The sooner this lovefest was over, the sooner she could dissect the remains of her car—that's where the answers were buried. Helplessness niggled at Tanner as he paced the gym floor. He'd failed to find anyone in the Newman circle willing to discuss the wreck or spot a single red flag in the video footage.

"You're quite a fighter, Frankie Newman," Mark said. "A lesser woman would not have come so far so quickly in her recovery."

Tanner gagged as Frankie smiled up at the pretty boy PT with his baby face, unbuttoned logo Polo shirt, and khaki shorts. She kept the smile for most of the next hour, even as he put her legs and arms through so many repetitive motions, Tanner grew tired and bored of watching this guy put the moves on her.

She'd nearly fallen out of her chair and instantly fallen in love when the therapist introduced himself as Mark Martin, the namesake of a racing legend. He could strangle Cane for sending this distraction. Her job was to focus on recovering and helping him find the person who tried to murder her. It was bad enough when she'd been dating online.

"Have you ever dated a patient?" Frankie's words were bold but she was blushing.

Mark, who had knelt in front of her, looked up suddenly and didn't speak for a moment. "I haven't dated a patient before."

Well, that certainly left the door wide open, didn't it? Instead of laying down a solid "No, such a relationship would be inappropriate," Mark stroked Frankie's foot and slipped on her tennis shoes like he was Prince Charming in waiting. Waiting to cross that line.

Tanner would be waiting too for the opportunity to get rid of Mark Martin.

"That's it for today, Supergirl," Mark cooed.

"Please, call me Wonder Woman, and I have plenty of energy left." The flirty twinkle in her blue eyes morphed into a glint. She swiped a towel over the sweat dripping from her arms and face. "Two hours more, three hours, morning, noon, and night if that's what it takes."

She'd said the same thing to the crew at the rehab center. When they'd pried her off the parallel bars, she'd wrap her hands around the rails on her bed and pull herself up morning and night for weeks, fighting for every inch of progress. When Selah fussed, Frankie had sent her home to Cane.

"Muscles require rest to repair themselves. In your off time, visualize the muscles and ligaments in your legs activating, walking, and running." Mark stepped back and studied her as she reached for hand weights and began overhead presses, despite his call to stop. "I see you're going to be one of *those* patients."

Frankie lowered the hand weights and shoulder shrugged at him.

Mark turned toward Tanner with a grin. "She always this hardcore?"

Tanner nodded curtly but had a feeling that Frankie would have a gooey heart and arms wide open for the man who finally got close to her. That man would not be this dumbbell if Tanner had any say in it.

"Since you're such a go-getter, let's start pool therapy sooner rather than later," Mark suggested.

That was actually a good idea, Mark Martin.

"No!" Frankie paled. Setting the weights down, she gripped the wheels of the chair, ready to split.

"Why not? The water will be easier on your body but still give you an intense workout and greater flexibility."

"I said no. No water. No pool." Her eyes flashed. She jerked the chair around, forcing Mark to step back. "You fix me right here or I find somebody else who is capable."

Tanner watched her closely. So, water was Frankie Newman's kryptonite. He could use it to tear down her walls. He just needed to learn the backstory.

"I don't understand. If you can't swim, we'll get a belt to assist you." Mark looked to Tanner for back-up. "Water is an incredible healer."

Frankie snorted, keeping her back to them both as she headed for the door.

"Frankie, let's talk about this." Mark caught up to her, slowing the wheelchair and leaning in from behind.

She lurched forward again. "As I told Dr. Pepper, if you're not on my team, then get out of the way."

If Tanner didn't know better, he'd say smoke came out of those tires as Frankie peeled out the door and down the sidewalk.

This was a side he'd never seen—a woman running from something and not to it. Strange that water would be the thing to put fear in Frankie Newman. If she couldn't swim, she'd find a way. She'd take a class or read a book and teach herself. Tanner had to admit that he was the same way. When he met a challenge, his curiosity and hard head wouldn't let him rest until he'd overpowered, overcome, and mastered it. Protecting her was the challenge to beat all challenges.

"Maybe she'll listen to you," Mark said. "Water therapy is a game-changer. Help me out, man."

Tanner barked out a laugh. "That's why they pay you the big bucks, Marky Mark. Good luck."

"I'm not getting good vibrations from you, Tanner," Mark retorted as Tanner shut the door behind him.

Idiot. Something about the familiar way Mark stretched out Tanner's name rankled Tanner more than it should have.

First things first, Tanner scanned the premises for Speedy Newman. Tanner was pretty sure he knew the destination. *Three guesses and the first two don't count.* His father's voice echoed. Funny how, when he was young, his parents' goofy sayings, words of wisdom, and teaching moments got on his last nerve with the constant repetition. Now, they returned at just the right moment with the impact of a football to the chest.

Frankie had indeed retreated to her happy place—the

barn where her "babies" slept, as she described it. He found her inside, slowly circling the wreckage of her stock car. One lap. Two laps. Three laps. On the fourth lap, she stopped at what was left of the cage. Reaching in, she caressed the steering wheel.

"I see your gears turning."

Frankie didn't look up. "If you're here to kill me, get in line. If you're Tanner Ashton, don't say a word. I don't want to hear it."

"A word about what?"

"Water therapy," she turned to face him and air-quoted "therapy."

"Not my business." However, he would make it his business. "Maybe you could use another kind of therapy."

He swirled his index finger around his temple.

"Did you actually make another joke?" she grinned. "What is the world coming to? You called me crazy though, so all humor points have been deducted."

"Figures," Tannner said, making sure not to smile. "The car jog your memory?"

"Working on it. Now, if I could have a little peace and quiet."

"I'm leaving you alone for three hours. Do not move from this location. Do not open the door until I return."

It was like telling her not to go near the cookie jar, but he had no choice. He'd installed exterior cameras everywhere, places she didn't even know about. Nothing creepy, but enough to alert him to trouble.

"Don't you trust me by now?" Frankie's eyes pierced him.

Could Tanner trust her knowing what her father had done? Knowing what she may have played a part in?

When he didn't respond, her face fell. Turning her attention to the car, she said, "Maybe by the time you come back, this girl will show me what happened that night. The answer is staring me in the face."

"If you leave this barn before I return, you have to babysit Kojak for a month."

"Shoot, I was planning to jump in the car or take a stroll down Main Street. Oopsie. I don't have working legs to go anywhere. I guess you win." Frankie began to tap a wrench on the mangled door frame, shutting him out with the noise.

She didn't even take the softball he'd lobbed and insult his cat. The water therapy discussion had rattled her.

"At least you haven't lost your sunny disposition." He locked the door behind him.

Tanner slid into the Escalade and headed out. He and Mario had stalked the Newmans on the Internet, her clean hard drive, and the Dark Web until he felt like he was a member of the family. Today, he'd dig a little deeper. He was going old school to find the missing link—the county library.

"Speak to me, baby. What am I not seeing?" Frankie rolled back from the car and over to the table displaying the accident model she'd constructed during rehab. Nothing registered. The last thing she remembered that night was feeling the car wobble as she turned a corner. It was like she'd fallen asleep at the wheel and awakened paralyzed.

She tapped the wrench on her thighs, visualizing the

muscles spasming and lengthening. Once again, nothing. She did notice a new stack of papers on her desk.

Lifting the top sheet, she read the title of a scholarly medical article, *Using Electrical Stimulation and Acupuncture to Restore Functional Use in Paralysis.*

Hmm. Mark must have sent it to her. Her phone dinged. A message from Thomas on an obscure dating app she'd forgotten to delete. She also had another DM from Kyle on Instagram. Both men were in their thirties and appeared sane. Was that possible? No weird bathroom pix or serial killer eyes. Well, it couldn't hurt to look.

She chatted back and forth for an hour with Thomas from the app. Miracle of miracles he didn't ask for nude photos. But she did send him a pic of herself in the new wheels.

Thomas: Ur in a wheelchair?

The butterflies in her stomach died. **That bother u?**

Thomas: Nah, I dig all kinds of girlz. Skinny, fat, ugly. Everybody got something to offer.

Um. Okay. Not sure how to feel about that answer, but it would do for now. Guys weren't exactly beating down her door and she needed a pleasurable distraction.

Let's do dinner and drinks, babe.

A date! Frankie had an actual date. Maybe she'd been too hasty in deciding all men were scum. Maybe God did care and was answering prayers.

The second prospect was Kyle, aka LovePotion#9. His older sister had a progressive supranuclear palsy, so he understood physical challenges. He was a Christian seeking a woman of substance to marry, worked as a financial advisor, and loved his family, his dog, and NASCAR. What more could she ask for?

Frankie set up a date the night after her date with Thomas. She sighed, imagining handholding, cuddling around a campfire, and sitting on the bleachers at the track watching fireworks.

Kyle: You're 2 good 2 b tru, Frankie.

So was Kyle, but Frankie's heart did a little dance.

Kyle: What r u wearing?

A familiar unease skimmed her arms like goosebumps.

Frankie: Shorts and a t-shirt.

Kyle: Underneath?

Frankie swallowed hard before answering: **Bra and panties.**

Kyle: Mmm. Prove it.

Frankie: Not sending naked pix. My body isn't going viral.

Kyle: Ha! UR so sexy you'd break the Internet. Just teasy pix. Show me ur who u say.

Who am I? She was Wonder Woman. At least she used to be before the wreck. Frankie looked down at her lifeless legs and across the room at her burned-out car. Selah was back in Los Angeles and her father was too busy for her.

Frankie: I'm honest as a girl scout.

Frankie had dropped out of Brownie Girl Scouts when she found out there'd be no actual brownies at the meetings.

Kyle: Ur all woman. Sweet, sassy, smart. There's a V-8 engine running hot beneath the surface.

Well, that was true enough. What could it hurt? Just something sexy. She wouldn't be nude.

How long could she be expected to be deprived of

pleasure? She hadn't slept with anyone. She tried to be good, but she wasn't a saint like Selah. She and Kyle were both unmarried, consenting adults, and she was only human.

The feeling in the pit of her stomach didn't feel pleasurable. She shook off the nerves and rolled to the door to check the lock. Could she drag a piece of furniture in front of it to keep Tanner out?

She transferred herself from her wheels to a stationary chair, hoping the sweat that it worked up looked hot on camera. Loosening a few buttons, she shrugged the blouse off her shoulder and used her hands to lift her legs onto the desk. She waited a moment for the sickening, stabbing pain in her back to subside. How was it possible to hurt so badly when you were paralyzed?

She didn't dare take her shoes off. This morning when she'd dressed, one shoe kept falling off her foot before she could pull it on, which meant a twenty-minute fishing expedition to retrieve it.

Frankie lifted her cell phone to snap some photos, careful not to show her face. The results weren't bad. Her body was soft, but muscular and toned. Maybe even beautiful.

The phone dinged again.

Kyle: Baby, please. I need to see u. Can't believe I found someone incredible like u on here.

Frankie smiled. Maybe he was "The One." *I am hurt. I am exhausted. I need this. I deserve pleasure. Why should everyone else get to have all the fun while I'm here suffering?*

She clicked send and there it went. No harm in showing a little skin.

Kyle: Wow! (googly eyes and heart emojis) UR the hottest woman I've ever seen. I want to touch u right now.

Oh my. The cold dread trickling through her veins dissipated. He wanted her. Somebody wanted her. No man had ever loved her except Daddy in his own way. He wasn't one to hug or engage in conversations, but he would give her anything and that was something.

Stop being so needy. When had she become the crying, wilting, singing Disney princess waiting in the castle tower for her prince to come—the damsel in distress she'd railed against?

Kyle: I want u to take more photos. You'll feel as amazing as you look.

Maybe she would. Maybe this paralysis wasn't the end of the world.

A knock on the door threw cold water on the fire that had overtaken her. She managed to close three of six buttons before the temp guard announced Mark's arrival. Frankie nodded, smiling as Mark peeked around the door.

She teased, "Go away, unless you're delivering those new legs I ordered."

"It'd be a shame to replace legs like yours."

Frankie smoothed her shorts and hair. "So, why are you standing there instead of coming in?"

"Keeping an eye out for the babysitter and his big gun."

Interesting that Mark noticed what she rarely did. Tanner kept it very well hidden, just like his emotions.

She snorted. "He'll be along soon."

Mark's face tightened as he ran his hand through a wave of sandy hair.

"Your place is cool though," he said, checking out the bay and the beater Mustang she was restoring to its former glory.

When he bent to grab a rolling stool, his Abercrombie polo shifted, revealing a small back tattoo of a Christmas bell. She hadn't seen tattoos on Tanner. *Focus on the man in front of you, not the dead-end.*

"The barn belongs to my cars but they let me stay here sometimes. What brings you by? Not that I'm complaining." Frankie smiled when Mark did.

Her hottie therapist plopped down on the stool, straightened his shirt, and scooched up beside her. "I wanted to apologize for pushing you in therapy and to see how you're feeling."

"I'm feeling great. All is forgotten." The soreness was unrelenting, but she'd never let him know that.

They chatted a while. Mark promised to teach her swing dance if she showed him how to line dance. He'd lost his mother as a child too and it had colored everything in his life. Frankie's only color seemed to be blue these days, but things were looking rosy tonight with the prospect of three nice guys who actually liked and respected her.

Preppy Mark was completely different than what she'd have picked for herself: he didn't own a TV or follow superheroes and knew nothing of NASCAR, despite his name. Unfathomable.

"How's the dating going?" he asked.

Had she mentioned that to him? Mark edged a little closer.

"There was one guy who stood me up."

Mark's eyebrow quirked. "Does that mean you had an awful night or a night of miracles?"

They laughed easily together.

"Definitely not my miracle, unfortunately." She waved

her hands over her unmoving legs. "As you can see, I'm still in the penalty box."

He took her hand and squeezed, unleashing a swarm of butterflies to perform figure eights and dive bombs in her stomach.

"You know, Frankie, as much as I want you to walk again, you will adjust in time. Many people live incredible, fulfilling lives from their chairs." Mark waved his hand through the air like Buzz Lightyear beckoning Woody to infinity and beyond. "Don't give up your dreams and your hard work, but, if you have tunnel vision, you may miss the opportunities this season of life offers."

What if you learn to fly? Maybe Angel's words of wisdom should be her new battle cry.

"I'm beginning to realize that," she nodded.

"Selfishly, I'm glad you still need me."

"Oh?"

"You're my favorite client."

"Your only client."

"Ha! True for now. Still the most beautiful inside and out." Mark smiled, rubbing her leg with his free hand.

"I knew it! You took one look at my muscles and fell for me."

She stilled as he gazed into her eyes. If she breathed or moved, he'd spook and run away.

"As your therapist, I shouldn't be here like this with you, but I can't seem to make myself leave you." He leaned in. "It won't be long before you can do the exercises on your own without me or with another therapist. Once you start water therapy, I can take other job offers."

She ignored the water therapy bit and tried to process

what he was saying. "So, if you're not my physical therapist, we can date?"

He grinned, running his thumb down her chin.

"That settles it. You're fired," she whispered.

"I'll take that pink slip," he said, looking so doggone cute. "But are you willing to risk your father and Tanner putting a hit out on me?"

A loud bang nearly sent her out of the chair and onto the floor.

Mark whirled around, throwing off his hand and her high hopes. "Speak of the devil."

Tanner stood in the doorway with the sun aflame at his back, like Samson ready to give the doorframe a shove and send the whole place down on Mark's head.

She fidgeted with her buttons as Tanner's eyes—heat-seeking missiles—roamed the room. Frankie was doomed.

"I wasn't aware you had a scheduled appointment with your *licensed* physical therapist."

The words were directed at Mark, but the look of sheer disappointment was unmistakably for her. Was it too much to hope that he'd be jealous? Leave it to Tanner to ruin her moment when she'd been thisclose to having an actual kiss.

"Ah, *Tanner Ashton*, what would we ever do without your loyal and trustworthy bodyguard services?" Mark winked at Frankie, but the sarcasm toward Tanner left her unsettled.

"No need to throw down, boys. I'm fixing to get ready for a date tonight, and y'all are not invited."

CHAPTER THIRTEEN

"Good cars get you from point A to B. Great cars get you in trouble."

–Unknown

"I CAN'T DECIDE if I'm impressed or weirded out that your bodyguard came on the date with us." Thomas pushed her wheelchair under their table and smoothed the red-and-white checkered tablecloth.

Tanner, to his credit, kept a respectable distance at a nearby table, but positioned himself so he faced them. He had insisted that the restaurant be at least thirty miles out of town and small enough so he could monitor comings and goings.

When she told him about the date, he simply asked for Thomas' photo, address, and number, saying, "You deserve better."

"Someone like you, I suppose?"

"You deserve better than me."

Tanner's dark eyes weren't the usual swirling black holes, but they penetrated her soul. Why should she feel guilty?

She hadn't betrayed him, really, she just hadn't obeyed him when his demands were unreasonable.

There was a world of thought behind those dark eyes. But Frankie'd never get close enough to be a part of that world. She swallowed a queasy feeling down with her Mountain Dew.

So… moving on to Thomas.

Bachelor number one was cute enough in his flip-flops, strategically-ripped skinny jeans, Khaki blonde hair, and blue eyes that made him seem younger than thirty. She was only a few years older but fought an overwhelming urge to tell him to keep his napkin in his lap and stop calling her bae, babe, hottie, and yo.

When his spaghetti came, Thomas dug in before Frankie's fettucine hit the table. Couldn't fault him for that though. She'd already plowed through half the garlic knots and two Mountain Dews.

"So, Thomas, you work at a nursing home? That must be rewarding."

"Nah, hot stuff. Old people are nasty, but it pays the bills until I can produce music full-time. We'll talk about the boring junk later." He twirled his spaghetti on his fork and waved it in the air, making choo-choo noises as it chugged a path toward her mouth. "You gonna eat tho?"

"Oh, um—" Frankie tried not to choke as he crammed the forkful in her mouth. She chewed quickly. "Sweet, thanks."

He grinned, queued up more spaghetti on his fork and made the same noisy choo-chooing track toward her mouth. He repeated the sequence in time to the lively song "Funiculì, Funiculà" playing in the background.

"Mmm. So good, dude," Thomas said.

What just happened? Was he for real feeding her like a baby or had Momma's reality show followed her for a candid on-camera practical joke?

Nope, Thomas cued up the train and fed her again. Were they were actually doing this?

When he set down the fork a moment, she rolled back from the table a foot and said, "Thomas, why ever are you single?"

She didn't have to look at Tanner to hear him thinking, "I told you so."

When her date ignored her question and came at her with a bite-sized piece of garlic knot, she blurted, "I have to use the restroom."

"Go ahead, boo. I'll be waiting to feed your face." His lopsided grin would have been quite endearing on someone else. She'd rate Thomas three stars on Yelp: Not a bad dude, but slightly off the rails, er, the railway.

She tried a different tack. "*Bae*, since you've been so helpful in feeding me, I hoped you would help me with the restroom. I can't get out of the chair and take care of myself."

She hated the little white lie, but it was for his own good. God had a sense of humor, right?

The train screeched to a halt as his wide blue eyes met hers. "You need me to help you go to the bathroom? Can't the bodyguard handle it?"

"He has to guard the door. You're a standup dude to help me with this. You must do it all the time in the nursing home."

Suddenly, Thomas grabbed his phone from beside his plate. Without looking at the screen, he said, "Sorry, I gotta take this. A patient has an emergency."

"Of course. You're a hero, Thomas." She smiled at him as if he was her light in the tunnel.

Thomas bolted from the table like a high-speed locomotive. Emphasis on loco.

Tanner was already at her side, the corner of his mouth turned up. "Thomas the Tank Engine coming back?"

Naturally, he'd seen and heard all.

"That train has left the station." She sighed and dropped her head in her hands.

The woman certainly could think fast. She'd derailed Thomas in under a half hour. If only Tanner had come up with brilliant excuses like that when he'd been on bad dates years ago. End it quickly and nobody gets hurt. After Danielle, he swore never to play the love game again. He always kept his promises, unlike Frankie who had already broken her vow to stay away from online dating for a month.

He steeled himself for hours of mind-numbing tedium as she embarked on a date with a second online loser in the same Italian restaurant the next day. The location was moderately secure. Frankie was the wildcard.

"Chill. I can take care of myself. I don't need you," she'd reminded Tanner.

He wasn't about to let anything or anyone harm her again, including Kyle Gordon, age 39, financial consultant, Rhodes Scholar, elder in the Henderson Baptist Church. Men who appeared shiny and squeaky clean were often rotten at the core.

Jealous? Tanner pushed the thought aside as he took his place at a table adjacent to the happy couple's. His mission was to protect the warrior princess, impress the king, bring down the kingdom, and never look back. The end.

❧

Kyle was going to be Frankie's happy ending. She just knew it. Tanner only thought he knew better. She cupped her hand beside her eye to block her bodyguard's grump and glare.

Her date, on the other hand… wowza! She could gaze at that smile forever. The man wore a business casual suit, but there was nothing casual about him. His eyes twinkled and his light brown hair greyed at the temples. He smelled like a candy shop—slightly sweet with all kinds of flavors and surprises. She'd seen pheromones and other musky men's fragrances online. Why did men waste money on that junk when all they had to do to attract women was dab Nutella behind the ears?

"Frankie, you are the most attractive woman I've ever met, honestly." Kyle's voice sounded even more masculine with Dean Martin as a backup and "That's Amore" playing in the background. "A talented driver and smart-as a-whip accountant. How did I get so lucky?"

What was behind his twinkly eyes? Could she trust him with her heart? Maybe she was overthinking.

When he reached for her hand across the table and brought it to his lips a moment, she dropped her head so he wouldn't notice the color in her cheeks. *You're not a 16-year-old girl. You can handle the heat.*

"I'm looking for a woman of substance, not friends with benefits. I could see myself falling in love with you."

Speaking of heat, he was coming in strong on the first

date. *Put a sock in it. He's perfect.* Perfect teeth. Perfectly warm hands. Perfect ability to express his feelings comfortably, unlike some other people.

She glanced at Tanner, who sat perfectly still, except for the pulsing jaw. She could see herself falling for someone like him. *Like Kyle, you mean.*

Her date leaned in, forcing her to crane her neck. The fatigued muscles in her upper body cried for mercy. Never in her own training had she experienced the kind of soreness that physical therapy induced.

"I want to see more of you, make you feel as beautiful as you are."

"Can't argue with that," her voice dropped to a husky whisper she'd never heard before and kind of liked. She'd waited so long to set free this part of her.

"If I distract your goon, shall we make a break for it?"

An adventure! Tanner wasn't a goon, but she would love to leave his frowny face behind for a few minutes while she got to know Kyle in peace. "The bathrooms are behind me, to my right. There's also a back exit past that. You handle the distraction and follow me in three minutes."

"How did you know all that?" Kyle marveled.

"I make it a point to memorize the location of the start and finish lines and the pit at every track."

Then why are you leaving this safe place for who knows where with a man you've only known for an hour?

"I'm utterly enchanted by you, Miss Newman." Kyle flashed a smile that brought out the light in his eyes and a Matthew McConaughey dimple.

That's why.

Frankie turned the chair and nearly wheelied toward

the bathroom. Out of the corner of her eye, she saw Kyle handing the waiter something. By the time she reached the exit, Kyle was right behind her, panting and grinning.

She hadn't had this much fun in months. At least since Selah's wedding last Thanksgiving when she and Tanner posed as Selah and Cane to help the newlyweds escape the paparazzi.

She gasped as Kyle picked her up and headed for the parking lot, leaving the wheelchair behind.

"I kind of need that." Frankie looked back at her wheels. "Where are we going?"

"Trust me, sweetheart."

After Kyle secured Frankie in the passenger seat of his BMW 330i, he slid into the driver's seat and gunned it. A thrill shot through her, along with a double shot of fear. It felt like race day, except she wasn't driving and she had no idea what she was doing or where she'd end up.

What if he's an axe murderer? What if he did something to Tanner?

"How did you shake my bodyguard?"

"Paid the waiter to spill a tray on him, which bought me some time to follow you."

Acid splashed in her stomach and it wasn't from the garlic knots. She'd liked that shirt on Tanner. Well, it looked like all his other black t-shirts, but it would be a shame to stain something that fit him just right.

Frankie pulled down the visor. No headlights following on this backroad. She sighed. They'd lost him.

But what if he can't find you?

They drove another ten miles before Kyle pulled into a gated high-rise that was impressive yet vaguely disappointing. Had she expected a mountain chateau? A walk by a sparkling lake? A fun round of roller skating? Actually, yes, was that too much to hope for?

"You brought me back to your place?"

"No better place to be, sexy." He reached over and unbuckled her seatbelt.

"I thought we were just going for a joyride in this spectacular car."

"How boring is that?"

Did he know her at all? Before she could catch her breath and get her head on straight to ask him, she was in his arms and inside his apartment. The last guy—the only guy—she'd nearly kissed had gone AWOL the day after. It had taken some time to get over the complex he'd given her about her allure. She must have been doing something right this time, though, because Kyle carried her directly into his bedroom.

Frankie still didn't get her first kiss, because Kyle moved straight to kissing her neck and collar bone. Her head hit something soft. His pillow! His bed! The tiny alarm bells in her head morphed into a tornado siren.

She tried to mirror his moves, but they weren't going anywhere she wanted as he danced to his own aggressive beat. She was turned on with curiosity, but shouldn't she be in love when she was in a man's arms like this? She didn't even know if she was in "like."

There'd been no kisses on the cheek, hair stroking, long conversations about things that really mattered in life. He'd shifted from neutral to fifth gear. Body parts grinding, searching for connection, but finding only emptiness.

"Kyle, mmm." When he didn't answer, she said more firmly, "Kyle, stop."

"So good, sweetheart." His body pressed her into the bed.

What happened to the man seeking a woman of substance and not a friend with benefits? The elder in the church?

"We can't do this." She tried to get a breath. When he kept going, she said, "We can't have sex."

Why did she have to say it out loud? He should know.

He continued to squeeze her like he was testing out fresh produce. "Those other guys online only want you out of pity or curiosity, but I like you for you."

That remark stung enough to jolt her out of this hormonal haze. He peeled his shirt off, revealing a bicep tattoo of a clown figure. The image clashed with his clean-cut persona.

"Let's keep our clothes on," she dragged in another breath. "Kyle, don't. I mean it."

Kyle was oblivious and apparently hard of hearing because his hands dove underneath her blouse and had it off before she could protest.

"Thank heaven for zippers," he groaned.

"Stop!" She tried to push him off but he was too heavy and fast. She needed to get out of here. *Please hurry, Tanner.*

He leaned back on his knees and pulled open the front clasp of her bra. She froze. He froze too, as his eyes roamed her nakedness.

He was silent as his breathing slowed.

"What?" She demanded. Her fear began to fade as confusion and irritation set in. If he was going to tear her bra off without permission, why wasn't he touching or kissing her?

She looked down, remembering the deep cuts and

burns she'd suffered in the wreck. She was in her thirties now and had the stripes to show for it—biopsy scars, stretch marks, and apparently a body that wasn't up to his standards. The heat of passion inside Frankie turned to hellfire and brimstone.

"It's a push-up." He sneered. "Things aren't always what they seem online."

When he raised up to shut the clasp, Frankie saw the opportunity to escape. "Well, *sweetheart*, did my online profile mention that I dabble in martial arts?"

CHAPTER FOURTEEN

“Girls that like fast cars and racing aren’t weird. They are a rare gift from God.”

—Unknown

TANNER LET OUT the breath he’d been holding and nodded heavenward. Frankie was alive and dragging herself by the elbows down the hallway of Kyle’s apartment complex.

When Frankie’s eyes met Tanner’s, she collapsed. “I knew you’d come for me.”

“I will *always* find you.” He holstered his weapon and helped her sit up against the wall.

Her face was drawn in a defeat he’d never seen, even when she’d lost her ability to walk. It sent a chill straight through the dark place where his heart had been.

“Is he still in there? Speak, Frankie, before I—” Tanner took a breath and lowered his voice. “Did he hurt you? Do I need to call the police? An ambulance? Selah?”

“No. Let’s just go.”

“I have to be blunt, Frankie,” Tanner swallowed, “did he rape you?”

Frankie hesitated a moment too long, then shook her head. "No harm done, physical that is. I had enough of his games and dragged myself out. He's still in there, licking his wounds, I guess."

He marveled at the strength of her will and her arms. Something more went on than she was saying, but Tanner'd leave it until she was ready to talk.

"Do you want me to shoot him?" He'd be doing the world a service.

Frankie somberly studied his face. "I took care of it."

"I figured as much, Wonder Woman."

A smile lit in her blue eyes, the color of a reef he'd seen on a job in Belize. "Let's just say that, tonight, Kyle gained a clearer understanding of what it feels like to be immobilized from the waist down."

"May I lift you up?" Tanner asked.

When she nodded, he scooped her up in his arms.

"Can you believe he left my chair and gear behind?"

Frankie rested her head on his shoulder, sending a ripple of warmth through skin already hot with rage. If Frankie hadn't finished off Kyle, Tanner would.

When he finally strapped her into the Escalade and started for home, the gravity of what just transpired settled thick in the air. Tanner had so many questions and needed to say his peace, but she probably wanted time to regroup, so they rode in silence until they rolled up to the main house.

Tanner put it in park, but he couldn't stop the scenarios spinning in his head. "Do not ever pull something like that again. He could have murdered you. He could have..."

"He didn't," she cut him off. "I am sorry for scaring you,

but it all happened so fast. I just wanted to have adventure and pleasure for once. I don't drown my sorrows in booze or drugs and I can't exercise all day or Mark will yell at me. Perhaps fun is a foreign concept to you."

"Is this what fun looks like?"

She paled. Seemed like every day, Frankie lost a little more of her spark, even as she regained her muscular strength.

"Good talk. Well, goodnight." She rummaged around in her purse, reached into the glove compartment and shut it again, then ran her hand down the sides of her seat.

Tanner kept one hand on the wheel while he fished her phone out of his jeans pocket. "Searching for this?"

"Oh! Thank goodness. I thought I'd dropped it."

"You left it on the table when you ran off with Mr. Perfect. Maybe you could have, I don't know, used it to call for help when he transformed into Mr. Hyde."

She reached for it, but he held it up and lit the screen.

"You'll never believe what I found on your phone when I used it to call his."

Frankie's eyes flickered and widened.

He tried to push the images from his head, but he couldn't forget. In one photo she'd texted that pervert, she wore a white lacy camisole top and stretched out on red sheets, her blonde hair fanned out across her pillow. Her daring pose couldn't hide her hesitance. Her eyes held such innocence and sweetness, it took his breath away. Tanner could see into her soul.

"You shouldn't have snooped." Frankie jabbed her index finger at Tanner.

"Excuse me for trying to save your life and not expecting

to find boudoir shots. You're giving yourself away bit by bit to a moron who doesn't care about or deserve you."

"It's just sexy photos."

"It's about you trying to escape your fear that you'll never do the thing you love most again. You're afraid you'll be nobody if racing's gone."

"Don't give me that dime-store therapy when you're just as broken."

He ignored the last remark. Venom burned his veins at the thought of Kyle looking at, touching her body. Tanner's hands came down hard on the steering wheel. "Do not ever post a photo like that again. Do you hear me? No one should see you like this."

Don't you mean, "No one else should see you like this"?

This was about her childish behavior, not what Tanner wanted. Didn't want. Tanner put his aching hands to his muddled head.

"I hear you and now you'll hear me." Frankie straightened, eyes blazing. "You will never speak to me in that tone again. You are not my master, my father, or my husband. Even if you were, you have no right to dictate to me how I will use my body and run my life."

Tanner's heart and head were pounding. He bit his bottom lip, breathing slowly through his nose as the minutes passed. "You're right."

He took another breath and handed her the phone. "It's your business. I overstepped."

"Let us never speak of this again. If you want to snoop, come back with a warrant." She tucked the phone into her purse, staring straight ahead.

Tanner swallowed hard. If she only knew the extent of his snooping.

"I have to ask, Frankie. Why?" Tanner shook his head, jostling the pain in his temples.

"I just wanted someone to love me and to love. Now, can we just leave it alone and you leave me alone?"

"You are so… and these men are…" There were no adequate adjectives. Tanner gave her one last glance before getting out of the vehicle and grabbing her wheelchair out of the trunk.

"I'm so what? Lonely? Exhausted? For a moment, it just felt good to escape *this.*" Frankie waved her hand over her legs as he helped her out and opened the door to her room. "My life right now is something out of a horror movie."

"Trust *me* to help you until we catch the monster who—

His words died on his lips as he caught sight of her bed. The monster had returned.

CHAPTER FIFTEEN

SITTING ATOP THE comforter that had covered Frankie last night while she slept was a Wonder Woman doll with a broken neck.

"That is not mine," she whispered.

Tanner turned her around quickly and practically threw her back into the SUV. "Lock the door behind you. You're not spending the night here."

Tanner braced for an argument, which never came. Frankie obeyed for once.

He swept the room before inspecting the doll. It sat on a note that said, "Daddy plays or Princess pays."

Tanner's blood boiled as he played back the security footage on his phone and found nothing. He'd been hacked by a professional, not some disgruntled employee or client. His boss was in it up to his eyeballs.

Tanner punched in the number to Newman's cell. He was tired of trying to do his job with one arm tied behind his back. "I'm aware it's 11 o'clock at night. If you don't come clean about the threats against Frankie, they will finish the job this time."

~

"Start talking. I need details. Is Kyle still alive? Did you report him? He had no clue the black belt he was dealing with."

Frankie could see Selah's face crinkle with worry over their video connection. The waves behind Selah's Malibu home rolled peacefully. Frankie would give anything to be there with Selah and Faith, feeling the sand between her toes and the sun on her face. Maybe it would burn Kyle's sneer from her brain.

Frankie shrugged. "Kyle was alive when I left him, and I'm fairly sure Tanner will pay him a visit to check his pulse."

Tanner would have finished off her date if she'd asked him. When he'd brought her back to the barn, he put his security head, Mario, to work installing new locks and cameras and then peeled out in a fury.

Tanner's mask had slipped tonight, and rage flared from the depths. What else was he hiding? *You can't trust anyone, not even Tanner.* Selah's advice was solid. Frankie just couldn't make her heart listen.

"Do you think Kyle was right?" Frankie asked her best friend. "I mean, the way he freaked when he saw my body."

"Are you seriously asking if a sex offender was correct in assessing your body? That's what you took away from the trauma you suffered and your heroic escape? Self-doubt?" Selah's violet eyes narrowed. "You are gorgeous. Gorgeous! Do you hear me? Even if you weren't, even if your body wasn't perfect, who cares? Looks aren't what we truly fall in love with. If it was, Cane might not have married me. Please don't turn into an obsessive body-hater like me."

"Maybe I should have a nice guy look me over and give me some pointers." Frankie turned her chair to one side, studying herself in the full-length mirror, then spun in the other direction to get a different angle.

Selah smacked her hand to her forehead. "I cannot believe I'm hearing this. You are the world's most self-confident, strong, powerful woman. One idiot will not ruin you."

"You're right. I know." She didn't know anything right now.

Selah sighed. "Would you lay off the online dating? It's messing with your mind. Just until you're back on your feet."

Frankie snorted at Selah's word choice. "Sure, whatever."

"You will get back on your feet, whatever shape or form that takes. Who is this woman I'm talking to? Are you giving up?"

"On dating? Absolutely." Frankie frowned. "With my injury, I have some control and I will fight to heal: PT from sunup to sundown, clinical trials, medication, whatever it takes. But with men, whoowhee, I feel so helpless and I hate it. Love's just not going to happen for me. At this point, I don't really want it to. I felt nothing but curiosity with Kyle."

Selah smiled with such compassion Frankie could feel it through the screen. Frankie ached for her mother.

"I wish I could hug you right now." Selah wrapped her arms around herself. "The reason you didn't feel anything was because Kyle didn't know how to lead you."

"Oh, he had the experience to take me where he wanted."

"I'm not talking about sexual experience or know-how or mind games to lead you astray. It's a different kind of knowing when you're in love."

Frankie did not want to hear about love—that elusive thing everybody sings about but nobody can hang onto.

Selah grinned. "Did I tell you about the Salsa boot-camp I took?"

"You're dancing again?" Frankie pretended to bite her nails. "Poor Cane. Time to up the health insurance."

"I took the class without Cane, because I wanted to surprise him with my skills and I hate stepping on his feet." Selah blushed. "I couldn't get this spin with my partner, another student who was as fresh as I was. He was sweaty and nervous and held me either too loose or too stiff. I concluded, naturally, that there was something wrong with *me*. I was the one who couldn't dance, not him."

Frankie nodded encouragingly but ached to hit the sack and not have to endure a heartsy-feely parable about love.

"Finally, the instructor came over and told me to shut my eyes. He said, 'Just move when I tell you.' He never spoke a word after that, but the hand on my back and the other hand in mine showed me exactly where to go. I opened my eyes, and he was smiling. I had performed the step perfectly on the first try with the right dancer—the one who knew where and how to lead me."

Selah continued, "The professional dancer anticipated my moves. I could trust him because he knew how to make the real me— the competent and confident dancer—come alive."

"So," Frankie was confused, "I just need to find someone I can trust? Good luck with that. I'm surrounded by people trying to kill me."

"One reason you weren't feeling anything for Kyle, why he made you feel afraid and doubt yourself, was because you didn't know what was in his soul. He didn't know your soul either, so he couldn't lead you and anticipate your moves. He hadn't been there before, danced the dance of emotional intimacy with you. You couldn't surrender to him without fearing what he was going to do next."

Selah rested her hand over her heart. "You should be able to trust that, whatever your man does, it comes from a place of love and of knowing you deeply and of looking out for your best interests and *your* pleasure. The man who moves you emotionally will be the one you can move with, eyes closed. You'll be connected by more than skin."

"Someone like Cane."

Gee, too bad he didn't have a twin. Oh wait, yes he did! And, lucky for Frankie, it was the evil twin.

"Like my husband."

The green light at Charlotte Motor Speedway didn't beam as bright as Selah in that moment.

"I love that man."

"Well, duh."

As they were speaking, a text from Kyle arrived: **I like a feisty woman. Call me and we'll finish what we started. U know U can't do better than me. You'll be lucky to do anybody in your condition.**

Frankie's cheeks burned. *Your condition* bounced around in her head. Like paralysis was some kind of disease or something to be ashamed or pitied for. She should have hit him harder.

Same goes for you in your condition. She texted back, then blocked him.

"I've always loved Cane, even when I was just watching him on TV, but now he's part of my soul." Selah was waxing poetic about the last amazing man on earth—the shirtless wonder. "When he's in New York and I'm apart from him either in Virginia or LA, I *feel* him and I long to tell him about my day: how our cranky head writer, Mason, complimented me on a script I wrote, how a seagull swooped down and pecked Faith on the noggin', or how I walked an extra mile, even without Cane pushing me. Silly stuff. I lie in bed and anticipate him bursting through the door with that steamy smile, calling me 'sweetness' and telling me how he flubbed up on air because he was distracted thinking about my mouth. Or, we'll sit on this balcony watching the ocean and holding hands, and he'll tell me how he loves this life we're building together."

Selah fanned herself. "There I go again. I've upset you with my long-winded love talk. Blame my husband. His picture is in the dictionary under 'the feels.' Don't get me wrong though. He chews so loud at times I think I've married Cookie Monster. Drives me up the wall."

Frankie laughed. She'd take Cookie any day to the monsters in her life. "I'm genuinely glad to have been a part of your miracle love story, Selah. I just can't help wondering…"

"When your miracle's coming." Selah squeezed Faith to her chest. "Don't lose hope."

Easy for you to say.

"Sometimes I wonder if I'm just the BFF in some romantic comedy whose sequel never gets written."

CHAPTER SIXTEEN

"THE WRITING'S ON the wall, Kojak, or at least in her pretty blue eyes. Frankie finally trusts me."

Kojak squawked as he scratched it behind its ears. The cat couldn't know Tanner was talking about her mortal enemy, could she?

"You don't trust her?" He grabbed a treat off the side table and Kojak snarfed it down. "How can someone work that closely with her father and not get her hands dirty?"

Newman had offered zero help in identifying who sent the doll. He'd simply said he wasn't going to let his enemies take what belonged to him again. The old man wasn't just talking about protecting Frankie—something valuable was buried beneath the casino and Newman refused to negotiate with his enemies for it, even if it put Frankie in danger.

Frankie acted clueless about the fact that her father's business was a front, but she was smart and had no qualms about keeping secrets. Look how easily she lied to him about the online dating and sexting and disappeared with Kyle.

"Women will betray you," he muttered as he strummed Kojak's throat.

"Ow!" A pain shot through his index finger. He looked down to find the cat's teeth wrapped around it. "Sorry girl, present company excluded."

The feline looked up at him, eyes shining with love or, perhaps, hunger for more treats. "You might like Frankie if you gave her a chance. You two have a lot in common—mischievous eyes, quick temper, bottomless stomach, soft skin." Aaand, moving on from that last thought.

Unlike the cat, Frankie had a feminine, but hearty laugh he didn't hear often enough and a smile that could get a man in trouble and begging for more.

He studied his quiet, minimalist apartment. It was dry bread and water compared to the warm buffet that filled Frankie's barn—the scents of grease and perfume greeting you when you cracked open that wooden door, Darius Rucker's "Southern State of Mind" playing on the radio, rust bleeding through the grabber blue fender of a Mustang she had dismantled and put back together, and takeout from Chinese Willie's, Good Company, or Ruby's barbecue joint in the refrigerator or placed strategically where she could grab them.

"You need to get a life, Tanner. Put down some roots," Cane had said at his wedding.

Tanner shook his head to banish the thought. Roots were slip-and-fall hazards. What did Tanner need with Frankie's wild and wacky little life in the country? What Tanner *needed* was revenge. A few more weeks and he'd have what he wanted and she'd be out of his life for good.

Vengeance belongs to me.

God's word knocked the wind out of his anger, pushing him back in the chair. Kojak took the movement as an invitation to crawl up on his chest, claws unfurled. Everybody was on Tanner's case tonight.

No. He shook his head at the ceiling. He couldn't hand over the reins to God. This was Tanner's fight.

I will repay.

Tanner sighed at the intrusive thoughts. The danger of reading the Gospel was that the truth always came to mind at the most inconvenient times. He couldn't recall a verse if he tried, but, if God wanted to send a message, Tanner would remember.

Without his mission, who was he? The minutes ticked by while the cat's chest rose and fell as it clung to its master, purring without a care in the world.

Finally, he relented. *Alright, God. You're in the driver's seat when it comes to vengeance.* But Tanner was calling shotgun.

Frankie averted her eyes from the gigantic shotgun, rifles, and animal trophy heads mounted on the walls of Daddy's windowless office. They had freaked her out since childhood, but Daddy, a skilled hunter, claimed they served a purpose.

"Kitten, what a surprise." He looked up from the file he was writing in as she rolled toward his desk.

"Is it? You haven't been around since my accident, and I missed you."

"I've been under a lot of pressure here." The dark circles under his eyes confirmed it. He returned to his file. No apologies or offers to make it up to her. Shouldn't Frankie almost dying bring them closer as a family?

"I thought business was good. Are you being pressured by the people responsible for my crash?"

Daddy stopped writing, pen mid-air, taking a solid minute to respond. "When you deliver a high-quality product, lesser men take notice of your success. They will use any means to steal your power."

"So, the answer is yes. Do they want to take over the casino and track?"

"Don't worry, kitten. No one will hurt our family again." He glanced at his watch. "How are things going with Tanner Ashton? Do I need to hire more security?"

"No. Nooo." One bodyguard was more than enough, thank you. "Why do you ask?"

"Since I'm increasing his responsibilities around here, I want to make sure he's treating you with respect."

"He handles me like fine china."

Tanner left Frankie cold and lonely on the shelf.

She frowned. "What kind of responsibility?"

Frankie had hoped that, when they discovered the cause of the crash and found her attacker, Tanner would leave town and leave her alone. What if he stayed and she was forced to look into those eyes for a lifetime of torment?

"Nothing you need to worry about. Concentrate on getting stronger."

"I will walk again. Don't *you* worry."

"That's great, honey."

The jaguar behind Daddy seemed to be eyeing her. Frankie hadn't noticed that one before. Maybe he'd bagged it on his recent Mexico trip. She shivered.

"You want me to walk again, don't you?"

"Of course! Don't ask silly questions. I want my best girl and my accountant back."

He smiled down at her. She'd give anything if he would cross the divide between them: come out from behind his desk, pick her up, and spin her around like he used to.

"Do you think Mom would be proud of me?"

He studied her with a look she couldn't pin down. Why did Daddy weird out about her mother? The death was tragic, but lots of folks died of cancer and their families didn't stop talking about them.

"She would." His tone was clipped.

Was he mad at her for asking or mad at her mother for dying?

"I tried to help her as I have tried to help you. The Newmans will come out on top. Don't forget that, no matter what happens. Always remember where your loyalties lie."

Frankie blinked at the dressing down. "I'm sorry I upset you."

His face softened a smidge. "No, Kitten, never. Come give Daddy a hug."

She rolled around the desk and wrapped her arms around him. His body was stiffer than hers. He quickly pulled back and returned to the file.

"Send Tanner in when you leave."

Dismissed! He had always made time for her before.

Frankie swallowed against the scratchiness in her throat and put it in turbo to get out the door and past Tanner.

"Hey!" He jumped back.

She called over her shoulder as she rolled down the hall, "Daddy summoned you. I'll be in the casino."

It was Daddy's baby. Maybe if Frankie got to know the place, she'd understand him.

She caught a chill as she glanced up at the televisions above the bar. They displayed feeds of every sport you could think of, including racing. The dings of the machines rattled around in Frankie's head like a loose bolt. It wasn't as big as Charles Town Casino, but it was busy.

It was most certainly not criminal, although he'd constructed it on the West Virginia side of their property so as to avoid the stricter Virginia regulations. The only thing amiss was Miss Pearl from Selah's church, who had fallen asleep with her forehead pressed against a Wheel of Fortune slot machine. The scent of prime rib and fried chicken drifting from the Grand Slam Buffet made her stomach rumble. An establishment boasting a delectable buffet that catered to blue-haired ladies couldn't be crooked.

It had been over six months since Frankie'd walked through the casino and lingered to chat with Selah's father. She smiled at the memory of how Russ hugged her, picking her up off the ground. He won a hand of poker and wanted to celebrate with his other daughter. Margo had come in and dragged him home by the ear, like some fifties sitcom couple.

The longing for her mother was so strong, her chest ached. Had Frankie lost her father now too?

CHAPTER SEVENTEEN

Brakes? You Mean the Coward Pedal?

"EXCELLENT WORK, CHAMP." Mark smiled at Frankie as he put her through the paces. "That's enough for the parallel bars for today. While you cool down, you can tell me all about the dating adventures."

She groaned. "Not for the faint of heart. One guy fixated on feeding me like a child while he made choo-choo noises. I might have put the second date in the hospital."

Tanner grunted from his spot at the window. "If only."

Frankie shifted on the bars. "Should my back hurt this bad?"

"Don't push past that pain, Frankie. I like you too much to allow you to hurt yourself." Mark eased her leg to the floor. "You've only got five minutes left. We'll do some laser treatment and massage and call it a day."

She flashed to Kyle and the countless men online whose profiles read, "I give the sexiest massages."

Nobody was putting hands on her body again if she could help it.

"I didn't say I wanted to stop." She continued to inch across the bars, willing her feet to follow her arm movements. Every flex felt like a bullet piercing her skin, worse than she'd experienced before. What fresh torture was this?

Mark must have noticed her grimace, because he grabbed her arm and said, "You are done."

Go away, mister. I don't need another man telling me what to do or who I am or what I should be.

"We're so close to a breakthrough, I can feel it." Her shaking biceps hadn't gotten that memo though.

"I believe you are too," Mark said, "but you'll set your progress back if you keep this up. Let's get you into the water in a few days and I promise you'll see a difference."

"No water."

"I have your best interests at heart. Why are you being so stubborn?" Mark jerked the bar and shook it.

Hot tears flowed to the surface. Really? How original. She didn't need them. She didn't need water therapy. She didn't need Mark. She would defeat this on her own.

"Are you deaf? I said no water, Mark. I'm already scheduled for the electrical spine stimulator implant. Isn't that enough? If you care about me, you'll let it go."

His hands were on hers as he tried to pry her off the bars. Tanner started toward her.

"Great." Mark whipped around, "Make yourself useful and help me stop her from injuring herself."

Frankie bit back a sob. They were ganging up on her. She needed to finish. Five more minutes could mean the difference between a life trapped in that prison on wheels or a life in her real wheels.

"Let her be," Tanner growled. "She knows her body."

"With all due respect, she does not know. Her spine is broken and fused. If this paralysis is temporary, further injury could make it permanent."

"I'm aware. She's aware. Why don't you step outside, cool off, and give her some space to finish on her own?"

Frankie wasn't stopping until she was walking or dead. She wasn't getting in the water. She wasn't going to be bossed around by Mark or by Tanner or by some online perv. No more. She had the power. Everything just seemed like it was falling apart. She wasn't going to fall apart.

Mark mumbled something, stomped to the door, and slammed it on his way out.

Frankie said, "I hear you breathing back there, Darth Vader. Thank you for defending me, but you can leave now, too."

"You know I'm not leaving." Tanner stood behind her, making her more determined not to give up.

"Please." Frankie's voice eeked out like that of a fragile, helpless soap ingenue on *The Winds of Change* and she didn't care for it one bit. "Leave me alone for a couple of hours or I'll have a nervous breakdown."

She couldn't look at him and see pity or anger or any emotion if he was capable of feeling it. Frankie'd love to catch Tanner asleep and inspect his skin for robot implants.

"I need a testosterone-free, grumpy-free, boss-free zone where I can breathe. Go home and play with the bald eagle. It must be missing the only person on this planet who loves it."

Tanner sighed. "I'll give you an hour."

He'd still be watching from a distance or by video. Maybe a giant telescope. Who knew? Who cared anymore? She'd have freedom, if only fleeting.

When the door banged shut, Frankie's arms gave out. She gasped when something or someone broke her fall.

"One hour… starting now." Tanner scooped her up and set her in the wheelchair.

He brushed her hair from her eyes and stared into them for a moment. She searched the darkness of the deep moats that protected the fortress around Tanner's heart. They were the eyes that had hovered over her when she'd awakened from her surgeries. The eyes of the man who'd held her on the dance floor. The eyes of the man who would never love her, probably never love anyone. She didn't know who to feel sadder for.

Tanner stood quickly and walked out for real this time, leaving her heart feeling like he'd vacated more than just the room.

Frankie exhaled so loudly, it echoed. She pushed the chair toward the door, her arms and abs screaming. With every push, she got slower and slower until she stopped.

She rested a moment, reading the motivational signs Mark had hung on the walls. *When you feel like quitting, think about why you started… No excuses, just do the work… Great things never came from comfort zones.* Duh. Nobody needed to remind her of that. It was the last sign before she reached the door that got her: "Those who keeping waiting for the Lord will renew their strength. Then they'll soar on wings like eagles."

Why should she wait on God? Seemed like He'd walked

off the job when He let someone paralyze and nearly kill her. How could she count on Him to heal her when He'd already proven he wouldn't protect her?

Ultimately, it was up to her to win, but, right now, she didn't have the strength to get herself where she so desperately needed to be. Time was a wastin'. She read the sign again.

What could it hurt to send up a quick one? *God, if You could send me some strength, wisdom, power, courage, love—anything You've got up there—now would be a good time.*

Tanner gave Frankie the full hour, but never let her out of his sight. He stood in the woods, watching her stare out over the abyss, a pond at the edge of the Speedway property. Her hair blew wildly in the breeze, doing all the talking for emotions.

No denying Frankie was tougher than the average human. The more pain she felt, the harder she fought. She had been determined to stay up on those bars until her legs moved.

When storm clouds began to cast shadows over her, Tanner drew closer.

"Hey."

"Hey," she said, her voice uncharacteristically serious and her face unreadable.

When he reached her side, he eased down to the grass and sat criss-cross. Sweet gum balls and magnolia seed pods dug into his behind.

"What if I can't race again? What will I do? It's all I know."

Didn't take her long to spill everything that had been whirring in her mind

"What if you can make it happen by getting in the water?" Sympathy wasn't Tanner's strong suit, so he took a different tack.

"Not you too. It isn't that simple."

Tanner was still for a moment, watching the trees begin to sway. A small flock of crows ascended from the branches and flew away cawing.

"Tell me about your mother and what happened here."

Her head snapped around then. "How did you… of course, you know about her. You know everything."

"Not everything. Researching something and hearing about it from the people involved tell two different stories."

The library microfiche provided a clinical account of the alleged accidental drowning. The 80-year-old librarian delivered a eulogy of the virtues of her friend Tanya Newman, her battle with cancer, and the precious toddler she'd left behind. The absence of a female role model had turned the poor child into a daredevil tomboy.

"My mother died here. Alone. At night." Frankie swallowed.

A speckled frog dove from a rock into the greenish-blue waters and didn't reappear. The ripples seemed to go on and on.

"I knew there had to be more to it when you said, 'I can't swim.' 'Can't' isn't in Frankie Newman's vocabulary. What's your father's take on her death?"

"Daddy doesn't reveal much. Like some other people I know." She squinted at him. "You're the human equivalent of a muumuu dress."

Tanner proved her point by snorting but revealing nothing.

"Daddy said she loved to swim and wandered down here to cool off one summer night. She was delirious and too feeble to save herself." Frankie cocked an eyebrow. "I guess we'll never know."

She was questioning her father's honesty instead of towing the party line. That was a good sign.

Tanner found no evidence of a police investigation or autopsy. Margo Morgan had organized a memorial service for Tanya that Kenny Newman didn't attend. Her clothing appeared in the local mission store within the week. Newman was either removing all traces of a crime or all memories of his wife. Either way, he couldn't erase the motherless baby and the heartbreak left behind, thirty years later.

"What do you remember about her?"

Frankie's eyes turned downward to the hands in her lap. "Warmth. I know from Momma, the church ladies, and my soul that my mom was a good woman. When I race, I feel her coursing through me."

"What would she say about you not wanting to go in the water and get a jump on therapy?"

A rush of wind blew Frankie's hair from her shoulders and sent waves across the pond. It was on the tip of his tongue to tell her to pack it in before the storm hit, but Frankie held up her hand, fingers spread, as if to become part of the wind. Tanner lifted his cheek to another gust, opening his lips to take it in. Kind of goofy. Kind of cool.

"Mom would want me to do anything I could to heal. She'd encourage me to do the scary thing, the brave thing, the hardest thing."

"And what is that?" When Frankie's eyes met Tanner's, he reached up and squeezed her knee lightly.

"To dive into this water and bring it back to life again."

He had a feeling this wasn't the first time she'd come out here and considered getting in the water by herself. Tanner could learn a thing or two from Frankie about courage.

"You don't have to start here. We can ease into the new pool, somewhere neutral. Clean."

"No, it has to be here." She reached up to pull her blouse over her head.

"Whoa! What are you doing?" Tanner jumped up, prepared to cover her with his body if need be. They were well protected out here from prying eyes, but who would protect him from the sight of her bare skin?

"No time like the present," she grinned, reaching for her shorts.

He let out a "whew" when he saw she had a swimsuit on under the shorts. The tension came right back as he realized how tiny it was and how the green and blue flecks turned her into a mermaid.

"I kind of feel like an overgrown Ariel." She smoothed the suit, tugging at the straps. "Selah sent it to encourage me to get in the pool with Mark."

Tanner didn't know whether to thank or strangle his sister-in-law for outfitting Frankie like the seductive sirens of yore who lured sailors to their doom.

Look away. Don't gaze into her eyes. Too late.

"It's nice, right?" She bit her lip, probably waiting for him to say something encouraging, to say anything.

"Nice," was all he could grind out.

Stunning was more like it—it had stunned all sense out

of him. He would find her some suitable fishing waders at the bait 'n tackle.

"Were you planning on getting in there by yourself if I hadn't come along?"

"I've worn it every day to PT under my clothes, hoping I'd get the gumption to try water therapy."

"Gumption? Try daredevil, danger—"

"Make it snappy with the lecture and let's do this." She pushed herself up from the chair.

"I'm getting hazard pay."

Tanner made a quick visual sweep of the area before securing his weapon and preparing for an unscheduled dip in the pond. If bodyguards worldwide held a seminar on the moves that could get you and your client killed, Tanner would qualify as a case study. If Kenny Newman, currently out of town, knew Tanner was about to lay hands on his half-naked daughter, Tanner would land at the bottom of the pond.

Tanner stripped off his shirt and shoes and left his jeans on. "You didn't ask me if *I* knew how to swim."

Her laugh turned into a gasp as he scooped her up in his arms. The shadows swirling in her eyes like the storm clouds overhead told the true story of her terror, grief, and excitement.

Tanner started down the bank towards the water, biting his tongue as his bare feet met hot, jagged rocks. When she buried his face in his chest, the pain dissipated. Her cheek rested against the scar.

"Secrets," Frankie murmured as she traced the scar's edges with the pad of her thumb.

"None you should worry about."

She rested her head again. No doubt the wheels were still turning. He should have left his shirt on. If she realized it was a bullet wound, she wouldn't be satisfied with the fact that his job was dangerous. She'd wonder who put it there and why.

Tanner was still figuring out the "why" as well.

His first footstep into the mud made a splash that caused Frankie to startle and grasp his neck tighter than a socket wrench on a lug nut. Now she had him thinking in car metaphors too.

"Tanner?" she whispered as he got waist deep and water splashed her arm.

"On my life, I'll never let you fall."

Who would keep him from falling? They were getting too close. It was imperative that Tanner pull back and regain distance and perspective. As soon as he got her in and out of the water safely, he'd bring her to pool therapy and establish boundaries again.

"I'll take a few more steps and you'll be at your shoulder level. Then, I can set you on your feet or we can get out of the water."

"Take me all the way."

"What?" It was Tanner's turn to be startled.

"I want you to dunk me in the water."

"Are you sure?"

Their eyes locked. She finally trusted Tanner as he'd asked her to time and time again. Tanner had Frankie Newman right where he wanted for the plan to work.

"I'm an all-in kind of girl. Go big or go bigger." Frankie's soft voice didn't match the bravado. Her eyes glazed with tears held back so tightly, they were afraid to fall.

A few years had passed since Tanner first saw Frankie's photo in Danielle's file. When he'd come to Shadybrook to find Cane, Frankie stomped into his life for real at Selah's hospital bedside. Cane's wife was a kind-hearted, nurturing beauty while Frankie was a blonde Wonder Woman in black leather boots. Her fire and fierceness hid a pure love and joy that didn't fit the dark world created by her father.

In that instant, Tanner knew: whatever crimes Kenny Newman had committed, Frankie was innocent. Like the mud under his feet, Tanner's footing changed.

"You alright?" Frankie touched his cheek. "You look like I feel all of a sudden."

Thunder rumbled in the distance as Tanner fought every instinct to throw her over his shoulder, jump in the SUV, take her away from this place, and never look back. There had to be a way to complete his mission and keep her safe too.

"Hold your breath when you go under. It's gonna shock your system."

Trusting her had shocked his system. The last time he'd put his faith in a woman, he took a bullet to the chest.

CHAPTER EIGHTEEN
There's No Crying in Racing

FRANKIE CAME UP out of the water like a baptism. The skies opened and water came from everywhere. As she coughed and sputtered, Tanner's words were ringing in her ears. *Don't let go.* She'd heard someone say it after the wreck and now it was her mother's voice coming back to her. Her heart knew the sound.

Don't let go, Francine. Stay beside me. Slow down, speedy. We have all afternoon to learn to swim. Look at those little arms and legs fly!

It was a memory, not a fantasy. Frankie was sure of it! One solitary memory that she'd cling to forever. Suddenly, she looked around and remembered where she was—clutching Tanner as he stood patiently in the muddy water.

"Now you can let go, Wonder Woman."

She could barely tell the difference between Tanner's rumble and the thunder.

When he hugged Frankie closer against his chest, the tears shook everything that wasn't already sore and quaking from physical therapy. She'd heard of but never experienced an ugly cry until now. With every torrent of rain that lashed against them, she moaned aloud for her mother and for everything she'd lost. Her body caved as an infant curling up in fetal position.

That's when she felt it. A tingle skimmed her thigh, but it might as well have been a lightning strike. Frankie tried to curl up and make it happen again. The twitch in her leg would have appeared invisible, imperceptible to a stranger, but she *knew*. Her leg moved! The thrill of hope rocked her entire body.

The sensation was gone in a moment. Like her mother's voice, it was so close and yet just out of her reach.

Should she tell Tanner? No, he might not be able to see the twitch and the disappointment would throw caution flags to slow her progress. Vaguely, Frankie felt him carry her out of the water. She didn't look up again until he scooted her into the backseat of his Escalade.

Wrapping a fleece blanket around her, he said, "Be right back."

Her mind raced as the rain pelted the windows. When Tanner returned, he stowed the wheelchair and slid in beside her. Unfortunately, he'd put another shirt on, covering killer abs and the mystery scar on his chest. He hovered over her, his brow furrowed and his breath jagged against her cheek.

"You've been working out secretly. It shows." She smiled up at him, longing to stroke the tension from his jaw. "But you need to work on the sweating thing."

Laughing, he shook out his soaked hair, sprinkling her.

"How you feeling after your first swim?"

"Actually, it wasn't my first. I flashed back to my mother teaching me to swim in that pond as a toddler. I heard her voice saying, 'Slow down, speedy.'" Frankie giggled. Discovering a piece of her mother had shown her a part of herself.

"Some things never change." Tanner gifted her a real smile, the corners of his eyes crinkling.

"S-she wouldn't take her own l-life in a place where we'd had such fun together, would she?"

"No. Not if she was in her right mind." He wrapped her in his arms so that her back was resting against his chest. Tanner's beard brushed against her cheek as he whispered, "It's okay. I've got you."

His soothing words and the strength of his embrace broke the dam. Every tear Frankie'd held back for 30 years made its way to the surface in front of Tanner of all people.

When Frankie came up for air again, he stroked her hair from her eyes. "Feel better?"

Nodding, she said, "I'm sorry for unloading on you and for acting like a brat in PT. There's no crying in racing. Daddy says it's weak."

Tanner scooted her around and tipped her chin up so she was looking into his eyes. "Crying means you have a heart."

Their faces were so close, heat radiated from his skin against hers. "I don't want to bring others down with my bad moods. Everyone has his or her own struggle."

"You aren't allowed to feel?"

His eyes were soft and searching. Who was this man?

"You are the most positive and genuine person I've ever

met. I've never once felt the happiness that comes naturally to you every day. I'm envious. I want some of that."

If only Frankie could give it to him and overpower the grief and darkness he'd experienced. She brought her hand to his chest. "What hurts, Tanner? Let me heal you."

When he didn't speak, Frankie lightened the mood. "I am, after all, the Grump Whisperer."

It was like watching the Northern Lights when a spark flashed in the deep blackness of his eyes, his lips parted, and his perfectly imperfect white teeth shown through.

"A beautiful one at that." He rubbed his thumb across her lips and leaned in.

This is it. This is it. Bring on the lovin'. Bring it home, baby.

A crack louder than lightning penetrated the steamy silence in the vehicle. Tanner turned, blocking her from the window, but not before Frankie saw the cause of the disturbance: Momma. Proof positive that, whenever things were going well with her and Tanner, it summoned the forces of darkness.

With her wild eyes and flapping gums and the rain bouncing off her auburn beehive, Momma made the phrase "madder than a wet hen" come alive. Even Tanner looked nervous as he set Frankie upright and rolled down the window an inch.

"What in this wide world are you two doing fogging up the windows out here?"

Frankie smiled with all teeth. "Making out like bunnies, Margo."

Momma clutched her chest with one hand and jiggled

the door handle with the other. Tanner, bless him, had sense enough to lock the door and made no move to unlock it.

"We took cover from the rain, ma'am."

"In the backseat?" Margo pressed her face against the glass. "In your drawers? With Frankie on your lap?"

Watching Tanner sputter was the most fun Frankie had had in a long time. She couldn't wait to tell Selah. But first, she had to tell Margo where to get off.

"We are above the age of consent, according to the law."

Margo said, "Not according to the law of God and the law of my house, Francine."

Tanner groaned and hissed, "Don't poke the bear."

Frankie huffed, bored with the interrogation. "Since you will hold us prisoner here until you get all the gossip, I'll just go ahead and confess that Tanner helped me into the pond so I'd be prepared for water therapy. Then, we got caught in the storm."

"The pond." The ire fell away from Margo's face. Her voice was deadly soft. "Be careful out there, you hear."

She turned back toward the water, gazing at it for a moment, before returning to Frankie. As Momma's eyes clouded, Frankie's welled up again.

Momma straightened and sniffed, wiping away the tears with a swish of her handkerchief. "Now, unhand my child, young man."

The rain had stopped and so had the waterworks.

Frankie's heart welled. Momma was nosy, demanding, and controlling, but she meant well. She'd always loved Frankie as her own, including doling out punishment and unwanted advice.

Tanner hopped to, jumping out of the vehicle.

"Land's sakes," Momma exclaimed, looking up at him. "You're so tall you could hunt geese with a rake."

"Thanks?" Tanner said to the woman whose hair was piled so high, you could play Jenga.

Tanner assembled the wheelchair in a jiffy and tapped on the wheel when he was finished. He'd make a fine pit crew… if she ever returned to the track. Doubt loomed as large as Momma. Frankie couldn't shake it, so she'd just deal with it.

"I done been all over this property looking for you," Momma said.

"How did you track us down, Mrs. Morgan?" Tanner was all business again as he helped Frankie into the chair.

"My husband proved himself good for something other than spending my money. He was leaving the casino when he spied Tanner turnin' in here."

"What's the emergency?" Frankie pulled her soaking hair out of her face to look at Momma, whose beehive was unmoved.

"I brought you dinner and one of the new pies I'm trying out." Margo handed Tanner two massive plastic bags from the diner.

"And?" Frankie knew a bribe when she saw one.

"And you're going to be on the show with me again."

"Oh no. N to the O. To the no, no, no." Frankie put her hand down to turn the chair. "The last time I helped you, I ended up mauled by a flying monkey."

She rolled her eyes at Tanner, who was trying to tamp down a grin on behalf of that evil bald cat.

Momma wrung her hands. "The ratings dipped when

you were recuperating. I may not get picked up if you don't come back."

The look on her face was kind of pitiful. Frankie should really show some kindness.

"The viewers loved me, didn't they?"

"No accounting for taste these days." Momma met Frankie's grin with a glower. "When word got out that you'd been in an accident, the viewers who enjoyed your special brand of humor got worried. People were rooting for you. They enjoy seeing crippled people happy."

Frankie slapped her palm against her forehead and dragged it down her face. Why did anything Margo say surprise her anymore? This is why Selah moved away.

"Differently abled," Tanner corrected. Angel had to teach Frankie the empowering term but he knew already.

"That's what I said. Handicapped. Incapacitated. All y'all who ain't quite right. The viewers eat it up. Please?"

Tanner steadied her chair. Maybe he was locking her in place to protect Margo.

"When you put it so kindly… Hard pass." Frankie turned the chair and headed begrudgingly for the passenger side. Now that she wasn't in the backseat wrapped up in Tanner's arms, the breeze and the clueless company were giving her a chill.

"Sounds like the perfect time to negotiate," came a deep voice. Tanner was right behind her with a glint in his eye.

"Hmm. Good point." She turned the chair around, pondering the possibilities. "I'll do it if, number one, you stop calling me Francine."

"But…" Margo held out her hand. "Your mother loved that name."

"Oh." Frankie reached out and squeezed Margo's hand a moment.

"She got so tickled by those silly movies starring Francine York—you know, swamp creatures, doll squads, and outer space. The actress had hair about the color of yours."

"She was a beautiful woman," Tanner said. "Guested on your soaps and *Bewitched.*"

New life bubbled up in Frankie as she added another piece to the puzzle that was her mother. "Tell me everything you know about Tanya Newman. All the secrets, all the stories. Everyone in Shadybrook gossips about everything and everybody, except her. Don't you dare refuse me—"

Margo nodded. "You deserve to know."

Well, that was easy. "I expect free food for life at Good Company."

Tanner snickered.

"Blazes, you'll put me out of business the way you eat."

"You can handle it," Frankie shrugged. "I demand you stop saying horribly insensitive things about people, especially your own child. And finally, I require one favor to be named at a future date. Those are the terms. Deal or no deal."

"That accident knocked some marbles loose." Margo shook her head and sighed dramatically. "If I must, it's a deal. Filming starts tomorrow at 3 p.m. Fix your hair. Clothing is not optional. I don't need ratings *that* badly. This ain't *Bachelor in Paradise.*"

Frankie waggled her eyebrows at Tanner. Oh, but it could be.

Without a thank you or goodbye, Momma marched off to her car.

"Wow," Tanner stood watching.

Frankie wheeled toward the door and helped herself in before Tanner could. "Don't stare or she'll turn you to stone."

"Free pancakes for life though!" She clapped her hands, slinging chilly water everywhere. "And I may find out more about my mom."

Ever the mind reader, Tanner pulled the blanket from the back and draped it over her. The closeness stirred her up again. His jaw clenched. Was he feeling it, too? Maybe they could stay here forever, a little oasis from the forces of nature surrounding them.

Another earthquake hit when Tanner laid a folder labeled, Tanya Newman, in her lap. "This should get you started. The librarian was friends with your mother. Take her research with a grain of salt—she told me you and I were married in a past life and are destined to be together. She said, if it didn't work out between us, she'd be waiting for me."

Tanner guffawed as he put the SUV in drive. Frankie was formulating a wisecrack about octogenarian Ms. Pearson and her poor taste in men when she opened the folder.

The photos of her mother took Frankie's breath away. She traced the long, light hair of a smiling woman who cradled a toddler reaching for her glasses.

"That's me!"

Her expressionless father squeezed her mother against him as they all stood in front of the Washington Monument. "I never knew we went there as a family."

Her father once said that Tanya Newman was the love of his life. Maybe that's why he'd never remarried in thirty years. A few years back, he'd entertained a brainy brunette. Like Frankie's mother, Dani left without saying goodbye and Daddy changed the subject when Frankie asked about her.

"The resemblance is uncanny. She looks happy with you in her arms."

"What happened to her, Tanner? How did she go from this beautiful moment to drowning in the pond?" Frankie closed the folder and took a breath. "Thank you for working on this, for always being honest with me."

Something flashed in his eyes. She could trust him, right?

"Everyone deserves closure." Tanner swung the vehicle beside the barn, put it in park, and turned off the engine. "Can you recall any memories of her or belongings that might be significant?"

"Daddy was so grief-stricken he got rid of it all or put it in storage. I was afraid to ask and upset him." Poor Daddy. What had he been like before this tragedy colored his life?

"I do have another photo of her. Margo gave it to me in a locket, but I'm not much on jewelry, so I keep it inside my helmet when I race."

"My helmet!" Frankie's hand shot out to grab Tanner's arm. "It could be the key."

CHAPTER NINETEEN

"Gotta work on the nut behind the wheel before you start fixing bolts on the car."

–Unknown

FRANKIE KNEW INSTINCTIVELY that the helmet would unlock the cause of her crash. "Did you take it after the wreck?"

"No," Tanner stiffened. "I never saw it again after they pulled you from the car."

"What about my fire suit?"

"I got distracted when your father decked me. I assumed the paramedics cut it off and discarded it."

"Daddy punched you?" He would never resort to violence.

"I didn't protect his kitten." Tanner rubbed his jaw.

"You couldn't have seen this coming, but I'm beginning to think I should have." Frankie's mind reeled. "This whole time I've been looking at the car—creating a model of the crash and consulting experts to determine what went wrong. Maybe the answer isn't in the car."

"Are you up to viewing security footage tonight?"

Frankie threw open the car door, lurched forward, and caught herself before she faceplanted on the driveway. She groaned, remembering she hadn't learned to fly yet. Had she imagined the new sensation she felt in her legs?

When Tanner rolled up with her wheels, she said, "I have never been more ready to find out who tried to kill me so I can move on with my life."

Gravel crunched behind them, causing Tanner to step in front of Frankie and draw his weapon.

A familiar voice said loudly, "Well, you have only to look in the mirror for that answer."

Frankie rolled her eyes at the man who tried to steal Good Company from the Morgan family and to cover up his sister's hit-and-run involving Selah."

"Cody Buchanan. Did the storm flood you out from the rock you live under?"

Cody guffawed, shining his flashlight in her face. "Good one, hot wheels."

"Stay away from my barn! Better yet, stay off the Speedway property." Frankie turned the chair and headed for the barn door.

"I have a standing invitation from your father. Hey," Cody hollered, "slow down there, you might get a speeding ticket."

Frankie backtracked at supersonic speed and rolled around Tanner, stopping as close to Cody's feet as possible without running over them. Tempting.

"Look at you, big man, picking on a woman in a wheelchair. I bet you're relieved I'm out of commission so I can't kick you to kingdom come like I did when we were kids.

Remember how you tried to bully Selah and you were incompetent at that?"

His smile turned into a sneer.

Frankie continued. "How about the time I shimmied up the rope climb in PE class and broke your record by a full minute? Wasn't that fun? Or that time—"

"Don't pop a wheelie, Frankie, I was just making conversation on my way to help Kenny throw some sore losers out of the casino." Cody pulled up his britches. "I saw you on the TV. You're looking sexy as ever, despite being paralyzed and all."

Cody put his hand out like he was going to stroke her hair. Tanner caught his wrist, twisted sharply, and shoved it away. "What can we do for you *Deputy* Sheriff?"

"You'll regret that," Cody ground out his words. "Frankie, I thought you'd like to know that the final accident report came back today. We confirmed our initial findings of driver error. Guess your glory days are behind you."

"I'm going to prove that creep wrong." Frankie's skin was still crawling from Cody as she scrolled through the videos she'd played hundreds of times.

"Your glory days have only just begun," Tanner said. "You worry about the car. I'll take care of our dear dimwitted Deputy."

"There's one more thing you haven't reviewed: fan footage of the wreck and immediately following." Tanner projected it onto the TV and paused the playback.

"What are you waiting for? Let's see it."

"I don't want it to affect your recovery." His frown was more grim than usual.

"I can handle anything."

"So you remind me every day. Silly me for trying to protect you." He pulled up a chair beside her. "Frankie, your car split in half when it landed on the guardrail. Pretty graphic, even for someone who's seen carnage."

Frankie studied his eyes and the hard lines that suddenly slashed across his forehead. Carnage? Who was this man? Rambo? Special Forces? An assassin for hire? She swallowed, remembering Selah's advice to be cautious of everyone, even her brother-in-law. What if he didn't want her to see the video because it would show that he was behind all this? What if her mortal enemy had been in front of her this whole time?

Tanner must have read her mind because he reached toward her, then dropped his hand. "I frightened you."

"No. Nope. I just realized how little I know about you." She eyed him. "My life was quiet and safe before you came to town."

"Ask me."

She was dying to watch that footage, but she couldn't pass up this opportunity to analyze him. "What carnage have you seen?"

"In my line of work, you learn quickly that the lust for power, money, and drugs changes people, causes them to commit unspeakable acts to get what they want."

"Like put a bullet in your chest?"

Tanner's hand reflexively went to his rib cage for a moment. "Like that. Next question."

"Who sent me research about treatments and self-care after paralysis?"

He was silent a beat too long.

She remembered the journal on his nightstand and Cane once calling Tanner a science nerd. "Why does a body-guard know so much about medicine?"

Tanner raised his palms. "You caught me. Shockingly, big, dumb thugs get college degrees these days, too."

"You are too good at answering questions without really giving an answer."

He shrugged. "All of life is rooted in science and chem-istry. That fascinates me."

"I understand chemistry." Frankie rolled her chair up until they were touching knees, which caused a chain reac-tion in Tanner's jaw muscle. Making him squirm never got old. "A piston compresses fuel and air into the cylinder head and ignites the spark plug. It's the same principle in humans. A woman's words touch something in a man's mind and it ignites a fire in the body."

Tanner's mouth opened and closed and opened again. He ran a hand through his thick black locks, which would have been curly if he let them grow. "Interesting theory. If twenty questions is over, we should get back to watching—"

"Last question," she leaned in and whispered, "Why shouldn't I ask Daddy to fire you for lying by omission?"

Tanner didn't flinch. "Maybe you should ask yourself where Daddy has been and where *I* have been since your crash, Frankie."

The hurt was still fresh after their one and only visit post-wreck when Daddy had practically pushed her out the door. He holed away in his office, preoccupied by a business that now threatened their lives. Had he made her mother feel this lonely?

"Tanner," she sighed, "don't make me regret trusting you."

He stroked her hair from her face and rested his palm lightly against her cheek. "On my life, I'll never let you fall."

She leaned into his palm. He'd said it when he helped her into the pond. Perhaps he was sitting on a secret and she had lost all common sense, but he would protect her when push came to shove.

"Let's nail this guy then. Roll the video."

Frankie forced her voice to sound confident. She needed to see this footage. The answers were in the tough places. The worst had happened and she'd survived. If she solved this mystery, her attacker could never hurt her again.

Tanner pulled back and turned his face toward the screen, hitting play on the video.

And there it was in color: the worst day of her life. Her car approached the turn. The new kid from Blacksburg came up too cozy from behind, stealing her line and pushing her to the outside. Then, a boom and the car went airborne. Frankie took a deep breath. The video jerked and vibrated and the image went to the sky as if the person behind the lens was running. So much shouting. A muffled announcement over the loudspeaker. Tires squealing. Sirens. And she'd slept through it.

She peeked at Tanner who had pulled up a chair beside her and was watching her. She nodded for him to go on. The next video showed Frankie on the stretcher. She studied the grainy faces of those attending to her.

She pointed at a uniformed man who had his head

down. "I know all our volunteer fire and rescue and he isn't one of them. He seems familiar though."

Tanner reversed the feed and set it in slow motion. Frankie's pulse quickened as they watched the man pick up Frankie's suit and helmet and disappear around the side of the ambulance.

Tanner's fist came down hard on a table. "I should have gotten there sooner. He could have killed you."

"Did you see him get in the helicopter with me? Was he at the hospital?"

"No. He must have left with your equipment before the others transported you." Tanner backed up the hazy video and pushed in on the face of the man who walked off with Frankie's uniform. He wore sunglasses and a mustache. "I'll send it off to a buddy to run facial recognition."

He had actual real-life friends? Interesting.

"Do you think he's the one trying to kill me?"

"Maybe. Or, he could have been hired to do piece work for the one pulling the strings." Tanner glared at the screen.

"Well, the work was sub-par, because I'm still standing. Correction, I'm still breathing."

She shook her head as anger combusted through any residual self-doubt. "How will we see him coming if we don't know who he is?"

They got no more answers that night, although they replayed the videos for so long, her eyes started to bug out. The ding of her phone proved a welcome interruption.

She glanced at the texts and showed Tanner a photo her physical therapist sent of himself lifting weights. "Mark apologized for pushing me so hard and said he can't wait for me to get in the pool."

"Great. Wear a full-body wetsuit."

"He's so cute." Frankie smiled at the screen.

"It's what's on the inside that counts." Tanner grumbled.

His words flipped a switch in her brain. "That's it!"

She reached over and grabbed one of Tanner's lock-tight shoulders.

"That's what?" He steadied her as she quivered.

"My wreck was an inside job! I've been looking at this from the wrong angle, trying to determine what happened to the car to make it swerve, but it turns out the car wasn't the problem."

"What failed then?"

As Frankie caught her reflection on a piece of chrome, she dropped her hands to her lap. "Me."

"Didn't we just agree that you aren't to blame? I know it in my gut." Tanner punched the side of his fist against his abdomen.

Frankie replayed that moment, imagining the weight of the wheel in her hand and the roar of the engine. "I felt a wobble and everything grew foggy, but it wasn't the air or the engine. I was already fading when metal sheered the car, so I must have passed out before the wreck."

Comprehension dawned in Tanner's eyes. "The helmet and suit went missing because they were lined with something to knock you out."

"You're the chem nerd. Is it possible?"

"The tox screen was negative for alcohol, of course, but drugs can slip under the radar if you're not looking for them." Tanner's knee bobbed as he typed something into his phone. "A compounded fentanyl or anesthetic would make you very sleepy if they could keep it from evaporating or drying out. Maybe they used a spray to lace your gear."

Frankie shut her eyes and re-traced the morning of the race. She'd pulled on the helmet, smiling at the thought that her mother's photo was tucked inside.

The helmet fit like it was made for her, but… Frankie gasped, "My helmet was damp! The scent was a little odd, but I couldn't tell you whether it was chemical or not. It's hard to smell anything over the odors from the car and the stands."

"Pesticides or bug spray could cause you to faint or have dizziness, especially if you have sensitivities." He nodded vigorously. "Allergies?"

"Shellfish. I've never had to use an epi-pen, but I've gotten ill before, even just from fumes." Frankie's heart raced as it had in the moments before the crash. "What does this mean? What do we do now?"

Tanner continued to type and then stood suddenly. "It means that, if he intended to kill you, you'd be dead. This is no disgruntled customer or employee of the speedway or casino. It's a professional poking your father to get what he wants."

"So, you and I just have to figure out what they want from Daddy." A new adventure to share with Tanner.

"*You* don't do anything." Tanner burst her bubble. "You solved the mystery of the crash, so your job is done. Continue the status quo. Go to water therapy. I'll take care of the rest.

"But who'll take care of you?"

CHAPTER TWENTY
Push It to the Limit

For one dangerous moment, Tanner considered letting Frankie Newman, with her vivid blue eyes and wild hair and squishy loving heart, take care of him. He jolted like he'd been jumped by a battery charger and headed for the door.

"It's getting late," he called over his shoulder. "Rest up."

"Ohhh," Frankie moaned behind him.

Tanner stopped hard, on alert, and turned. "What's wrong?"

"It's been a long day between the mystery-solving and the swim and Momma."

He puffed out a breath, his heart rate returning to normal. He'd abandoned his smart watch when he met her, because it kept alerting him to a cardiac emergency whenever Frankie was around.

"I'm so tired, I can't move another inch."

Tanner headed for the door again.

"Aren't you going to help me into bed?"

Ignore her. Keep walking. Turn the knob. Don't look. It's a trap. Wonder Woman doesn't need help.

"Tanner?"

He glanced back at the woman whose coy smile had somehow become his Achilles heel. "Whatever you need."

That was the wrong thing to say. Frankie's smile widened as she locked her wheels and lifted her arms toward him. He seemed to be rooted in place, a tree resisting hurricane winds.

"Uh. Sure." It was all part of the job. Tanner was helping meet a client's needs.

"Are you going to sleep in your clothes?" Also, the wrong thing to say. He dug himself deeper and she was loving every minute of it.

"Now that you mention it, you may undress me."

"Do you want your father to murder me?"

There would be no removal of clothes now or ever. He suddenly needed a gulp of fresh air… outside… in another state. Back in Minnesota. That was far enough. Mountain man, chopping wood in a desolate cabin, away from all women sounded like a dream profession.

Frankie tapped her iPhone, unleashing Brian McKnight's "Back At One," a not-so-subtle reminder of the steps to love and the tenderness of her heart. Tanner was losing whatever game she was playing with his mind.

He sighed heavily, hoisting her from the waist. "Up you go."

Frankie clung to Tanner's neck, as she had at the pond, watching him with those eyes. "Dance with me, Tanner. It's good therapy. I miss it almost as much as I miss racing."

"Dance," he repeated. Her perfume and the closeness

of their faces left him with the speaking capacity of a caveman. "I'm not much of a—"

"Please?"

He wasn't sure what she was really asking for or if he could deny her anything as her hands rubbed the back of his neck and her eyes searched his. He set her down so her feet rested on top of his and their bodies pressed together. She was so light and this was too easy. He waited for the alarm bells, but they never came. He breathed deeper, feeling his shoulders relax beneath her.

"This is just for your therapy." Who was he kidding?

"Mmm hmm." She hummed against Tanner's chest as he moved them across the floor. When the singer reached the "make you fall in love with me," Frankie started singing along.

The muscles in her arms and abs strained as she swayed with him. She was trying to walk again, even in her down time. She was always working and fighting to win. Without a doubt, she would do so eventually, or she'd go down swinging.

She looked up suddenly, her blue eyes shining like rays from the full moon through the sky light. They connected with his as intimately as their bodies. One step, two steps, and he backed her against the wall. Wordlessly, they breathed each other in, lips hovering, anticipating.

Something flickered in Frankie's eyes. Behind the sweetness and strength was a vulnerable woman afraid of being rejected again. She was wise to be afraid of Tanner.

He put out a hand to steady himself, but it slammed against the wall beside her head. She gasped at the impact.

"Stop. Making. Me. Crazy." He issued the warning

against her ear, but it sounded more like a wounded animal than a threat. He willed his body to pull away from her and set her down somewhere like Siberia, maybe?

All he could manage was one step back.

"Tanner, wait!" Her hands moved from his neck to his biceps and held on.

She'd gone from warm and flirty to ashen in a heartbeat. The only thing this brilliant mission of his had accomplished so far was hurting the woman he'd promised to protect and defiling the memory of the woman he'd failed to protect.

"No, Frankie. I have to go. This is madness."

"My foot moved again."

"It happened before?" He scanned her legs and feet. She must have moved given how much she was shaking.

Tanner transferred her over to the bed and propped her up against the pillow. He wrapped his hands around her feet, massaging.

She nodded, half-laughing, half-crying. "There it is!"

He couldn't help but laugh, too. "I see it now. I feel it. What did I tell you? Never give up. You just need time to heal."

"It happened once before when you dunked me in the pond and I came up out of the water. I wasn't sure, because I was so emotional, I thought maybe I'd dreamed it."

"It's a dream come true." He stood over her, not willing to risk sitting on the bed.

"I can't wait to tell Selah and Daddy. Oh, and Mark."

Mark. Dark clouds rolled in over Tanner's surprisingly hopeful mood. "I need you to do something for me."

She raised an eyebrow.

"Let's keep this development to ourselves for now."

"Why? Aren't you proud of me?" She morphed from victorious to vulnerable in a heartbeat.

He knelt in front of her, grasping her wet cheeks in his hands. "I have never seen anyone work harder to achieve a goal than you, Frankie Newman. You are a force to be reckoned with. Be proud of *yourself*."

"But…"

"The person who put you in this chair is still out there and he believes he's neutralized you. We'll use that to our advantage."

Frankie snapped her fingers and pointed at Tanner. "If they realize I can walk, they may try to hurt me again!"

"Affirmative. Continue your therapy as usual with Mark, get stronger, but try not to move your legs there. Something tells me you're already doing leg work on your own time anyway."

When she nodded, he rose slowly to his feet, creaking and groaning.

"Maybe you should get in some leg work, too." She laughed when he rolled his eyes. "I want to help find this guy. I do trust you, Tanner."

And I trust you. The game had changed. The pawn had become his queen. Laying down the betrayals of the past and allowing her in was risky but liberating.

"I'm headed out for the night for real this time," Tanner said.

"You're still going to help me get undressed though, right?"

CHAPTER TWENTY-ONE

"I don't run away from challenges. I run over them."

–Frankie Newman

FRANKIE WAS RIGHT about one thing, Tanner needed to put in a leg day at the gym. Pulling himself away from her felt like slogging through mud left by the spinning wheels of her race car.

Desperate for space from her face, he sent an emergency SOS to Mario, who agreed to guard Frankie a few days. Not that Tanner didn't see her face when he closed his eyes at night.

Rebuilding the protective wall between them would be easier with Selah in town. She'd flown in for a quick trip to check on Frankie and watch her and Margo film a special live episode of *Momma's Family.*

Distracting Frankie meant more time to nail Kenny Newman. Maybe he should hire mercenary Momma to do it for him. For now, he could only depend on Russ Morgan and a hacker friend Mario used as backup.

Beady eyes followed Tanner's every move. Ignoring the stares, he picked up the pace. He had a job to do. The animals on the walls of Newman's office were alive and free once, but Newman snuffed them out, just as he had—

The toe of Tanner's boot caught on a cord stretched across the floor, sending him face first into a lion's head. He bit back a growl as he dislodged himself. Wouldn't Frankie have loved witnessing his little trip through wild kingdom? She wouldn't be too thrilled that his target was Daddy. Soon, he'd show her solid proof that her father wasn't the man he claimed to be.

When Tanner's chest finally stopped pounding, he went to work. Mario's co-hort had re-routed the security system so Tanner could slip into Newman's office undetected. Tanner nudged a USB into Newman's computer and set up the DIY robot built for safe cracking. If Tanner was a betting man, he'd say Newman would go old-school and store his important papers in the safe rather than trusting the newfangled computer.

Tanner had enlisted a distraction that should take just long enough for him to find what he was looking for.

"Here we go," Russ Morgan's drawl crackled in Tanner's earpiece.

Tanner glanced at his phone and refreshed the videos of Russ and Kenny Newman sharing a drink at a private gaming table in the casino. As they chatted, Tanner skimmed through files and drawers, felt along the walls for hidden panels, and periodically checked on the safe and Russ.

"How long have I put up with you?"

Newman's voice sent both ice and fire through Tanner's

veins. It had been the last sound Tanner heard before he took a bullet to the chest.

Russ chuckled, smoothing his bushy white hair and mustache. "Forty years? Why put a number on friendship?"

Newman snorted, taking a sip of bourbon. "We've had our ups and downs, mostly your downs. But you did save my backside in high school, and I pay my debts."

Russ was saying, "You owe me for introducing you to Tanya. Wasn't it something how Frankie crashed July 4, same day Tanya passed?"

Newman set the drink down hard but said nothing.

Russ's head swiveled when a slot machine ding-ding-dinged for a winner.

"Focus," Tanner whispered. "Your family's depending on you."

Russ cleared his throat. "That's why I wanted to talk to you, Kenny. The wife was cleaning out our attic and found some articles and photos about Tanya. She thought you or Frankie might like to reminisce."

Newman took an envelope from Russ, glancing at the documents Tanner had procured from the library and the school's yearbooks.

Newman downed the drink and motioned for a hostess, who promptly brought him another. "Memories are overrated."

"She'd be surprised, wouldn't she, of the success you've made for yourself? From pig farm to penthouse?" Russ slowly turned up the heat. "The rest of us just ain't that smart or lucky."

Newman dropped the photos back into the envelope but kept the article about her death in front of him on the table. He swirled the bourbon before tracing the article with the glass bottom. "What you mean is she'd be disgusted by the life I've made."

Tanner glanced at the safe. The robot was taking too long. Tanner had an idea for the combination, but he'd have to get it right on the first try.

Newman's voice dropped an octave. "The irony is that I did it for *her*, not for the money."

"How's that?" Russ asked.

"Tanya got so sick so quickly. No warning, just a few fainting spells. The doctor brushed her off with a death sentence and hospice, rather than pursuing a cure. He was more anxious to get back to his golf game than to save my wife."

"Whatever happened to young doctor Gibbs?"

Tanner looked up as Newman stretched his thumb and index finger into the shape of a gun and tapped the glass.

"Dead. Sheriff Cody Buchanan, Sr. found him at one of those seedy bars on the outskirts of town. You just never know who you'll meet up with in an alley, Russ."

Now they were getting somewhere.

Russ swallowed, scratching at his neck. "No. No, you don't."

Stay cool. Bring him back around again.

"She died too young, Kenny," Russ patted him on the forearm. "But you did what you could to save her."

Newman leaned away. "She was in so much pain. Cancer had spread to her bones. Liver failure caused dementia. I found a clinical trial in Mexico, but Government red tape blocked us from getting our passports expedited. The drugs weren't FDA-approved, so we couldn't bring them into the country. I arranged to drive her myself, but…"

"But she passed before you could."

"The bureaucracy killed her. Keeping Americans from what they need, what they have a Constitutional, God-given right to. You ever heard your wife crying in pain and nausea and losing her mind as her organs shut down?" Newman looked down at his open palms.

Russ shook his head slowly.

"Has the woman you love ever begged you to call the game warden and catch the imaginary goats and llamas in front of her window so they don't get cold or fall in the pond?" Newman's iron mask fell away for a moment to reveal a tortured soul. "Do you know how it feels when your wife says, 'Dr. Kenny, will you make that baby stop crying in the next room, I can't sleep?'"

"Reckon it'd make me feel pretty helpless." Russ' voice cracked. "Less of a man."

Tanner's gut wrenched at the thought of Frankie's mother suffering while her toddler cried helplessly. Watching the love of his life die in such a traumatic way had caused a part of Newman to die. Hearing his parents' screams as another car hit them head on had forever altered Tanner's DNA.

Newman suddenly leaned forward and pounded his fist, causing the table, Russ, and Tanner to jump. Despite their "friendship," Russ had taken some fists to the face over the years from Newman employees when he didn't pay his debts.

"I decided to take back my power."

"You did at that," Russ said. "How'd you manage to become the most powerful man in the county when I've worked like a dog for Good Company and we're barely hanging on?"

"I vowed that no one would ever go without what they need, regardless of government strictures. I would find a way."

Boost his ego, Russ. He's high on this power trip.

"Breaking the law to bring relief to the needy. Sounds like Robin Hood to me."

Yes!

Newman smiled blandly. "I'm a simple concierge. I see a need and I help fill it. Like you, I provide my customers something special. My product is a bit more specialized than cornbread and meatloaf. No offense to Margo."

Newman drained the glass and began to straighten his coat.

C'mon. C'mon. Tanner eyed the safe as he pulled the USB from the computer. Russ wouldn't be able to distract Newman much longer. Tanner would have to crack it himself.

"Hard to beat that cornbread," Russ chuckled.

"None of my business concerns the sweet little family you've got there, *friend*." Newman's iron walls locked in place again. "A beautiful daughter living in an isolated beach house with a three-legged dog and a baseball bat to protect her while her husband travels 3,000 miles away for work in New York City. A dutiful wife in a dilapidated home with no security system or smoke alarms."

Game over. Tanner's spirits plummeted and his pulse raced as his time ran out. The photos had rattled Newman, but not enough for him to let his guard down with his oldest acquaintance.

Russ drew his shoulders back. "No need for talk like that. I ain't about to give away your secrets. I might not be perfect, but my conscience is clear. Can you say the same?"

Newman calmly tucked the article back into the envelope and pushed it toward Russ. "Drink's on the house."

"Rolling your way," Russ huffed into the microphone. "Be careful, son."

Tanner pulled the robot off the safe. He didn't have time to wait for modern technology. If he didn't risk it, he might not have this chance again. If he did risk it, he might not live to take the chance again. He punched in the combination—the date of Tanya Newman's death—and said a prayer.

CHAPTER TWENTY-TWO

"They should change the name of the *Momma's Family* show to *The Betty Crocker Massacre.* The cooking always ends in disaster."

–Tanner Ashton

"Why isn't Tanner here?" Selah's eyes locked on the massively-muscled suit who had no hope of remaining inconspicuous in the downhome diner.

"I don't know. The replacement is cute with his little mustache." Frankie waggled her fingers at Mario, who nodded curtly.

Frankie did know and the truth stung. Her dance with Tanner last night had rattled him. She seemed to have that effect on men. He'd split and picked the largest bodyguard in the state to overcompensate.

"Hmph. That isn't like Tanner to bail. Well, I'm happy to take you out alone for a girls' day—lunch and pampering at the nail salon." Selah flipped her hair out of her eyes, posing like a diva. "Plus, we can gossip about him behind his back."

"Everything's perfect now that you're here. Who cares about Tanner?" Her skin warmed at the thought of him holding her, stroking her cheek and hair. Frankie held her arms out for an embrace that was more reliable. "Come give me a hug."

Selah jokingly put Frankie in a headlock before squatting and giving her a real, vanilla-scented squeeze. When Selah pulled back, they looked at each other, squealed simultaneously, and embraced again. Best friends were the best medicine.

Selah raised up and took stock of the diner. Momma pranced in one corner of Good Company, teasing and plastering her bouffant before her closeup. A producer, who was arranging huge biscuits on the countertop, frowned as another producer swiped one, shoved it in his mouth, and casually proceeded to adjust the lights. All of the crew were looking fluffier after weeks of sampling Momma's cooking.

"So, what's new with you?" Selah asked.

If only she could ignore Tanner's advice and announce that she had moved her foot and identified the cause of her crash. She would trust him this one last time.

Frankie said, "I'm dying to know what's happening at *The Winds of Change*."

"They've rehired Eva, and guess who hears about it when she doesn't take a shine to her storylines?" Selah put the back of her hand to her forehead.

"I hope her little one doesn't turn out to be a big fruit loop. That drama queen is living proof that looks can be deceiving."

"Shockingly, she's pretty good with baby Rich," Selah shrugged. "Rick has been a positive influence on her and loves to babysit."

"Rick?" Frankie searched her memory. "He was the hot tatted photographer who crushed on you? I question his choice of Eva as a girlfriend, but I'm grateful he saved you from wackadoodle dancer Lacey."

A flare of envy and sadness shot through Frankie—Selah had an exciting new life and lots of new friends on another coast without her.

"Lacey will be in a mental institution for a while." Selah nodded, her eyes and mouth downturned, ever compassionate. "Cane has stopped visiting. It upsets Lacey too much to be reminded of her twin sister's death."

"Well, it upset me when Lacey tried to murder you," Frankie said. "How awful for Cane, Tanner, and Lacey's sister. One night, one car accident scarred so many lives forever."

Was that what happened to Daddy? Had her mother's death broken something inside him that Frankie could never fix, try as she might to make him happy? She refused to allow her wreck to destroy her future.

Selah squeezed her shoulder and slid into a booth beside Frankie's chair, seeming to read her thoughts. "You'll get through this and you'll be behind the wheel again."

"I would give anything to race competitively again."

Selah said, "I saw a huge change in Cane after you helped him overcome his fear of driving. He said you're a natural teacher and intimidator. Maybe you should consider other options. Maybe God has a bigger plan."

"Can we not talk about God today? Why should I count on anybody other than myself? God's already proven He won't protect me. The more I pray about dating, the more losers who show up on my doorstep."

"God allowed the crash, but He didn't bring it down on you."

"Semantics," Frankie tossed her hand.

"Have you given up hope in God and in love?"

Frankie was silent.

"What do you feel like when you know you're a half a lap before the finish line and you're in the lead?"

"Like I'm flying," Frankie mused. "Like it's the best day of my life. Like everything has led me to this moment. Like anything is possible."

Selah smiled. "Well, that Frankie fire is still burning after all. Fan those flames. Don't let it die inside you. Someday soon you'll walk or you'll find something that gets you fired up in a way you never dreamed of."

"What if I never see victory lane again?"

"You'll land yourself somewhere better. I'll hold onto hope for you."

Suddenly, there was a devil of a commotion as a producer hollered "Quiet on set!" in her ear and tried to yank the wheelchair. Mario was the one who did the yanking, bending the guy's arm back until he squeaked.

She smiled her thanks and used the diversion to spin away from Selah's rose-colored advice. Frankie quickly took her place in the spotlight beside Momma.

"Could you not have taken a moment to fix your hair and put on some lady lips?" Momma picked up a strand of Frankie's hair and dropped it like a French fry into grease.

Momma turned to snap at her own hair and makeup artist, who was actually an overworked camerawoman pulling double-duty with a giant toolbox of colors, brushes, and a mirror.

The woman, who appeared to be the same age as Frankie, looked her over, and handed her a small tube of lipstick. "You don't need fixing. You are already gorg, girl."

Frankie dabbed on the lipstick and winked at her. "Time to shock and awe."

In a few moments, the cameras and Momma were rolling.

"Welcome y'all to *Momma's Family*. Margo Morgan here and my sidekick, Frankie Newman. I'll be cookin' and she'll be eatin', I reckon."

Frankie grinned as Momma filibustered.

"We're fixin' to have a Q&A before the angel food segment today. Seems like a waste of time when we could get straight to cooking, but I aim to please the viewing audience."

Momma reached for a stack of cards containing viewer questions, but Frankie grabbed the deck and announced, "I'll start. Thank y'all for sending your support on social media after my wreck. I could feel your prayers."

Frankie swallowed hard against the lie but couldn't shake the unease that Selah's advice had left behind. "Now, for questions: Irma from Idaho wants to know how Margo gets her hair so big and pretty."

"Plaster of Paris." Frankie answered before Margo could.

Margo patted her coif, cheesing for the camera. "Thank you, Irma. I just tease it to Jesus."

"Her ego inflates the hair, Irma. Don't make it any bigger." Frankie rolled her eyes.

Margo grabbed the cards and began to read. "There's a bunch for you, Francine. Question Number 1: 'You're really pretty and normal for someone in a wheelchair.'"

"Um, thanks? Next."

Her mind went to Franklin D. Roosevelt, Joni Eareckson Tada, Christopher Reeve, Michael Zaslow, Stephen Hawking, Frida Kahlo, and all the other heroes on wheels. It was just a piece of rolling metal, people, not the scarlet letter A.

Margo flipped through the cards. "These seem to be from male viewers, 'Can I get a ride?' 'How fast can you go?' 'Can you do it?'"

Frankie willed her face not to flush, which is what she wanted do with these question cards. The producers, who had obviously stacked this deck, looked pleased as punch.

"Well, I ain't never!" Margo pointed a finger at the camera. "I might be old, but I ain't dumb."

Aww, Momma was defending her again.

"You boys should be ashamed of yourselves saying such things to a poor woman confined to a wheelchair."

"I'm a wheelchair user, Margo!" Frankie smacked her forehead. "Think before you put your mouth in gear."

If only she could smack Momma without getting arrested for assault. Frankie needed to go on the offensive.

"Look folks. There's no shame in being different. Maybe you're in a wheelchair, maybe you wear hearing aids or have a guide dog, or maybe you have a skin condition or chronic pain or you're losing your hair. Rock it!"

Frankie looked over at Selah, who was smiling back, hand over her heart.

"A dear friend reminded me that you must find a way to live your life to the fullest, whatever the circumstances. It's not what you look like, it's what you fight like. Everyone else can deal with it. You don't have to answer to anyone else but yourself."

"Amen!" Momma said, fanning herself with three cards. "Now, are the sex ed class and the sermon over so we can get cooking?"

Frankie laughed, picking up a knife and fork and banging them on the counter. "Do your thing, Chef Momma."

Momma sighed dramatically, then launched into a spiel on the joys of angel food cake. She stirred egg whites, flour, sugar, and cream of tartar in a bowl as she gave her TV audience the measurements and baking tips.

"Some uninformed Yankees claim it originated as ice cream cake, which was a Pennsylvania Dutch wedding cake. We know better. It was invented in the South by slaves and included as silver cake in the cookbook of former slave Abby Fisher."

Momma poured the ingredients in a pan, swatting Frankie's hand.

"Don't never eat raw eggs or you'll turn into a deviled one." Momma popped the pan into the oven and moved toward the pre-prepared baked cake. Frankie already had a fork in it and tasted the slightly bland stuff.

"Maybe it needs butter?" Frankie put the fork down and leaned back in her chair, thrilled when Momma looked befuddled. "Why is it called angel food cake? I mean, is this really what angels would choose to eat given all the options out there?"

"It's supposed to be light and fluffy like angel wings. I bet when the Israelites ate manna, it tasted like this."

Frankie's nose turned up. "Every day for 40 years? And then all they get to eat in the new kingdom is..."

"The promised land."

"All they eat in the promised land is milk and honey?

No wonder they protested and got mad at Moses." Frankie pushed a palm against the plate. "Hold the manna, Momma."

Momma jerked the plate away and set it aside. She gathered other ingredients, including sugar and chocolate sandwich cookies, and whipped up a cookies and cream concoction. She spread it over the cake and doused it in melted chocolate and strawberries before plunking it in front of Frankie.

"Is this more to your liking, madame?"

"Mmm," Frankie savored the first bite, then quickly added two more. Food always tasted better when her mouth was completely full. "Muth betther."

"Oh no," Momma said suddenly. "Oh no, no, no."

Frankie looked up but kept eating as Momma trotted over to the oven, grabbed some mitts, and flung open the door. Black smoke rolled out as Momma unveiled an equally black cake and the smoke alarm began to clang.

"*Now* the angel food is devil's food!" Frankie observed.

And, oh boy, did Momma's face resemble Lucifer. Frankie glanced over at Selah who pressed one hand to her mouth and the other to her shaking belly.

"Where in tarnation is that spray stuff?" Momma shouted as she threw open doors and cabinets.

Once again, the producers and camera people didn't lift a finger to help. They had signed on as mere passengers in Momma's train wreck.

"The fire extinguisher?" Frankie offered, pointing to the big red canister that had been hanging in the same spot for twenty years.

But there was no need for it because the sprinklers initiated. Now, the Hollywood people, who had no interest in protecting human life, began to scramble to cover their equipment.

Mario grabbed the handles of her chair. "Never fear, Miss Newman, I'll chariot you to safety."

"Aww, Mario, the entertainment is just getting started. Wait, my food!" Frankie turned around and grabbed her plate and the bowl of cookies and cream.

Selah snuck out with them as they left Momma batting at the smoke and giving orders. "You come back here. Francine, this is all your fault!"

Selah shook her head. "Another show, literally up in flames."

Frankie had to yell over the approaching siren of the Shadybrook Volunteer Fire Department. "Good cake though."

Frankie crammed in the last mouthful as they strolled the sidewalk toward the nail salon. "I don't know why we're doing this when no one will see my toes. They better have Wonder Woman blue.

Selah tugged Frankie's ponytail as she pushed the chair. "That cutie physical therapist will notice in pool therapy, and you might get a date."

Frankie scoffed. "My dating days are over. Kyle drove a nail in that coffin."

"Did I hear my name? My ears are burning."

As the speaker came into view, Frankie's stomach sloshed like a shaken bottle of Pepto pink polish. She started to back up, but Kyle's smug face made her hold her ground. Kyle wasn't going to ruin a perfect day.

"I accidentally summoned a demon when I spoke your name," she said. "What are you doing here?"

Mario moved in, blocking Kyle as he edged closer to Frankie. Bandage tape stretched across Kyle's nose and he walked with a limp. Good. That would slow him down before he tried to take advantage of a woman again. What if she hadn't been trained to defend herself? What if Tanner hadn't found her? What if she finished off Kyle right now?

"Glad you haven't lost your sense of humor. To answer your question, the owners are friends of mine." Kyle carried a box labeled acetone under his arm. Since he didn't wear polish, he must be an OCD clean freak. "I'm happy to see you again, Frankie. I apologize for our misunderstanding. Please give me another chance."

She'd blocked his number, but he'd continued to text from other numbers, begging for forgiveness. "Misunderstanding? You tried to force yourself on me and then insulted me when I didn't meet your standards. That sent a pretty clear message."

"*This* is Kyle?" Selah marched herself right between the clown and Mario. "He's as plain as grass. I was expecting more of a man given the size of his ego."

God bless her best friend.

"Charmed," Kyle said as he flashed a smile at Selah. "Frankie, you're as beautiful as ever. I've got to run, but don't let my one mistake keep us from finding happiness."

"The nerve of that guy!" Selah huffed. "Shoot him next time, Mario."

Mario gave her the thumbs up before ushering them inside. Frankie's heart was still beating in her ears as Selah got the attention of the nail techs who took them back to adjoining pedicure spa chairs.

Kyle'd seemed surprised to see her, so he hadn't been stalking her. It was just rotten timing. Was it awful that she was disappointed he wasn't dead? Was it really awful that he'd gotten to her a little, calling her beautiful and begging for another chance? Her head spun like the lavender and pink lights in the bubbling foot bath.

She glanced at Mario, who stood guard in place of that chicken Tanner who ran away when she got too close.

Selah the mindreader said, "Someday the right man will pursue and love you with everything he's got. All the rejection and losers will be forgotten."

CHAPTER TWENTY-THREE

Be Fast or Be Last

If only Tanner could forget. He didn't know how long he sat in his apartment staring at those pictures and reliving the night he'd almost died. He'd guessed the July 4 combination on the first crack and logged the contents before the boss caught him. The photographs Kenny Newman had locked away pierced Tanner like the bullet that changed the trajectory of his life.

The cold bottom shelf of the safe—Newman's personal morgue—held a stack of papers, a golf tee, and two photos. Tanner swallowed hard against the lump in his throat as he traced the first image he'd captured and printed from his phone. She was smiling through a tooth gap as she decorated a Christmas tree he'd never seen. But he had observed the cherry wood panelling behind her on the walls of Newman's home. Her long, silky brown hair with eyes to match were unmistakable.

"Danielle," he whispered, willing her to explain herself and clear up her betrayal as a misunderstanding.

In an instant, he was transported to their last night together. He'd just returned from a job in Asia. He didn't need a welcome-home party or anything special, but he certainly hadn't expected to find her D.C. apartment locked up, covered in dust, suitcases missing. He tracked her cell phone to the alley of a bar in Cleveland Park, figuring he'd find her hanging out with friends. Danielle always loved surprises.

"Hey," he'd said simply in case she was still undercover.

She spun to face him, her mouth stretched in a wide "O". She'd shut down the shock quickly, blanking her features and shrinking from his outstretched hand. "What are you doing here?"

What are you doing with another man in a dark alley?

"Who's the vagrant?" The man's face was obscured by shadow, but his voice clear and unforgettable.

Tanner hadn't had time to change, shave his foot-long Professor Shaggy beard, or cut the even longer curly hair. He just wanted to come home to his fiancée and thought maybe she'd even dig his new look.

"Just an old friend." Danielle put her hand on the man's bicep and tried to turn him in the other direction.

Tanner backed away. She was working and he'd interrupted.

"Get rid of him."

"What? No!"

"Now, Dani. Show me that I can trust you or you'll join him at the bottom of the Potomac."

And just like that, the woman who'd suckered him into a June wedding with froo-froo pink flowers and a matching cake and a huge guest list drew her weapon and shot him in the chest. He could still feel his ribs crack with the impact.

The icy water on the pavement seeped through his clothes as her high heels clacked away and slipped into a town car.

Tanner inhaled sharply when Kojak jumped on his lap, jarring him into the present. She curled up in a ball on his lap and purred, as if the world wasn't spinning out of control. He stroked her neck, desperate to believe it too.

Grandma would be so excited to meet this cat. She had a small herd of them who kept her company while she painted. After the shooting, she'd flown in to care for him. When he was well enough to travel, they'd driven back to Minnesota to keep her and the furry monsters company while he pieced together how the woman he loved and trusted had become a murderer. Grandma encouraged him to date again. His chest might have healed, but his heart had hardened permanently.

Tanner glanced at the second photo and threw it onto the coffee table. It was all the confirmation he needed that the Newman family was responsible for setting dynamite to his life. He just couldn't believe that the one to light the match had been Frankie.

Frankie was burning rubber to get to her bed. She hugged her best friend goodbye at the airport, said goodnight to Mario, and slammed the barn door shut behind her. What a day! She couldn't wait to tell Tanner about it. If he was still talking to her.

When Frankie flipped on the lights, she startled at the sight of a figure on the couch. She caught herself from tumbling out of the chair.

"I've been thinking about you all day." Tanner's voice echoed off the rafters.

She'd been dying to hear those words since she met him, but the ice that dripped from them sent chill bumps down her arms.

"What are you doing here?"

He grunted. "Where have I heard that before?"

She hit the gas to the couch where he sat, hunched and staring straight ahead at the photograph lying on the table in front of him.

"Where have you been all day? What is wrong with you? You're scaring me."

"I've been waiting for you. Waiting for the truth." He looked up at her then, black holes swirling with a menace she'd never seen there before.

"You done lost your mind. Last I knew, we shared a special night together. You couldn't handle the heat, so you found a replacement bodyguard. I don't deserve this anger. If you don't like me, leave for good."

"Soon enough." He nodded, then dipped his head in the direction of the photo. "First, I need answers. Take a gander."

Frankie picked it up, smiling, relieved to see a familiar face. "Dani! I have missed her. Where did you get this? Is she back in town?"

Tanner straightened, studying Frankie like a mutating virus under a microscope. "Tell me about Dani."

"It's been a while since I've seen her. She was Daddy's lady friend for a few months."

The muscle in Tanner's jaw jumped. He rubbed it slowly.

"I never saw them kiss or anything. I just assumed. I certainly loved her. She joked that I could call her Danica, because, you know, NASCAR." Frankie smiled. "She talked to me like we were besties, but she always seemed a little lonely."

"Have you ever seen the necklace she's wearing?"

Frankie instantly recognized the little pink racing flags that read "Speedway Princess" and dangled on a silver chain.

"Oh, I'd forgotten about that old thing." She looked up from the photograph and wished she hadn't. The intensity of his stare could blind a person. "Daddy bought it for me from one of the vendors at a big race. As you know, I'm not exactly princess material."

"Warrior princess," he muttered, a chink in his armor cracking. "Speedway queen."

She wanted to reach across the table and touch him, but she'd get burned. "I wore it once just to please him and Dani admired it. I gave it to her later because she was cool and I was kind of hoping she'd stick around and make Daddy happy."

Tanner squeezed his eyes shut for a moment and took a breath before opening them again. Frankie longed to wrap her arms around him and ease the despair that had set in. He was supposed to be her rock.

"What happened to the necklace?" Tanner asked.

"I don't know. I guess she kept it." Frankie tried to remember more details. "As sweet as Dani was, she didn't talk much about herself or spend time outside the casino. She and Daddy went to D.C. a lot for business. After Christmas, I never saw Dani or the necklace again."

Tanner leaned forward again, putting his elbows on his knees, as if he needed assistance carrying the weight of their conversation. He interlaced his fingers and rested his forehead on his fist.

"Tanner, please, let me in. What is so important about that necklace? What happened to Dani?" She hugged the photograph to her chest, fearing the worst.

Tanner slid his hand over the sofa cushion and picked up another photograph, handing it to her.

She gasped, shaking her head from side to side rapidly. "No, no, this isn't…"

"Yep. Danielle Undine Khouri. Cause of death: *Accidental* overdose. Found in the back alley of a bar in Washington, D.C."

Frankie grabbed a wrench from the workbench and pointed it at him. "How do you know all this? Who are you, Tanner Ashton? And your answer better be the truth."

"You first," his eyes challenged her, but they'd softened since Frankie first came through the door.

"I have told you the truth since day one. I have given you everything I have and everything I am." She shook the wrench. "Are you accusing me of something? Spit it out. What happened to Dani? She wouldn't have overdosed like that."

When Tanner hesitated, she yelled, "Speak! I'm spinning my wheels here. What is it you want me to say?"

"Look closely at the photo."

"I'd rather not." She glanced at it and looked away. Frankie couldn't even watch *NCIS* for all the blood, gore, and violence, let alone study the body of a friend.

She tried again, because, for some reason, that's what Tanner needed. Then, she saw it. Dani, her beautiful skin marred with bruises, was clutching Frankie's pink necklace.

"You don't think that I…" Frankie searched his face. With all they'd shared, he couldn't believe she'd ever hurt someone, let alone kill her.

He took the photo from her hands and set it on the table. Reaching across the divide, Tanner enveloped Frankie's hands in his. "No. I don't believe that you killed Danielle, but, when I saw that necklace, *your* necklace, in her lifeless hand… I have been betrayed by a woman before."

"You loved her, didn't you?" Frankie's eyes filled. Dani was kind and attentive to her father, but she wasn't in love with him.

He smiled weakly and shut it down. "Danielle was my fiancée."

Frankie's heart broke for him, but then her senses kicked in and sympathy turned to questions, endless questions about the man she'd trusted to protect her. "You were engaged to Dani? Before she met Daddy?"

Tanner nodded. "I found those photographs in his safe."

She froze, dropping his hands. "Why were you poking around in Daddy's office?"

"*Daddy* kept a photograph of his girlfriend's dead body locked away in his safe. That photo was not logged into evidence. The necklace isn't in the official crime scene photos that were logged into evidence. Do you understand what I'm saying?"

Frankie's brain did gymnastics for so long Tanner piped up. "Someone snapped a photo of her dead body then took the necklace before the police found her. Your father has that photo in his safe."

Why didn't Daddy tell her Dani died? Did he know she was using drugs? Maybe he hadn't wanted to upset Frankie with such grim news and he'd sheltered her like he always had.

"There must be some explanation for why he has it. Maybe

the police lost the necklace and the photo. He would never hurt her. He's not evil. Why would he kill an innocent woman?"

"Because she wasn't innocent." Tanner turned over the photo of Danielle's body and looked away. "Because she didn't give him what he wanted, and he figured out she was a drug enforcement agent working undercover."

"Agent? Drugs? You just told me she died over an overdose. This is ridiculous. Daddy certainly doesn't do drugs. He runs a speedway and a casino."

"Both of which are a front for his real business."

Frankie rolled away from him, two feet, five feet, then behind the car. "I will ask you again, who are you? You didn't come to town because you heard Cane was here with Selah and wanted to connect. You didn't stay in town to legitimately work for Daddy and protect me from the boogeyman. You came on some revenge mission."

Tanner didn't move, didn't threaten, just sat there looking like a man who'd had his heart torn out of his chest and came to town to break hers.

"Was it you who tried to kill me, Tanner? You're the chemistry nerd. Maybe you laced my helmet. Were you planning to kill my father? And for what? Some misguided belief that we doped up and dumped your fiancée? Do you think I'm a monster?"

"No."

He was infuriatingly still and monosyllabic. Of course, Tanner would be calm, he had known every detail about everything and everybody in Frankie's life from the first moment he strutted into town. She had trotted along behind him like some dumb puppy believing that God had finally heard her prayers and sent her a playmate.

"The Tanner I knew… The Tanner I *thought* I knew wouldn't have kept me in the dark while he followed his own agenda. Explain yourself or I am calling Daddy and the police and Selah and putting an ad out in the *Shadybrook Squealer* that you are a liar."

No answer.

"You know, sometimes I wonder if I knocked on your heart, would your chest be as hollow as the Tin Man's?"

Tanner stood slowly then and held his palms up. "I will explain. I owe you that. But first, I'm laying down my weapon."

Frankie clutched the wrench tighter. Tanner drew his weapon, pointed it away from her, and unloaded the bullets, placing them and the gun on the table in front of her. He eased out of the holster, setting it aside. His eyes never left hers as he pulled his shirt over his head.

"A strip tease will not distract me." It already had, but she wasn't about to let him know that.

Frankie's anger lost its steam as real emotion filled his eyes and his face for the first time since she'd met him. He inhaled deeply and let it out slowly, his shoulders sagging on the way down. As much as she wanted to hate him and run, she couldn't.

Tanner dropped his hands by his sides, walked over to the car, and stood bare-chested before her, the circular scar emblazoned on his chest. It had lost its fascination. Had he been shot because he deserved it or because he was committing a crime? Perhaps another gullible woman had finally had enough.

"What on earth are you doing, Tanner Ashton?"

"Showing you where my heart used to be."

CHAPTER TWENTY-FOUR

TANNER HATED THE fact that, for a moment, when he'd seen the photograph of Danielle clutching Frankie's necklace, he'd doubted Frankie. He hated that he'd put fear into fearless Frankie's eyes and that he might lose her too.

"I just don't understand, Tanner. Help me understand."

"I came to town for the truth."

"What truth?"

"The truth about why Danielle shot me in the chest and left me for dead in an alley a few months before our wedding. The truth about who murdered her not long after. When it looked like I'd never get answers from your father, I wanted to leave town, but I stayed to protect you."

Frankie stared at his face, then his chest, then his face again as she jerked the wheels on the chair back and forth, back and forth. The clock behind her ticked 11 p.m., 11:01, 11:02, 11:03, as he broke out in a cold sweat. Would she hear him out or run to Daddy and the police?

Finally, she set the wrench in her lap before turning the wheels toward the couch.

Pulling herself onto the seat, she waited, arms crossed. "Sit down and start talking."

Tanner hadn't talked this much in years. The fury that had fueled him dissipated into exhaustion. He sank onto the other end of the couch.

"From the beginning," she said.

"The beginning was you, Frankie."

He didn't restrain the smile that came to his lips. Emotions got you killed in his profession. Now that he could be honest with her about a few things, he didn't have to hold back.

"It all started with a photo of you. Danielle, Agent Khouri, left a file on a desk in her apartment a few years ago. I knocked it onto the floor and a photo of you and your father fell out. Apparently, the FBI and ATF had never turned up anything concrete on him, so the DEA and Danielle took a crack at the case."

Frankie frowned. Would she ever fully realize the kind of man her father was?

"She couldn't discuss the specifics of the case, so I didn't press her on it. That image of you stuck with me. Something inside me longed to protect you, even then."

Her bright blue eyes widened. That revelation was a surprise to Tanner too. From the moment he saw that photo, he was hooked by Frankie, a perfect stranger. And she turned out to be perfect: kind, smart, wise-cracking, tenacious, with a natural beauty.

"So, uh," he tried to refocus but Frankie was distracting him again. "A few months after we got engaged, I left the country on a job for nearly a year. Danielle and I hadn't been on solid ground for a while and I thought absence might make the heart grow fonder. Big mistake. I wasn't there for Danielle when she needed it."

"She could handle herself."

"Sometimes," he agreed. "We all need a little help when we're staring our demons in the face."

Frankie's eyebrow quirked as she stared him in the face.

"I am sorry, whether you believe me or not." Tanner began to reach for her and stopped. "If I had told you the truth earlier, it would have jeopardized your safety and everything I'd worked for, everything I'm still working for."

"Blah. Blah. Blah." Frankie rolled her eyes. "I don't need another rallying cry about your ridiculous secret mission to bring down my father. Just tell me the story. Tell me about Danielle's demons."

"Like my brother, she struggled with addiction from an early age. When she got clean, she went to college and joined the DEA as a chemist and later trained to be an agent, believing she could save the world and help take down the dealers."

"Was she using when she died? I didn't see a trace of it when she was here."

"Maybe. She was fine when I left, but she'd had a couple slips. It doesn't take but a few grains of fentanyl to affect you or to be lethal, it's so powerful. One person's high is another's overdose, especially if you add in other medication. She had a special interest in counterfeit opioids and fentanyl and bringing down clandestine labs and their chemical suppliers. I assume that's why the agency chose her to infiltrate your family."

"For what? We live in a small country town, not Miami.

I repeat: Daddy owns a casino and a speedway. He's not a criminal."

"He's got people to run the casino. He's got you to run the speedway and keep a clean set of books. That frees him up to run the real enterprise."

"You have no proof."

Tanner fiddled with his phone and cued up the audio of Kenny boasting to Russ about his business and explaining how bureaucratic red tape kept Tanya Newman from receiving cancer treatment. "Straight from the horse's mouth."

Frankie listened, her face etched in pure agony. "What my parents must have gone through when she died! It breaks my heart how much they suffered."

"That's the message you took away from your father's words? Frankie, he bills himself as a concierge. He procures stolen artifacts, weapons, petroleum, rare animals, prescriptions, illicit drugs, whatever the buyer wants. He's made it his life's mission to swindle the government every chance he can get. He's got Cody Buchanan and loan sharks shaking down good people like Russ Morgan, the man you consider a second father."

"Even if he did those things, it was only because he was so broken by her death," Frankie cried.

"Your father had already made connections with organized crime and tussled with the law before your mother's illness."

"I don't believe it."

"You saw the jaguar head from his recent trip to Mexico? He's been dealing with the cartel there and chemical companies in China and India. My guess is that he's ramping up to fund or build a clandestine lab somewhere and his business is ready to explode.

Frankie choked out a laugh. "This is… I always knew you were insane, Tanner, but this takes the cake. Daddy would never hurt me like this. He's a good—"

"You can't say it with a straight face, can you? Where was this good man when you were having your surgeries and going through rehab? Has he stopped by the barn once to see how his daughter is doing after she was paralyzed? How about after you received the threatening doll? Did he greet you at the door with a big hug and flowers and an 'I love you, kitten?'"

Tanner paused a minute, letting that sink in.

She looked down at her hands.

"Ask yourself what kind of man hunts endangered species for sport and keeps them as trophies on his wall. He'd display the photo of Danielle's dead body right up there beside them if he could. Along with the golf tee from the doctor he had murdered, because he wouldn't treat your mother. He'd string me up there too if he knew that I was the one he'd ordered killed."

"What?"

"You want proof?" He pointed to his bullet wound. "How about this hole in my chest? He ordered Danielle to shoot me."

"I understand why Dani shot you." She pulled her hair with both hands. "You are crazier than a dog in a hubcap factory."

"What I'm telling you is the truth and, deep down, you know it."

"No! He's not a murderer. He loves me. Daddy wouldn't

do this to me or to the memory of my mother. I admit he's not some 80's sitcom dad doling out hugs and advice, but he's taken care of me. Someone is setting him up. Maybe it's you. Maybe it's the people trying to kill me."

"The people trying to kill you are connected to Danielle's death. They want something from him, and they're not afraid to destroy his family to have it."

"Get out of my barn, Tanner Ashton. I never want to see you again." Frankie pushed up on the sofa, straining, her feet moving, but not enough to propel her forward. She dropped back into the seat, banging her fists against the armrest and cushion. "I have to warn him. He needs to know who you are and what you're trying to do to us."

If she exposed Tanner, he was a dead man. Newman would shut down the operation, flee the country, and no one would ever hear from Frankie again.

"You can send me away, but your father is going down. The feds are closing in. If you back him, don't be surprised if he takes you down with him. It's only a matter of time. If you somehow escape criminal charges and don't go to prison with him, this speedway, this barn, and this home you love so much will all be gone, property of the government. So, you better decide what you're going to do with your life when you're no longer the speedway queen."

The sun had gone down hours ago, but Frankie's eyes seemed to harness its power, hurling solar flares at him. Tanner'd hoped she'd come to her senses or put that college education to good use and intelligently analyze her father's true motives. If she could just remember all the times Tanner had helped her and realize he would protect her at any cost. She was Kenny Newman's little girl after all and blood was thicker than water.

"Open your eyes, Frankie. You *know* me. Yes, I've kept secrets to safeguard you, but I've always been by your side. Can you say the same for your father?"

She opened her mouth but was interrupted by a loud bang that shook the front door.

Tanner jumped up, striding towards the entrance, as he checked the cameras. He chuckled at the interloper.

"Your fan club is here." Tanner grabbed his shirt and pulled it over his head before opening the door.

Frankie's death glare changed instantly when she saw her visitor: Angel. The kid stopped her door pounding mid-air. Her mother stood behind her, trying in vain to hold her back.

Angel wheeled in and stopped in front of Frankie's chair, their feet touching.

"You're a sight for sore eyes." Frankie said.

Tanner extended a hand. "Janet, right? Tanner Ashton. Good to see you again."

The redhead, looking like her daughter's twin, ducked her chin and shook his hand.

"Oh, don't mind him, he's always pushing me around and talking behind my back," Frankie grinned at Angel, whose neck strained in every direction, trying to take it all in. "Why don't you come check the tire pressure on this clunker I'm working on?"

The girls, hair flying, raced to the car, zipping around boxes and carts until they nearly slammed into the trunk of the old Mustang. Tanner removed the photographs from the table and sofa and motioned for Janet to sit. She smiled up at Tanner and relaxed into the cushion, looking like a weight had been lifted. Frankie had a way of doing that. When he was with her, he could forget the outside world existed, forget why he'd come to Shadybrook in the first place.

"You should charge admission, Frankie," Angel said, cranking the gauge. "It's so cool. My friends would love to see this place."

"They can come for free," Frankie handed her a rag. "We'll tour the barn and the infield."

"What? Free? I thought you were a businesswoman." Angel rubbed her palms together quickly as if she was gonna make it rain. "*I'll* charge them and you give them a show. We split the profits, 60/40."

"Angel," her mother tsked.

"Kid makes a good point, Frankie," Tanner said. "After you show her and her friends around, maybe you could give them a safe driving demonstration."

Frankie scoffed. "And after that, I'll fly them around on my spaceship."

Tanner winked at Angel's mom. "I was thinking Frankie could use the car with the hand controls."

Angel and Frankie lifted up from the tire they were working on.

"I saw Lefty testing out a little Nissan on the track. Electronic brakes, throttle, clutch, and some gearbox thingamajig. Eh, you probably wouldn't be interested. Too complicated."

Frankie looked like she could levitate out of that chair. The joy on her face sparked in the place where Tanner once had a heart. Maybe Frankie was the adaptive equipment *he* needed to get his paralyzed soul running again. If he was capable of love, only Frankie could take him there.

"Of course, she's interested!" Angel answered for her.

Frankie gripped the rails, speechless for a moment, looking at him as if he had two heads—one who had lied to her all these months, the other who knew her better than she knew herself. "This doesn't let you off the hook."

"Didn't think it would." He ventured a smile.

She huffed, but at least she wasn't threatening to bludgeon him with a wrench, out him to her father, or call the police anymore.

"Lefty and I wanted to surprise you. Just keep it under the speed limit. Wouldn't want to reverse all the progress you've made."

"So, are we going to take it for a spin or not?" Angel squealed.

"Baby, it's past your bedtime, and we don't want to wear out our welcome." Janet rose from the couch. "We only stopped by to see for ourselves that you were okay after rehab."

"I'm more than okay," Frankie nodded. "Race car drivers never die. They just find another way."

CHAPTER TWENTY-FIVE

Summer Nights and Dirt Track Lights

Frankie found a way alright—she convinced Tanner to take them all to the track at midnight, Angel's mother to let the kid sit in the car, and Frankie's mechanic to turn on the speedway lights and teach her how to operate the assistive devices on the car. It was almost two when Angel went home and Frankie turned the key for a few laps of her own in the Nissan.

"Thank you for the surprise," she said, cinching his seatbelt tighter.

Was she trying to cut off his oxygen supply?

"I sense you're still angry."

"If, in some parallel universe, what you're telling me is true, this may be my last night on the track."

"Maybe you should consider taking your career in a different direction." Tanner suggested.

"What do you mean?"

"Racing encompasses so many more areas than just burning rubber. You're an accountant with drive, pun intended, and a positive attitude. You have a way with kids and you made one's dreams come true tonight. What if you could use your talents to help someone else?"

"How?"

Tanner shrugged. "That's up to you, Wonder Woman."

Frankie looked down at the hand controls and shifted into gear. "I'll think about it, and I know something that always helps me think."

Twenty "slow" laps in, Tanner groaned and gripped the dash as his stomach and head switched places and flipped back again. Sweat beaded on his forehead and arms.

"Whoa! Don't hurl in the car." Frankie's voice sounded like she was in a tunnel as they slowed to a stop. "Squeeze your muscles and put your head between your knees."

He obeyed mostly, but rested his head against the vent as she blasted the AC. Her hands rubbing his back and massaging his shoulders was the only healing balm he needed.

"I should have known you'd be dizzy. I got so caught up in being behind the wheel again, I forgot that it takes a while to get used to going in circles."

"Here I was worried about *you* having PTSD." He turned his head gingerly to face her, cool air whooshing into his ear.

"Riding at high speeds must take you back to the crash that killed your parents?"

"Stupid, huh? Some bodyguard I am, almost passing out in your car."

"I don't see how anybody could ever really get over a trauma like that." Frankie's voice was soothing as she unlatched his belt and brushed his clammy cheek with the back of her hand. "Cane couldn't even drive a car for 17 years because of it. I guess that makes you the stronger brother."

If he could muster an ounce of energy, he would marry this woman right now. The thought made his stomach flip again, but he didn't push it away. He didn't push her hand away either, even though the spinning had dissipated, and Tanner was feeling better.

"I like you this way," she said, tilting her head.

He raised up an inch, looking at her sideways. "What way? Nauseous? A hot mess? Do they call men that?"

"Smiling. Joking. Human." She laughed and smacked him lightly on the back before dropping her hand. "I was checking you for an on/off switch."

He coughed out a chuckle, took a deep breath of cold air, and sat back, sagging against the headrest. "I was human once."

A tap on the car window made him sit up straight. Lefty stood outside, right eyebrow raised, left eye covered by a black eye patch as faded as his salt-and-pepper hair.

"Don't worry, he doesn't move as fast as Momma and he's probably not as dangerous." Frankie winked as she rolled down the window.

Tanner knew better. Lefty had taught Frankie martial arts.

"Everything alright, Miss Frankie?"

"Rookie couldn't handle the G-Force. Can I drive this baby out of here?"

Was she talking about him?

"She's all yours. We'll customize her when you're ready."

Lefty patted her on the cheek before loading up the wheelchair. He rapped on the roof and waved her on.

"I know it's late, but I don't want to stop driving and go home yet. Are you feeling better?"

"We are not going line dancing." Tanner said when Frankie passed the barn and headed for the main road.

"Not tonight, but I need to show you something." Frankie drove towards the mountains. "Take my phone and put Ruby on speaker. I deleted all the photos you got so huffy about."

Tanner did as she asked. He would never snoop her phone again. Aunt Ruby appeared to be as kooky as her older sister, Margo Morgan. Owned a BBQ joint and a pet store right next door. Walked a pig and a parrot around Shadybrook like that was what normal folks did.

"This better be good," Ruby cackled. "It's after midnight, young lady. I'm already in bed and you should be too."

"Don't story me, Ruby." Frankie's drawl got deeper. Seemed like, when Southerners got together, their accents showed out as well. "I know it's poker night with the girls and you and Pearl will be up till dawn."

"Eh, you're too smart for your own good." Ruby chuckled. "What can I do ya for?"

"Would you turn on the lights over the mill for an hour or so?"

"Bringing your sugar over for some necking?"

Frankie shot him a sideglance. "Nah, it's just Tanner. I may break his neck though."

"Ooowee. Escort that fine bodyguard in here for a visit after. We need some entertainment." Female voices hooted in the background. "The best lookin' thing our age in town is Willie at the Chinese place and that dried-up mechanic of yours."

Tanner snorted quietly.

"Just flip the lights, Ruby, and I promise to send Lefty over next poker night, okay?"

"That'll do. Love you, badness. Try and behave or at least be careful." With that, Ruby disconnected.

Tanner wasn't trying to keep a straight face anymore. Frankie looked at him again and laughed. "They're actually really sweet, God-fearing ladies."

"*They* think I'm handsome. Although, they might have to fight the librarian for me, because she and I were betrothed in another life."

Frankie rolled her eyes as she brought the car to a stop at the edge of a tree-lined field. "In spring, wildflowers fill that field."

Tanner got out and helped her into the wheelchair, even though she needed no assistance. The fatigue he felt in his bones reflected in her pretty face. She led him around a gazebo and picnic tables and over a little bridge until they came to an old grist mill that looked like it had been around since the first settlers. The Blue Ridge Mountains towered in the distance; their azure tones had faded to deep purple in the moonlight.

"What do you think?" she motioned him toward a bench at the base of the mill.

"Enchanting," he said, looking into her eyes.

She sipped a breath before looking away. "That's what Dani said."

Would he ever conquer the wave of nausea he got when he heard her name? "She was here?"

"She wanted to see the countryside, so I took her on a road trip and we ended up here. She said she'd finally found the perfect place. Do you know what she meant?"

He stepped back quickly, dropping onto the bench seat. Danielle had taken over planning the wedding of her dreams, initially researching venues in the District. Tanner wasn't crazy about an uptight reception in a hotel, horns honking outside, people rushing past, going home to their families, not caring as he and his bride celebrated the most important day of their lives.

"She must have wanted us to get married here. She was anxious because she hadn't found the perfect place." He dropped his head in his hands. "If she was still planning on marrying me at that point, why shoot me?"

"Maybe it was an accident?"

"Not a chance." He shook his head vigorously. "She could have shot a hole in a quarter on the top of that mill. She was infinitely better than I was."

"Don't cops or agents shoot to kill? If she'd wanted you dead, you'd be dead. Since you're alive, she obviously hoped to keep you that way."

Tanner froze. How had he never thought of that? The bullet entered his chest without nicking arteries or damaging organs. He'd been so blinded by his anger and physical pain, he'd missed the truth right in front of him. "She saved my life. All this time, I thought she turned against me because she'd fallen for him."

"Who?"

"Kenny Newman."

&

Frankie pressed her mouth into a thin line. She'd let him explain himself, but no way would she ever believe Daddy murdered sweet Dani. Of course, she would never have thought in a million years that Dani was an undercover DEA agent. Frankie tried to push the doubts from her mind.

Tanner took her silence as an opportunity to dive in, detailing the night he was shot.

"I will never forget that voice, telling Danielle to get rid of me or we'd both end up in the Potomac River. She followed his orders," he said. "You know your father's distinctive voice—as loud and powerful as a gunshot."

Frankie whacked a mosquito on her neck, then another on her arm, and growled in frustration as they kept coming, relentless as Tanner's accusations. "Daddy would have recognized you when you came to Shadybrook if he'd already met you."

"I had a full beard, dark tan, long hair when he saw me with Danielle. *You* wouldn't have recognized me. I had a different name then, too."

"Disguises. Fake names. Who's the real criminal here?" She spat and moved to unlock the chair. "I'm leaving."

He loosely ringed her wrist, rubbing his thumb against the sensitive underside and erasing her thoughts.

"I changed my name from Tanner Ashton when I turned 18 and left Minnesota. I wanted a new life and identity separate from my twin's."

"What was your new name?"

"David Banner."

"Ha!" Frankie's mouth quirked. "David Banner? Now that I believe. Cane was right. You are a nerd."

"I'm insulted," he said, but he looked rather proud of

himself. "You know you loved that show. Banner was a man of science."

"A man who morphed from one personality into a hulk, while hiding a giant secret. Fits you to a tee."

She pinned him with her eyes. Maybe Frankie had morphed too—Wonder Woman was a mere mortal now, wondering how she got here. How had she let her guard down and allowed a man to take her for a fool? Her life had been just fine before Tanner Ashton came to town.

"Sometimes life imitates art." He nodded. "I lied about my purpose for coming to town, but I have shown you parts of me no one has ever seen. I never lied about wanting to protect you or help you walk again."

"Sure. Whatever." She sighed long and loud. Poor deluded fake bodyguard. She'd play along. "What happened after Dani shot you and left you for dead?"

"I went home to Minnesota. Grandma helped me get back on my feet, mentally and physically."

Would Frankie ever get back on her feet? What would her life look like when she did? Was there a way back into racing or would she be sharing a prison cell with Daddy?

She shut her eyes a moment, tuning out the tales spun by Tanner. A soft breeze from the lake carried in the jug-o-rums of bullfrogs and the scents of mud and grass and a distant (hopefully) skunk. Laughter and BBQ drifted out of Ruby's house as if everything was right with the world. Frankie opened her eyes, focusing on the faint star specks above the lights and the mountains. *Make everything right with my world again.*

She guessed it was a selfish prayer, but Selah said God

listened to all prayers. If only Selah was here to help her discern truth from the lies.

Tanner's voice rose above the frogs, startling her. "Not long after the shooting, Danielle was found dead in the same alley. The DEA wrote her off."

"Did you?"

"It's too convenient that she died of an OD from tainted fentanyl while investigating opioid dealers and labs. She was an outstanding agent, but, suddenly, negative performance reviews popped up in her file and everyone turned against her. So, I started digging."

Tanner looked up at the stars a moment too. "I can't help but think Danielle might have left something behind. What happened to the evidence she was collecting? Did she hide it before she died? Do you remember her giving you anything? Did she hang out anyplace else? Does anything stand out? Even something insignificant might be the answer."

"Only this place and the necklace."

His questions jarred another memory of something Dani said in confidence. Frankie filed it. It would come to her later, like a word on the tip of her tongue.

Tanner rubbed his mouth and beard. "I never had anything to go on except the photo of you and your father I found in her files. When I received the letter that my brother wanted to patch things up, I came to Shadybrook, curious about Cane's motives and about yours. I had no choice but to use my real name. There's no hiding from the Ashton legacy and an identical twin."

She watched him for an eternity. "You are such a hypocrite. Cane begged you time and again to forgive him for an accident that happened when you all were minors, and you still can't let it go. But you are a grown man now, and *you* lied to Cane, to Selah, to Russ and Margo, to me, and to my father, who entrusted you with a job guarding our family. How could you?"

Tanner dropped down in front of her, positioning himself at eye level and taking her hands in his. Muscles strained against his black t-shirt as though he was prepared to give chase when she split.

"I did it for you and Danielle. Her killer must be brought to justice. If Kenny is the kind of man I think he is, you are in grave danger living on his compound. If he murdered Danielle, what will stop him from hurting you and the Morgans? You heard him threaten Russ."

"What I heard was Russ, a compulsive gambler, babbling while Daddy told him to go home to his family. They've been friends since they were kids. How much did you pay Russ to get mixed up in this cockamamie scheme?"

"Russ wouldn't take the money. Said he'd do anything to keep his wife and daughters safe. It was time to step up after the mistakes he's made."

That revelation pushed her back against the chair. Selah was her soul sister. Margo loved to brag about how she'd "practically raised Frankie". But Russ… He considered her a daughter?

His "aw shucks" smile warmed the corner of Frankie's heart that her father had left cold.

She shook off Tanner's hands. "Get up. This nice guy act is not like you. You talk a good game. You seem sincere, but I cannot snap my fingers and trust anything you say after you've deceived me all these months."

"I'm not getting up until you believe me."

"Why? So, you can use me to take down my father?"

"Because," he knelt on the cobblestone path, looking up at her, "I care more about you than I care about justice."

Months ago, she'd prayed Tanner would come around and admit he cared about her, that he would stop pushing her away. Now, here he was, the swirling pool of his dark eyes beckoning her to test the waters. He stirred some untouched feminine place inside her.

"Who are you?" Frankie whispered the question she'd asked herself a hundred times in the last few hours.

"You *know* who I am. I am more myself with you than I've ever been."

He was the man who sat vigil in the hospital, waited outside her room at rehab for months, baptized her in the pond where her mother took her last breath, and held her while she cried to the depths of her soul. The man who'd helped install a roof on Momma's house. The man who'd stood up for his brother at his wedding even though he still held Cane responsible for their parents' deaths. The man who'd rescued the ugliest cat on God's green earth and was as dorky about old TV shows as she was.

The man she was in love with.

Frankie gulped in a breath and let out an "oh." She didn't know what love was. This couldn't be it. Nope. She was just sleep-deprived.

"It's late. Let's go home." She unlocked the chair, backed away, and punched it toward the car, not waiting to see the expression on his face.

"Night, Ruby," she hollered as she passed the house. "Hope you enjoyed the show."

Laughter erupted and a door slammed. Multi-color Christmas lights girding the old farmhouse illuminated the white hair and grinning faces at the window. Those lights stayed up all year until the holidays when Ruby added a manger beside the mill and a menagerie of gaudy blow-up animals skirting the lake.

Christmas! Dani spent Christmas with her and Daddy. She even gave Frankie a small present. Not long after that, she was gone. Frankie teared up at the memory. Dead. Had Dani feared she was in danger when she gave Frankie the gift?

Frankie couldn't wait to ditch Tanner and find it. Maybe then, she could prove to him that her father was innocent.

CHAPTER TWENTY-SIX

"I never lose, I only run out of laps, gas, or time."

–Unknown

FRANKIE COULD HAVE cried when she spotted the tub of Christmas ornaments in the back of a storage closet. Rescue and recovery presented a teensy problem. The box lay buried under two other tubs, a tree, and a wreath. She couldn't exactly ask Tanner for help digging it out. Buck up buttercup, and get 'er done.

She dragged the tree with one hand, backing up with the other, until the tree crashed to the floor, bringing the wreath with it. The other heavy tubs tested her strength. She knocked them to the floor, spilling their contents into one giant red and green tinseled mess. Frankie locked the chair and lowered to the floor, dragging her legs to the ornaments and throwing aside the plastic top. She rested a moment, huffing and puffing, with a new appreciation for Paralympic athletes who broke speed and strength records with less limbs than she had.

She hadn't collected many decorations on her own, just fun NASCAR trinkets her friends had gifted her. Add that to the mental list of things she would ask Margo about her mother—did Tanya Newman go all out for Christmas or was she kind of Grinchy like Frankie?

The best part of the holidays was Gingerbread cookies and eggnog cookies and sugar cookies. She even liked fruitcake. Her stomach growled. She hadn't eaten since she left Selah at the airport last night. She couldn't believe it but solving this mystery took priority over food.

Frankie got her second wind and dug into the box. There it was! At the very bottom of the barrel lay a kitschy plastic Wonder Woman ornament whose face looked like it been painted by a drunk factory worker. The black circles for eyes had run down into the big red open mouth, making her look more like the Joker. Dani had giggled over that ugly thing and told Frankie to treasure it as Dani treasured their friendship.

Frankie twisted her brain trying to remember, but Dani had said something like, "someday you'll understand." She'd seemed bona fide sweet but was hiding a badge and a sinister plan to betray Frankie and her father.

Frankie fished her phone out of the wheelchair pocket and took a photo of the ornament to remember it by. The ornament rattled when she shook it.

"Sorry, Wonder Woman," Frankie said before picturing Tanner's face and smashing the ornament.

It took a couple swings before the plastic gave way and a thumb drive clinked onto the floor.

"Gotcha." Frankie snatched up the Holy Grail.

She dragged herself back into the chair and rolled to her desk, sweat dripping, muscles screaming, and mind racing. The laptop took an eternity to come to life. By the time she slipped the drive into its slot on the side of the computer, her heart was pounding. She longed to fall into bed, pull the covers over her head, and pretend she wasn't about to detonate a grenade.

She rubbed her eyes and started clicking. A folder labeled "financials" appeared at first glance to hold copies of the speedway books, except those weren't the numbers Frankie had inputted on her spreadsheet. Dani's data was obscenely high, and there were payments to accounts Frankie'd never dealt with and currencies she'd never seen. It didn't make sense.

Another document "Synthetic Test" looked like a science textbook with formulas and 20-letter gobbledygook words like 4-anilino-N-phenethyl-4-piperidone (4-ANPP) and N-phenethyl-4-piperidone (NPP). She clicked out of that one when she flashed back to her chem final.

The schematics in a folder called "Lab", however, looked very familiar to Frankie. What would Dani need with a map of the tunnels under the property? Frankie and Selah had played in those passageways until Daddy put a stop to it. Some of the walls were crumbling and could fall on them. They could get lost or drown in a flash flood. She figured he'd walled them off by now, but the graphics showed entrances by the airstrip, the pond, and a few more she didn't know existed. A red x marked a spot underneath the casino and his office.

What had Dani been doing under there? Did Daddy know about it?

Frankie opened a gallery of photos of her father shaking hands with strange men. A list of contacts included China, India, and Mexico. Tanner said those countries were hubs for supplies and chemicals used in clandestine fentanyl operations being investigated by the DEA. Dani was lying to Frankie's face and setting Daddy up. But why?

The last doc was entitled "D Banner." The love letter from Dani begged for the forgiveness of Tanner's alter ego. Frankie teared up until she got to the part where Dani accused her father of causing her to return to drugs. She slammed the laptop shut. Hogwash. All of it. Danielle and Tanner Banner deserved each other. Professional hoodwinkers, the both of them.

Frankie wouldn't stand for this kind of attack on her family. She was going to end it once and for all. If the answers weren't in the tunnels, Daddy would tell her the truth.

She glanced at her watch. Six a.m. already! Time to get ready for her PT appointment with Mark. She texted him.

Frankie: Can't make it today

Mark: U can't duck out of water therapy. Pun intended!

Frankie: Need to take care of something. See u tomorrow I hope.

Mark: Coming 4 you.

She added a kissy-face emoji, then changed it to a hug. Future dates would have to earn her kisses. She silenced her phone so she wouldn't be bothered by his questions. The only question that needed answered right now was what part her father had played in this mess.

Frankie started to open the front door to the barn. Agh, the cameras! Tanner probably received an alert when anyone approached or left. Back door had one too. How could she get away by herself without him busting a gut to come after her? She could call someone to pick her up. Mark, maybe? No, if Mark came around, Tanner would giddy up, guns blazing.

She snapped her fingers. Tanner only trusted one person in town. She made a quick call.

"Russ? I need a favor."

"Anything for you, darlin'."

Frankie warmed at the smile in his voice. "Are you at the casino?"

When the Wheel of Fortune slot machine jangled in the background, Russ mumbled an excuse. The sun had just come up and he was already gambling. Russ was a good man, but he needed to get back into a program. Somebody could fix him, but it'd have to wait.

"Would you swing by the barn and give me a ride?"

"I'm up $300."

She didn't have time to argue. "Take your winnings, tithe your 10 percent, and come get me in the next five minutes, or I'll have the host cut you off permanently. Then, I'll send you home to listen to Momma complain about, well, everything."

Maybe she should have laid down the law on Russ years ago. This property was her inheritance. If she'd taken more of an interest in the business, she'd have shut down Dani's interference and kept Daddy on the straight and narrow.

Russ groaned and grumbled about his ungrateful family, but, in five minutes, he rolled up in his roulette-red Dodge Charger. After they stowed her chair and headed for the airstrip, Frankie gave Russ's rumpled jacket and hair a once-over.

"Have you even slept?" It was a wonder Momma didn't divorce him on grounds of abandonment.

"Have you?" He quirked a bushy eyebrow her way before steering the car west of the main house.

Frankie jerked down the visor and gasped at her finger-in-a-light-socket hair, the mascara etched into the creases under her eyes, and the smudge of chocolate on her chin. Turned out Snickers was the true breakfast of champions.

She rubbed off the smudge, put the visor back, and ran her hand over the dash panel. "This car is a work of art."

Lifting a gnarled hand from the wheel, he gently smoothed her hair. "It was nice to see you and Selah laughing and gossiping in the diner yesterday."

Frankie hadn't noticed him at Good Company and he hadn't come around to greet his daughter. Selah kept a stiff upper lip, but it had to hurt when she flew in from Los Angeles and her father wasn't there to greet her.

"Were you watching us from outside?"

He kept his eyes on the road as they pulled up to the strip.

"I'd give anything to be with my mother, Russ. Wouldn't matter if she'd made mistakes or done things she wasn't proud of, I would still love her."

Russ sniffed and coughed, turning his head to the driver's side window and shutting down the ignition.

"You fixin' to go somewhere?" He was quick to take a turn at her game of change-the-subject.

"Yep." Not a lie. She was going to get closure.

He creaked out of the car and helped her into the chair. Frankie about came out of her skin as she waited for Russ to dally and dawdle, lumber back to the car, ease in, adjust the mirrors, stare off into space, and, at last, turn the key to leave. Tanner was probably on the move by now, so she'd have to get rolling.

"Watch yourself," Russ hollered out the window as he drove away and she turned to find the entrance to the tunnel.

Frankie's heartbeat shifted a few gears as she scanned the deserted area. A black helicopter sat on the airstrip. Did it belong to Daddy? As she got closer the SS logo for the speedway came into view at the base of the aircraft. That expense was not included in her set of books. One more thing Daddy had kept from her. And for what reason?

The wheelchair became harder to push as a heaviness settled onto her shoulders. What if Tanner was telling the truth about her father?

Frankie expected cobwebs, overgrown bushes, and crumbling stones hiding the entryway to the privies of an era long past. What she discovered was a maintained walk, modern brick, and a shiny metal gate blocking her path to the tunnel.

"Huh," she muttered as she twisted and shook the locks on the gate. If only she had her toolbox, she could get after the locks.

Her high hopes for solving this mystery and saving the day on her own were shot. She'd have to wheel it back home or call Tanner and admit defeat. The puff went out of her chest.

As she considered her options, the crunch of gravel and a slamming car door turned her head. "Russ, I'm glad you're back. Do you have a crowbar?"

It wasn't Russ.

Mark, flashing that golden boy smile, was in her space before she even had time to move. Frankie's skin gasped with a shiver that hadn't blown in on the breeze.

"Need some help?"

Judging by the size of the pistol in his hand, she just might.

Alarms sounded in all directions and a sharp pain stabbed his nose, but it took Tanner a good two minutes to shake himself awake. Everything was hazy except Kojak sitting on his face, claws unfurled. Tanner must have fallen asleep on the couch as he rehashed his trip to the old mill. What a gift Frankie gave him when she showed him the spot Danielle had fallen in love with and helped him realize that his fiancée hadn't shot him intentionally.

Frankie! What time was it? He peeled off the cat, checked his watch, and groaned. Last night's clothes would have to do. Frankie needed to get her therapy appointment over with so they could initiate the next phase of his plan. He didn't have enough evidence yet to bring to the DEA, but, if Frankie agreed to act as bait, they could reel in her father.

When he arrived at the barn, Frankie's car was in the driveway, but she didn't answer the door, which was unlocked.

"Frankie? Are you home?" Tanner poked his head in and glanced around. The room was dark, but her perfume lingered.

He must have just missed her.

The security feed showed her leaving with Russ Morgan. She was safe at least. A pulse throbbed in his temples. Why wouldn't Frankie drive herself in the new car? Why hadn't she texted to give him a hard time about not showing up?

He got on the horn to Mario. "How soon can you make it to the pool and check on Miss Newman's physical therapy session?"

"I'll be there in a few minutes. I've had artificial intelligence doing a deep dive on the tattooed guy who took Frankie's helmet after the race. So far, no luck. He's a ghost, and you know what that means."

Tanner squeezed his cell phone, fighting the urge to hurl it at the wall. "It's a fed."

"I got your back, man. I'm a certified ghostbuster." Mario cackled.

"Get it done. Just don't get caught."

"Back atcha."

Tanner ended the conversation when he noticed red plastic shrapnel littering the floor and a flash drive lodged in the laptop.

He gave the mouse a good shake and stepped back when he saw the last line on the screen: *Love always, Danielle.* How had Frankie gotten her hands on Danielle's files?

My Delbar-am, the letter began with a Persian endearment. Dani always said he'd stolen her heart. She'd obliterated his.

This job has taken me far away from you and from myself. As you've probably already figured out by now, while you were in Asia, I went undercover to investigate Kenny Newman. I know you left because I was unfaithful. If I survive this, I will spend my life making it up to you.

You'll find everything you need on this drive to prove that he has been trafficking just about everything he could get his meaty hands on: artifacts, endangered species, and, now, counterfeit opioids. I'm hoping his increasingly bold grab for power will be his downfall.

I don't trust my task force contacts in Juarez. They seem more interested in the market for what I'm creating in the lab for Newman than in shutting down his distribution chain between the U.S., China, and Mexico. The file contains photos of who to steer clear of and who to trust. I know you'll get this evidence into the right hands.

I'm in over my head with Kenny. The highs are more than I've ever felt.

Sucker punch. The drug addiction she tried to overcome fueled sex addiction like a vicious cycle. He'd been a fool to think she'd beaten it.

Frankie is as innocent as they come. She is too busy playing with her cars to play a part in his business. Take good care of her.

Please forgive me, my love. You told me once, "Run from temptation," and you were right, as always. I wish I'd gotten on a plane to elope with you. I miss you more than I can say. I will die loving you.

Danielle

Tanner's chest constricted as if the mounting heat and pressure of a nuclear reactor had finally exploded. He hunched over the desk, face in his hands, wracked with dry shudders. She'd asked for *his* forgiveness when he should be asking for hers. He'd left her for too long and hadn't been there when she needed him most.

When the rush of guilt had calmed to an ache, he pulled himself back to the investigation, clicking through her other files. The financials alone would be enough to indict, but the laboratory notes, wow!

What have you done, Danielle?

Newman had asked her to perform the impossible and she had done it, creating a powerful new product that would take his business to the next level. The analog drug could be completely sourced and pressed in this country while cutting out foreign chemical suppliers and manufacturers.

No wonder someone was threatening Newman. They

wanted access to Danielle's formula. The only people she'd share it with were DEA.

As he scrolled through the file of contacts, the hair stood up on the back of his neck.

I knew it. He should have trusted his instincts.

When Mario's phone went to voicemail, Tanner's head began to pound. He made another call.

The person on the other end hesitated before answering. "Well, this is a surprise."

"I want to know everything about that physical therapist you sent Frankie."

Cane grumbled something about 'hello to you too' before responding. "I'm sorry about what happened with Joe. Something came up last minute, and he couldn't fly out there. Selah said the new guy is working out though."

"Joe?" Tanner groaned. "You didn't send Mark Martin?"

Everything he'd discovered on Mark appeared on the up and up, but identities could be manufactured, and websites and social profiles planted.

"No, is something wrong? Is Frankie okay?" Cane's voice was strained.

Everything was wrong and Tanner didn't have time to calm his brother's fears when Frankie's life was on the line.

"That's what I get for trusting you to handle something important." Tanner hung up, exhaling a prayer to save her life.

He tried calling Mark and Russ with no luck.

Tanner clicked the last file on the USB drive: a schematic of the speedway, main house, and casino grounds popped up. Someone had highlighted the intricate maze of tunnels undergirding the expansive property.

That was it. Frankie had gone to the tunnels. Always

determined to play Wonder Woman and save the day, she'd risk her life to protect the people she loved. If only she had chosen Tanner over her father.

Danielle's genius in creating a game-changing drug had gotten her killed. No way would Frankie meet the same fate.

Tanner's phone buzzed as he started up the Escalade and hit the gas.

"Mario, where have you been? Did you find Frankie? Did you get the files I just sent?"

"Miss Frankie isn't at the therapy pool." Mario puffed as if he'd been jogging. "Took me a few minutes to get here. I got a lock on the person who stole Frankie's fire suit and helmet after the crash."

"I already know. Mark Martin."

"The therapist?" Mario faltered. "I'm texting you a photo from his DEA file. You're not going to believe who it is."

Tanner choked on the name. It had been under his nose this whole time. Frankie was in more danger than he'd feared.

"Call it in. Now." Tanner ordered as he stomped the accelerator. "Danielle found all the evidence the DEA needs to bring Newman and this rogue agent to justice. Send it up the chain to the people we can trust."

"Oh yeah! I'm on it chief."

"Also, contact Deputy Gina Santiago in Shadybrook and have her bring local backup. We need all the help we can get. Russ Morgan is AWOL, but I'm assuming he drove Frankie out to the tunnels you'll find on the blueprints."

"What's your plan?"

"Heading to the tunnels. I'm bringing Frankie home."

Maybe for good, if she'd let him.

CHAPTER TWENTY-SEVEN

Smoke Tires, Not Drugs

FRANKIE JUST WANTED to go home. Instead, she was handcuffed to her wheelchair in Frankenstein's lab. Life had taken her into a blind curve and thrown down spikes on the road.

"Do you understand these rights as I've read them to you?"

"I understand that you have lost your ever-loving mind." She studied Mark's face. He looked angry and disappointed in her.

"I'm placing you under arrest for conspiracy to manufacture and distribute and for the murder of Special Agent Danielle Khouri."

"This gets better and better."

"You really should have opted for pool therapy this morning." Mark said, locking her chair in place. He stood, whistling as he looked around the tunnel at countertops lined with beakers and vials. "I would never have believed until today that you played a part in your father's business.

You were on your way here to meet him in Danielle's old lab, weren't you?"

"You've read me my rights. I'm not speaking to you." Frankie choked on a cough. "I thought you were here to heal me, not spy on my family. You and Tanner are cut from the same cloth of liars."

"There's nothing I wouldn't have done to help you walk again," Mark said, "But I had to take action after one of my agents was murdered and your father continued to thumb his nose at the government."

The vapors in the room tickled her nose and throat, causing her to cough again.

"Where are the masks located?" Mark asked, pulling out a pair of plastic gloves from his back pocket and slipping them on.

"How should I know? I haven't decided what I want to be for Halloween yet." Frankie rolled her eyes.

"Seriously, we need to mask up and get out of here. It's not safe." He pulled open a few plastic storage bins, rooted around, and produced two masks.

He secured a mask on his deceptively handsome mug and moved to help Frankie put one on. She grabbed the mask and slapped his hand away, struggling to loop it over her ears using one hand. Mark's face fell. Maybe he still cared about her and there was hope of getting out of this.

Mark knelt in front of her and stretched the mask over her ears. "I believe you're a good person. Save yourself and give up your father."

"Are you even a real therapist? Did you ever care if I walked again?"

"I cared so much that I was going to walk away from

this job for you. You are one of a kind, Frankie Newman." Mark touched her leg, then drew back, his eyes soft. "I tracked you here to tell you that. Little did I realize you'd lead me straight to what I've been searching for."

"I don't even know what this place is. I haven't been to the underground since I was a kid." Frankie waved her arm around the room, her eyes tearing. "I only came to prove Tanner wrong about Daddy. I loved Dani, Mark."

"Tanner wasn't wrong about your father," Mark frowned as he typed something into his phone and mumbled about cell reception. "I finally found a witness who saw Kenny with Agent Khouri on the night she died."

"Of an overdose," Frankie thwacked the chair with her free hand.

Mark offered a sad, half-smile. "That is the party line on her death. The agency ordered me to drop it, so I took leave to try and scrounge up evidence before the case goes cold. You wouldn't happen to know about the chemicals someone has been sending to this address, *your* address?"

Rattling the handcuff, she pleaded, "You know me. You know I'm innocent. If you'd uncuff me and let me go, we could have such a beautiful relationship."

Temptation flickered in his eyes. She'd lose a race on purpose before she let Mark lay a finger on her, but he didn't have to know that. She wasn't exactly sure what feminine wiles entailed, but now was a good time to muster some.

He nodded slowly, holding her gaze. "Help me help you, Frankie."

"What can I do to prove myself?"

"Where is the USB drive on which Danielle kept her files?"

Behind Mark, a shadow grew larger. A tall figure in a lab coat emerged from behind the glassware and said, "I'd like to hear the answer to that question as well."

He wore a mask and safety goggles, but Frankie recognized that voice from her nightmares.

ꕥ

Tanner held his breath as he crept along, weapon drawn. He exhaled a prayer of thanks when he heard Frankie pleading her innocence.

With his back to a crumbling wall, he edged a few steps more and caught sight of her. She sat upright in the wheelchair with Mark beside her. Tanner had encountered quite a few brazen criminal operations, but this surpassed them all. Generators, beakers, tubes, funnels, stacked bags and boxes, and scales filled a room that could be described as Willy Wonka's drug lab. Tanner was used to a filthy, chaotic basements with burned-out wall panels, stoves littered with boiling saucepans and Tupperware containers, and chickens or dogs wandering in and out.

Everything paid for with Newman cash seemed clean, fresh, and under control.

But those chemical odors were not from Lysol or Windex. Something deadly was cooking.

Holstering his weapon, Tanner started the voice recorder on his phone. He fished a handkerchief out of his jacket pocket and wrapped it around his nose and mouth, thankful that Frankie was covered too. The fact that Newman was creating poison underneath a casino full of people evidenced his callousness for human life and thirst for power at all costs. No one would ever suspect it or hear the machines over the noise upstairs. Who would ever believe that a good ol' boy was running a clandestine lab in rural America?

Tanner's blood boiled as he realized Mark had handcuffed her to the chair. Mark, one of Danielle's contacts, must be working with the person who contaminated and stole Frankie's uniform and helmet. Was he planning to murder her down here and steal the drugs? More likely he was going to use her to force her father's hand.

When a man in a lab coat crossed the room, headed for Frankie, Tanner grabbed his gun. The man pointed a Glock at Mark. Mark returned the favor.

"Kyle!" Frankie exclaimed, her voice like a strangled animal. "It can't be."

"Indeed, it is! Mr. LovePotion#9. You meet the most interesting people online, don't you, sweetheart?" Kyle chuckled.

Tanner's thumb twitched on the safety. He'd hoped Mario had been wrong. Kyle's joker tattoo, popular among the Mexican cartel, had identified him as the perpetrator who walked away with Frankie's tainted gear after the accident.

Kyle's rubbed his bandaged nose as he moved stiffly. Frankie had really thrashed him. *That's my girl.*

"Special Agent Kyle Gordon?" Mark rested his weapon a moment, but Kyle didn't.

"Agent? They hire rapists at the DEA?" Frankie spat. "Unbelievable."

Mark eyed Frankie as he steadied his weapon again. "Special Agent Marcello Martinotto. I wasn't informed that you'd been reassigned here."

"I knew it!" Frankie said. "Mark Martin was too good to be true."

"It wasn't a lie, just a shortcut," Agent What's-His-Name looked penitent.

"Right! Martinotto!" Kyle seemed genuinely surprised. "You're the cowboy who rode in to clean up Danielle's mess. The physical therapist for the poor, broken race car driver? Brilliant. I wish I'd thought of it. I'm a free agent now."

Tanner's mind reversed course. He'd assumed Kyle and Mark were working together to find Danielle's formula and sell it or create an empire of their own.

Kyle limped toward Frankie. "Were you playing Nancy Drew today, sexy? Sniffing out Daddy's dealings?"

"I caught her trying to break into the gate." Mark said.

"The gate on *my* property where you are trespassing." Frankie's face betrayed no fear, but her arms were sweaty and shaking. She was trying to come out of that chair.

Be patient, Wonder Woman.

Kyle got within a foot of Frankie and leaned over.

Frankie threw a right hook, which landed inches from Kyle's face.

He laughed in hers. "Not this time, tiger. I do enjoy a woman with fire in her veins. You and I will make a good team. Run your father's business and take a little honeymoon to Isla Mujeres, after your plastic surgery of course."

Kyle turned the gun on her, making a sweeping motion toward her chest. Tanner clenched his weapon, lining up a shot. The chemicals were explosive. Her life was too precious to risk. He'd have to move in closer.

"Maybe you should consider going under the knife yourself." Frankie swept her free hand toward Kyle's lower half. "Set me free or my father and Tanner will perform the surgery themselves."

Kyle stroked her hair. "Like they protected you when you crashed your little race car?"

"Back off." Mark grabbed Kyle's arm.

"You're dismissed, Agent Martinotto." Kyle turned suddenly and smashed his gun into Mark's skull. "This is my show."

Frankie screamed, a sound Tanner never wanted to hear again. Mark fell back against the wall and slid down beside her. Kyle grabbed Mark's gun and stuffed it in his coat.

Frankie reached down with her free hand and tugged at the lock on her chair. Kyle kicked her hand away.

"It was *you*. It was *all* you." Frankie lunged for his face. "You drugged me so I would wreck and then you toyed with me. Only someone as sick as you would have put that doll in my room. Why not just kill me? Or kill Daddy?"

"To put the screws to him and have a little fun with a beautiful woman. You are his Achilles heel. I offered my services to build up his lab here until I could find Danielle's formula or force his hand. He claims he doesn't have it, but I know she left it with him and he's shopping it around to the highest bidder."

Picking up a notebook, Kyle slammed it down on the counter, causing Frankie to shrink back. "I have made zero progress on unraveling her research notes. I am sick of trying to recreate this new drug and searching these mold-infested tunnels."

Kyle unlocked the chair and pushed Frankie toward the work tables. He stopped, walked in front of her, and adjusted a lever on a pill press. "It's perfect timing, because the big guy is coming down to inspect my work."

"So, your plan is to hold a gun to my head and force my father to give you the drive?"

"Such a smart girl!" Kyle tapped the top of her head with the weapon. "I turn up the heat, he hands me the keys to the kingdom, and you and I run this place ourselves. I've put out some feelers and the payout will be quite substantial. Even had a few offers from Big Pharma."

Frankie barked out a laugh, then coughed. She was too close to the chemicals, which had obviously gone to Kyle's head. Time was running out.

"Don't be looking at me all judgey. I'm not money hungry, Frankie. Taking care of my dying sister has depleted my resources. An agent's salary is a pittance for what they put us through."

"You were actually telling the truth about your sister? I didn't realize she'd gone down so quickly." Frankie studied him. "Let's work together to give everyone what they want. If you found Danielle's formula, would you let me go and leave my father alone?"

"I'm willing to negotiate." Kyle spun to face her.

"I have the USB drive containing the formula." Frankie blurted. "I've had it all along. Tanner doesn't know about it and neither does Daddy. I'll take you to it."

Frankie was offering herself up to save all of them. That was not going to happen.

"You minx. You'd do anything for Daddy, wouldn't you?" Kyle bent over and whispered in her ear. "Let me tell you all the things I'm going to do to you once I get you alone."

A single tear rolled down her mask as she said, "You'll get everything that's coming to you."

The blood in Tanner's ears pounded as Kyle stepped away from the glass and Tanner lined up a clean shot.

When the light flinted off his gun, Frankie turned, her eyes widening. Tanner motioned for her to stay back and took aim again.

"What are you looking at?"

When Kyle turned toward Tanner, Frankie shouted a Hi-yah! like the Karate Kid and kicked out her foot, tripping Kyle and sending his weapon to the floor.

Kyle regained his balance and stood a few feet away. "I thought you couldn't move!"

Tanner fired, shooting Kyle's legs from under him. "Now *you* won't be able to."

For a moment he considered putting that animal down for good, but he couldn't shake the pestering voice in his head that said the Lord would repay.

Frankie didn't scream this time, but Kyle did. She backed away from Kyle, who started crying and cursing. In the moment Tanner moved in front of Frankie, Kyle made a grab for the gun in his pocket.

Mark rose up with a groan and got there first, wrestling away the gun and taking aim. Tanner let out the breath he'd been holding when Mark pointed the gun at Kyle, not him.

Frankie sighed. "Thank goodness you're okay, Mark whatever your name is. I thought that clown had killed you."

Tanner fished his keys out of his pocket, unlocked Frankie's handcuffs, and secured Kyle with them. Always be prepared. A lesson drummed into him from Boy Scouts and a father who preached the warning in Matthew 10:16 to "Be as cunning as serpents and as innocent as doves."

"You carry handcuff keys?" Frankie quirked an eyebrow.

"Only for special occasions." Tanner winked.

He never had a problem holding back a smile unless she

was in the room. Kyle putting his hands on her and dimming that smile was Tanner's worst nightmare.

"Thanks for the assist, Special Agent Banner," Mark glanced up at Tanner. "Hard to tell who the good guys are around here."

"Don't thank me yet. I haven't decided whether I should shoot you for cuffing her. Let's get Frankie out of here, and you can explain how long you've known about my past."

"*Agent* Banner." Frankie repeated monotone, her face hard. "DEA."

Tanner locked eyes with her, willing her to forgive him again. The mischievous twinkle in Frankie's eyes had chilled. This was not the way he'd wanted her to find out.

"I resigned permanently after Danielle shot me," Tanner said.

"I heard we had a rogue agent bumbling around in the sticks, avenging Danielle's death." Mark wiped at the blood streaming from his forehead onto his mask. "Didn't have to dig much to discover corruption top to bottom in this case."

Tanner moved to grab the bars of Frankie's wheelchair when he caught the odor of acetone and noticed vapors rising from a container on the stove. It was a miracle the shooting hadn't sent up a spark. "C'mon, they'll be digging up our bodies if we don't get out of here."

"I'll handle Kyle and you get Frankie to safety," Mark said.

Frankie had already turned and was pushing herself away from Tanner toward the exit by the pond.

Echoing footsteps caused them all to look back. "What is going on down here?"

The creaking of the rusty door hinge grated Tanner's nerves less than that voice.

Frankie did a 180 and shouted, "Daddy!"

Oh no you don't. Tanner stepped in front of her and aimed his piece at Newman's heart as Frankie tried to push by him to get to her father. He should have left the handcuffs on.

Kenny Newman stood behind the cooktop. The vapors rose around him as if he'd ascended from Hades.

"Son, would you explain to me why you just shot my chemist and why you've brought my daughter into the center of it?" He flicked his empty hands toward the security cameras but kept his gun within reach under that white seersucker suit.

"I'm sorry, Daddy." Frankie pushed at Tanner's back. "I came down here to prove them wrong about you. It's Kyle's fault. He caused my crash and tried to rape me and wants to kill you. And Mark, he—"

Tanner turned slightly and held up his hand to stop her before she revealed details that would get Mark killed. Kyle was on his own.

"Turns out your chemist here is a dirty government agent who has been threatening you to get Danielle's formula," Tanner explained. "He set up the accident that left your daughter paralyzed."

Darkness shrouded Newman's face as he focused his death glare on Kyle. "These feds are like ants. Just when I think I've stomped them all, another one comes crawling in. They're expendable."

Venom filled Tanner's veins like a quick hit of that

liquid death on the stove. He tightened his grip on the gun as Frankie's soft hand tightened around free hand.

"Good work, my boy. Clean this up. I'm taking Frankie out of the country for a while."

"What?" She cried out.

As Newman took a step toward them, Tanner stood taller, stretching his body to its limits to shield her.

Newman stopped. "You can put the gun down now, son, and I'll take over from here. I only hired you to protect her."

"I *am* protecting her." Tanner blinked repeatedly. He couldn't see straight as every memory of Frankie's accident and the day he had to identify Danielle's body came flooding in. "Was Danielle expendable too? An ant that you crushed?"

Newman's hand drew closer to his pocket.

Mark's safety clicked behind Tanner. "I wouldn't try it."

"I don't know what game you're playing here, but my daughter is coming with me." Newman held out his hand, beckoning for Frankie to follow him into some portal to hell.

Over my dead body.

CHAPTER TWENTY-EIGHT

"Race car drivers never die. They just find another way."

—Unknown

FRANKIE SQUEEZED TANNER'S hand, grabbing for some piece of reality to center her as the world shifted beneath. "What happened to Dani, Daddy? I loved her. I thought you did too."

"She was a troubled young woman who overdosed. Very sad. I assume these two are among her unfortunate lovers." Her father glanced over his shoulder at the door where he'd entered. "We need to go, Frankie."

Tanner ground out, "You need to tell the truth for once in your miserable life."

"Daddy, what is this place? Tell them it's all Kyle's fault. Tell them you didn't kill Dani."

Her father stood there, looking fresh in his new suit and smiling benevolently down at her while the machines hummed and, according to Tanner, the beakers dripped out drugs that obliterated people's lives. He took his sweet time answering her while Kyle whined behind them and Tanner breathed like a grizzly ready to attack.

Finally, Daddy spoke with a pleading tone that didn't match the stiffness of his body and the coldness of his eyes.

"Everything I have done has been for you, kitten."

And there it was. Her hand dropped to her lap. Her father was a murderer. Her childhood, her devotion—all based on a lie. The Daddy Frankie loved had died along with her mother.

"The government tried to break us from the very beginning. They killed your mother. Dani and the rest of them tried to steal your legacy. These medications we're creating here will help those suffering as she did. No one should be in that kind of pain."

"Aww, the long-suffering cartel needs more pills." Tanner scoffed. "Don't blame your actions on your wife's death or protecting Frankie. *You* built this empire for *you* because you crave power and money. Did you ever notice your daughter didn't want any of it? She only wants to race. Ultimately, your little concierge business here robbed her of that."

Daddy really looked at her then. "Francine… I only wanted the best for you. Come with me now and we'll find you another specialist. We can spend more time together, live the life I worked so hard to give you."

"All I ever longed for was your love." Frankie swallowed down the pain and smacked her hand on the rails of her chair. "Well, that's that. Please arrest him so I never have to see his face again."

"Not before you confess your crimes. You killed Tanya's doctor in some back alley. You ordered Danielle to shoot me, a vagrant, in an alley. You murdered Danielle and dumped her in an alley like she was trash. That's your M.O. isn't it? You're nothing but a serial killer masquerading as a Southern gentleman."

Her father backed up as Tanner stalked him with every accusation

"Agent Banner." Mark's voice was even. "Stand down."

"Tell me the truth!" Tanner roared, his voice echoing into the tunnels.

What would it be like to have a man love her so fiercely?

Sweat beaded on her father's chin as he quaked under Tanner's rage. "People who are disloyal to me pay the price. Danielle didn't suffer and obviously you haven't either."

Frankie clutched her stomach as it heaved. She felt Tanner's suffering to her core. He'd shown her the hole in his chest where his heart had been. If she'd taken a bullet to the chest, it wouldn't hurt as much as her father's betrayal.

Mark's voice penetrated the tension. "Kenny Newman, you're under arrest for the murder of a federal agent, conspiracy to traffic a controlled substance, and—

Frankie watched in horror as her father grabbed his gun.

"Everybody down!" Mark yelled.

Frankie froze.

Daddy fired multiple shots at the containers and machines beside Mark. Glass shattered and sparks flew.

Tanner dove for her as Mark and Kyle took cover. When the gunshots stopped, Tanner scooped her up from the wheelchair. Kyle fought off Mark's help.

Frankie pushed back. "Put me down and help them."

"Let me save *you* for once." Tanner said, coughing as he

shielded her face with his jacket. "Go after Newman, Mark. I'll come back for Kyle."

As smoke and flames billowed from the lab, Frankie couldn't see a way out. Adrenaline surged as her heart beat in her throat. "Tanner? What are we going to do?"

"Don't let go," he said, squeezing her closer as he pressed ahead in the darkness.

As the air grew thinner and hotter, she shut her eyes against a wave of dizziness and sagged against his chest. *Please, God.*

The light broke through as another explosion and sirens pierced the air.

"About time," Tanner grumbled as he sank onto the ground outside the tunnel.

Once Frankie's stinging, runny eyes cooperated and opened again, she could see that he'd brought them to the pond. A hacking cough shook his body as he tore off his singed jacket, mask, and t-shirt and slung them to the ground.

He lay beside her a moment, taking her cheeks in his hand as he stripped off her mask and searched her face. "Are you okay? You're breathing. You're okay."

He sighed and pulled her toward him, wrapping her in a tight embrace. "Thank God, you're alive."

"Barely," she wheezed as he squeezed the life out of her.

"Sorry," he said, releasing her.

He jogged to the water's edge, soaked his shirt, and winced when he swiped it across his face.

As he dropped down beside her again, she got a good look at the streaks on his forehead and neck. "You've got some nasty cuts and burns."

He held her chin while he gently rubbed the wet shirt across her face, neck, and arms. He croaked out. "Can't let the poison sink in."

Daddy had already poisoned everything in their lives.

"Guess I got my water therapy in after all."

"Always looking on the bright side, Wonder Woman." He stroked his thumb across her cheek, searching her eyes as if they were the only people on earth and their lives hadn't just burned to the ground. "You okay? Really?"

She nodded. "Thank you for saving me. When I said I wanted to torch that wheelchair, I didn't envision this."

Tanner cough-snorted. He sobered when she said, "You lied to me, Agent Banner, again and again and again. I understand your motives, but this is *me*. You could have trusted me with the truth."

"Like you trusted me when you found Danielle's flash drive?" He turned away a moment to cough. "I protected *you*, not Daddy, throughout this whole mess, but when push came to shove, you left me behind so you could prove him innocent."

Frankie recoiled from the bite in Tanner's tone.

Reaching for her hand, he took it in both of his. "You might not trust me yet, but remember who is still here by your side."

The beating of helicopter blades caused them both to look up. The black helicopter with the speedway logo rose above the treetops.

"Daddy." Her voice caught as she buried her face in Tanner's chest. No tears came. Her eyes were as dry as her throat.

She pulled back suddenly. "Go after him. Don't let him get away with this."

"I'm not leaving you alone again. Ever." Tanner wrestled his phone from the pocket of his jacket and cleared his throat before putting it to his ear. "This is Tanner Ashton. I'm on the southeast grounds of the Shadybrook Speedway, beside the pond. Do not approach the underground tunnels without Hazmat. Evacuate the casino and garages. We're going to need at least five Narcan units to counteract possible opioid exposure."

Frankie's head buzzed as he continued to give orders. *Clandestine lab, fentanyl, murder, attempted murder, escape. Special Agent in Charge in pursuit of the suspect at the airstrip. Helo headed south.* This was not her life. Surely, the producers of Momma's TV show would show up any minute and say she'd been punked.

CHAPTER TWENTY-NINE

The Road is Calling, and I Must Go

THE ONE WHO showed up for her during the next few hours was Tanner. He kept his promise and never left her side, although he must have been chomping at the bit to capture her father. While Frankie sucked down oxygen, sat in a borrowed wheelchair, and got probed and prodded by EMTs, Mark drug in, blood caked on his face and shirt, clothes tattered and singed.

"Thank goodness you're safe!" Frankie reached out and hugged him gently.

"What's the word?" Tanner rested his hand on Frankie's shoulder.

Mark took the hint and backed up. He waved off an EMT coming at him with bandages. "I've got to get back to the manhunt. I thought I was never going to find my way out of that crazy labyrinth alive. Newman had his exit carefully planned and threw some booby traps in the way."

"I'd start with his safe houses in Mexico and Saudi Arabia." Tanner said.

"Safe houses?" If Frankie's mind kept blowing these circuits, they'd have to bring in a fire truck for her as well.

Tanner handed Mark a flash drive. "It's all on here. I'm sorry Dani had to die to finally nail him."

As Frankie watched the men, faces cut and burned, the gravity of Daddy's deeds sunk in, making her heart heavy. The blood of two good men and her strong, funny Dani was on her father's hands. How had Frankie been so blind?

Mark said, "Frankie, I hate to tell you this, but I found Russ Morgan laid out on the airstrip. I'm hoping we don't have another casualty."

Frankie's heart went to her throat. Russ must have come back looking for her.

"He had a concussion and a heart attack, but he's conscious. Tried to stop Newman from getting away."

Tanner's hands massaged the knots in her shoulders, but there would be no relief from this pain. Daddy had nearly killed the one man who'd truly been a father to her and tried to be a friend to Daddy. Poor Selah.

"When Russ fought with Newman," Mark continued, "a piece of paper fell out of Newman's jacket. He's headed for Tangier."

"Tangier Island?" Frankie was confused.

"Morocco." Tanner corrected. "No extradition treaty."

"Did you find Kyle? I was hoping I'd be the one who'd roast him over an open spit." She joked, but the thought of him burning to death because of her family was too much to take.

Mark smirked. "Found him alive, high as a kite. He

used Frankie's chair to take cover in one of the passageways. Maybe I'll volunteer as his physical therapist."

"The idea of you stretching Kyle over a therapy torture rack is intriguing. Does this mean you won't be mine anymore?"

"I was never yours pretty lady." Mark's eyes flicked from Frankie to Tanner.

"Are you really a therapist? Or did you lie about that too?" She folded her arms in front of her.

"Truth. I was a therapist in another life," Mark rubbed the gold band on the chain around his neck.

She groaned. Sounded like something vague Tanner Ashton/David Banner would say. Maybe fuzzy answers were an occupational hazard.

"I would never have compromised your recovery. I'm sorry I deceived and doubted you, but it had to be done to put your father behind bars. Consider yourself un-arrested."

Frankie sank back into her chair. "You came through for me in the clutch. I guess that's what matters."

Tanner suddenly stopped rubbing her shoulders. Tanner had come through in the clutch too. But he'd seen her at her most vulnerable, taken that soft opening, and put a knife through it.

Mark squatted down and did some therapist voodoo on her legs, bending them and smiling when she kicked him playfully. "You're obviously making progress on your own, unbeknownst to me."

"I have a long way to go before I can walk."

"Nah, you're on the final lap," he said as he stood. "I wish I could be here to see it, but you're in good hands."

Frankie smiled up at him and squeezed his hand.

Tanner cleared his throat. "Aren't you supposed to be out apprehending Newman?"

"You know, I am still your superior, Special Agent Banner."

"You know, I am still retired from law enforcement. Call me Tanner."

"Riiight." Mark slapped his shoulder. "Enjoy your new life as a professional babysitter."

A familiar face strode across the lot to the ambulance. Sunlight bounced off the badge on Gina Santiago's uniform.

"Hey superstar!" Frankie held out her arms for a hug.

"You're like a moth to the flame when it comes to danger, aren't you Frankie?" Her childhood friend squeezed her and then pretended to knock on the top of her head. "And I'm always two steps behind."

Mark quickly extended a hand. "I'm Special—"

"I'm aware of who you are." Gina said drolly, but Frankie felt the heat when Gina's eyes connected with Mark's. "Your compatriots are already up in my business."

"It *is* a federal investigation, Deputy Sheriff."

"No offense, *Special* Agent," Gina's mouth quirked, "but your federal investigation just went up in flames and you look like you should be put out of your misery too."

Unlike Tanner, Mark didn't try to hide his amusement. "Did you have any information to share, ma'am, or did you just come to beat me up some more."

Gina snapped her fingers at the EMT who'd tried to help Mark earlier. "Petey, please hogtie this one and clean him up."

As the paramedic approached timidly, Mark relented. The smile lingered on Mark's lips, even as Pete sanitized his wounds. Frankie rubbed her hands together. Selah was going to eat this up. Gina had actually found a man she liked enough to banter with.

"Now here's what I know," Gina said. "Russ is at county hospital, stable condition. I've notified Momma and Selah. We've safely evacuated the casino and speedway. They will be closed indefinitely, Frankie. You can stay in the barn tonight, but I would advise you to find a new place to live."

Frankie's spirits took a nosedive again as she looked around. What would become of the magical place where she'd grown up? Sometimes magic was just an illusion.

"You're always welcome to bunk with me." Gina must have sensed her mood, because she gave Frankie another a tight hug, then glanced back at Mark. "When you're finished standing around, I have a lot of questions."

Pete, the EMT, interjected, "Since he lost consciousness, he should go to the hospital for brain scans."

"I doubt they'll find anything up there," Tanner said.

Mark ignored him, eyes still on Gina.

"Well, come on then," Gina said. "There are plenty of other special agents here to finish up what you started. I'll write you a permission slip and take you to the hospital."

Mark watched her walk away. His eyes twinkled when he turned back to Frankie. Saluting Tanner, he said, "I guess I have my marching orders."

"She's single. And you're single, right?" Frankie grinned with all teeth.

Mark chucked her under the chin. "I'll take that under advisement. Someone will be around to debrief you both forthwith."

"After you're finished making a love connection at the

hospital, find Kenny Newman before he finds Frankie." Tanner grabbed the bars of the chair. "I'm taking Frankie home."

⁂

Where would that be exactly? Tanner brought Frankie back to his apartment and the barn long enough to pull up stakes, packing up suitcases and that caterwauling demon of his. Frankie took one last look around the barn. The old Mustang she was restoring, the burned-out car that had nearly killed her, and her powder puff trophies. She was a stranger in a world that didn't belong to her anymore.

"Ready?" Tanner heaved her weekender bag on his shoulder.

"For what? Is there anything left?"

She looked up into his eyes, which shone with a warmth and ease she hadn't seen there before. His face and arms were streaked with cuts, burns, and dirt, but he was different. Lighter. He'd gotten the answers he came for.

Well, goody for him. He could go back to D.C. or Minnesota and leave her alone to pick up the pieces. He'd said Frankie was the most joyful person he knew, but only sadness, dread, and guilt swirled in the pit of her stomach. Wonder Woman had left the building.

CHAPTER THIRTY

FRANKIE HAD NEVER looked so lost. Tanner must have clenched his fist twenty times to keep from stroking her downcast face. Even after her accident, a steady spark had lit her up. But now, she sat in the back seat of the Escalade beside Kojak's crate, shut her eyes, and leaned her head against the window. Having the rug pulled out from under you by the people you trust took a while to get over. He wasn't sure how long of a while, since he hadn't gotten there himself.

They checked into a suite with separate bedrooms at Rendezvous, a mountain resort, called Frankie a lawyer, and spent hours with Tanner's former superiors, regurgitating the details of her accident, Danielle's death, Kyle's double-dealing, and the confrontation in the tunnels. Frankie never backed down when the feds put the screws to her about her involvement in Newman's criminal enterprise. Why yes, she'd be happy to testify against her father and against Kyle, who was in a wheelchair now himself.

They tried to visit Russ Morgan, but visiting hours were over and Selah's plane hadn't arrived yet. Tanner positioned a guard outside Russ's room, although, with Momma around, it was superfluous. By the time they'd reached the resort again, Tanner could have sprawled out on the floor and slept. Even Kojak was so knocked out on Tanner's bed that she didn't lift a paw to terrorize Frankie.

Frankie, however, seemed keyed up, rolling around the living room, inspecting the knickknacks and paintings. "Poor Russ, huh? Maybe I should warn the doctor that having Margo Morgan at his side increases his risk of a second heart attack."

"He might choose that over being nagged to death." Tanner chuckled as he grabbed two waters and handed her one before sinking down on the couch.

"Wouldn't Momma blow a gasket if she knew we were 'living in sin' up here in this hotel room?" Frankie joked, but her face was blank.

"She'd definitely flip her pancakes."

A swig of water calmed the coughing that threatened to erupt again when Tanner laughed. Inhaling smoke and chemicals seemed a small price to pay for shutting down that lab before it cost more lives. He'd spent years infiltrating pill mills in Mexico and supply operations in China and India, but how could anyone stop the epidemic when businessmen in the Bible belt were getting in on the action?

Watching Frankie rub her bloodshot eyes and then wring her hands, he vowed that life would never touch her again. He'd left Danielle behind for it. He was done with moving from job to job, lying, and pretending to be someone he wasn't in the name of justice.

"Have they found my father yet?" She opened the water top and closed it again.

Tanner shook his head 'no.' "I imagine he's had a fool-proof escape plan in place for quite a while."

She looked up then. "You're no fool. Go find him. Your duty to me has been discharged, Agent Banner. In fact, I think it would be better if you left."

"I don't care about him. I care about you."

As tears filled her eyes, his heart squeezed. Turned out, it was still in there. Frankie had brought it back to life.

"Don't do me any favors," she snapped. "I'm busy. I need to focus on rebuilding. I've got a casino and a garage full of employees to repay somehow. I have to find a new place to live, a new job, and new friends once they hear I've been aiding and abetting a criminal all these years. You are not my friend, so you're fired."

Tanner stood, every muscle screaming. He closed the distance between them and dropped to the floor in front of her. How many times had she brought him to his knees?

He rasped, "I. am. not. walking away from you and I won't let you walk away from me."

Her blue eyes widened for an instant before she narrowed them and turned the chair toward her bedroom. "Someday soon, I will. Watch me."

When the door slammed, he rose up and leaned against it, breathing in her perfume, like exhaust she'd kicked up when she threw it into fourth gear to get away from him.

Kojak jumped down from his bed and trotted to him, rubbing his ankles with her whiskers. "What are we going to do, buddy? I can't lose her, but the tighter I hold on, the faster she runs."

Only one person could help him now. He pulled his phone from his pocket and hit speed dial.

"Hey little sis. How soon are you getting here?"

"Tanner Ashton," Selah said. "I could wring your ever-living neck right now."

He held the phone away from his ear a few moments while she raked him over the coals for running a sting on her best friend. He had to smile though. That accent. The more animated she got, the deeper the drawl. Frankie's was the same way.

Finally, Selah sighed. "Thank God you and Frankie are okay. I was so scared when Cane told me you called asking about Frankie's fake physical therapist. Thank *you* for saving her life."

"If Frankie had died in that fire, I would have died with her," Tanner admitted. One thing he and Kenny Newman had in common. "Did you make it to the hospital yet?"

"Just got here. I'm trying to get Momma to go home and give my father some peace tonight. Mr. Newman beat him up pretty badly, although he's taken worse punishment from loan sharks over the years." Her voice caught. "He's going to be okay though."

"Good news."

"Did he really help you bring down Mr. Newman?"

"Your dad came through when it counted. He secretly recorded the old man for me. Then, he took it upon himself to try and stop Newman from escaping. I'll give you the details when I see you."

"I… It's hard to believe." Selah sniffled. "Maybe after all these years, this will finally be over, and we can get my father the help he needs."

"Russ Morgan has put you and your mom through the

wringer, Selah, but, when somebody threatened his family, he acted as a hero."

Selah was quiet for a long moment with only the sounds of beeping and Momma chattering in the background.

"I, however, messed up," Tanner groaned.

"Well, duh."

Selah made Tanner want to straighten up and fly right.

"I need your help to fix what I've done."

"What *exactly* did you do, Tanner?"

"I broke Frankie's heart a thousand times." Tanner smiled down at the photo of Frankie he'd carried in his wallet since day one of this adventure. "Then I fell in love with her."

Frankie rubbed sleep from her eyes and startled as she noticed someone in the room with her. Daddy?

Sunlight snuck in from the closed curtains of the hotel room, splaying across Selah's bowed curly head. She was probably praying as she sat in a chair across from Frankie's bed, just like she had day after day when Frankie was in rehab. Somewhere in the room, Faith was snoring.

Frankie's scratchy throat and eyes filled. "You always show up when I need you most."

"I took a best friend's oath," Selah said. "Where else would I be?"

"Maybe with your dad?"

"I left my parents to duke it out." Selah stretched. "Her film crew arrived at the hospital and I escaped before Momma put on a woe-is-me show. She'll complain he's the laziest, orneriest old man on earth until the camera is rolling and she can cry about how worried she is."

"How will they survive now that he can't escape her and spend his days in the casino?" Frankie's stomach clenched as Selah's face fell. "I'm sorry. I'm sorry. I shouldn't have brought that up. I'm so, so sorry about all the things Daddy did and how he treated Russ. Did I mention how sorry I am?"

Frankie's hands covered her face. "How could I have been so oblivious to the things he was doing and all the pain he was causing? Will you ever forgive me? I don't think I could forgive me."

Selah plunked down on Frankie's bed and tugged her hands from her face. "Quit all that carryin' on, ya hear?"

"You sounded so much like Momma just now, it was terrifying."

"Now I'm crying," Selah covered her eyes playfully. "Family messes with your head, especially, in your case when that person is intentionally manipulating you. No one knew the depths of his evil. You were a loyal and trusting daughter. There's nothing to forgive."

Frankie reveled in her Selah hug—soft, strong, and cotton-candy scented. "I've missed you."

Selah pulled back and gave her a once-over. "Rise and shine so I can see you move your feet!"

Frankie kicked off the covers and wiggled her feet, eliciting a woo-hoo and a bark.

"Tanner left for more meetings, so you and I are going shopping and out for breakfast and anything your little heart desires." Selah tossed Frankie the bathrobe by the bed.

"Cane is bringing up the Charger so we can get it detailed for Dad. Cane is dying to see you."

"I love Cane!" Frankie clapped her hands. "Don't worry, not as much as I love—"

The words tumbled out before she realized what she was saying.

Selah cocked her head, violet eyes twinkling. "Yes? Finish that sentence, please."

"That's not what I meant."

"You fell for Tanner the moment you laid eyes on him in my hospital room."

Frankie flashed back to the moment Tanner had come in like Terminator, scanning the corners of the room with laser eyes. His black jeans and black leather jacket and his even blacker hair and eyes melted everything that got too close in that blindingly white room.

Why did her best friend have to know her better than she knew herself?

"I tried loving Tanner, but it only left me empty. He admitted that his obscenely muscular chest is sadly empty too. He doesn't have a heart to love me with."

"Hmm. Interesting."

"Stop grinning! Tanner is a government thug, a hired gun. Even if he did deign to love me, he'd run off on his next assignment first chance he got. Danger is in his blood."

"Wow, that's fresh coming from someone with engine oil in hers. You know everything about him, do you?"

"Pretty much, yep." Frankie knew enough to steer clear. "I can see you're planning to educate me."

Selah got up and opened the blinds, then stood in front of the open window, the sunlight casting her in an ethereal light. "Tanner is just a corn-fed kid from Minnesota. He was good at football, but he didn't love it like Cane did. He cared more about bringing home science projects and stray animals. You remember that Cane wigged out on a date with demented Lacey back then? Tanner felt so bad for her that he went in Cane's place and let her down gently."

"You extol his virtues all you want, but that was high school. He graduated into a professional liar."

"We've all changed since then, but aren't you, at your core, the same person you were as a teen?"

Frankie never cared what people thought about her then either. She'd held her head high and grown a tough shell to hide the gaping hole of loneliness inside. When she was around normal people doing normal things, she felt very vulnerable. When she raced, she was safe.

"Look at who Tanner became as an adult." Selah continued her Tanner for President PowerPoint presentation. "He majored in chemistry at MIT because he wanted to help cure addictions like Cane's. He met a pretty girl who wanted the same things and joined the DEA when she did. He almost got himself killed trying to solve what happened to her. He could have died saving you, running through smoke and fire like some action hero. Doesn't that count for something?"

"It means he's got a savior complex and I don't need saving." Frankie scooted out of bed and into her chair. "How soon until breakfast?"

When Selah groaned, Faith woofed. Frankie looked around for the mutt, spotting her in a dog bed on the floor.

Frankie's eyes widened in horror. Faith wasn't alone in the bed. "Selah! Grab Faith."

"What?" Selah gasped, running over to the dog. "What's wrong?"

"That swamp rat is wrapped around your dog. Get Faith out of there before it sucks the life out of her."

Selah looked down and then back at Frankie. "You mean, Kojak? Such a loving kitty. She adores Faith. Instant best friends. Isn't it crazy?"

Selah bent and rubbed the cat, who rolled over, purring, and let her scratch its belly.

"Crazy." Frankie muttered, as she wheeled over toward them.

As Frankie approached, the cat began to growl. Frankie growled back and turned toward the bathroom. "There had better be a heavy dose of sugar and coffee in that breakfast you promised."

His nutty cat was just one more reason to put Tanner Ashton in her rear-view mirror.

CHAPTER THIRTY-ONE

Ride It Like You Stole It

"TANNER," A VOICE as familiar as his own stopped Tanner as he slid behind the wheel of the Escalade.

The irritation that rippled over his skin and jabbed his temples were familiar too as Tanner watched his brother roll out of Russ's vintage Dodge Charger. Cane had a spring in his step as he jumped onto the sidewalk in front of the lodge and headed for Tanner.

"I was hoping to run into you."

And Tanner was hoping to avoid running into Cane. He'd left Mario to guard the ladies until Cane got there.

Cane didn't do anything specific to get under Tanner's skin, he just did. His brother displayed no Hollywood pretense—jeans, sneakers, and a too-tight "Shirtless Wonder" tee Selah had given him as a wedding present. Cane had gained a few pounds since marrying a woman who baked cakes and pies that rivalled her Momma's. He'd switched to a new MS drug that seemed to be helping. Cane was living the dream. But hadn't he always, while Tanner cleaned up his messes?

When Cane flashed a crooked grin and waved his left hand, wedding band glinting in the sun, Tanner slammed the door and put the key in the ignition. He didn't have time for this.

Twins take care of each other. Grandma's voice rang out as if she was in the car with him, swatting the back of his head with her paintbrush. Make-nice-with-your-brother small talk expended a lot of energy, but so did anger.

Tanner heaved a sigh, sent up a quick prayer, and creaked out of his vehicle. Every inch of his skin seemed to ache or burn from yesterday's little tunnel run. If Frankie was still speaking to him, maybe he'd hire her to whip him into shape. First, he had to pitch an idea to his former bosses this morning. He'd fight for her future, even if she didn't want him in it.

Before Tanner got a word out, Cane met him on the sidewalk and crushed him in a hug. Tanner groaned at the impact but dug deep and patted his brother a few times on the back before pushing him off.

Cane stepped back and dropped his hands, pushing them awkwardly into his jeans' pockets. "I'm grateful you and Frankie made it out alive."

Tanner nodded curtly. He didn't enjoy seeing Cane shifting uncomfortably, but he had no desire to make him comfortable and no clue as to how to bridge the divide between them.

"I hate to think what could have happened because of the mix-up with the physical therapist," Cane said. "When

Selah told me this Mark guy conned his way in and I was somehow responsible... again... I couldn't have lived with myself if you or Frankie had died."

"We didn't."

Cane shook his head, scrubbing his hand violently up and down his jaw. He looked away and then finally made eye contact. "I'm sorry."

The apology went beyond Cane's failure to doublecheck the identity of the physical therapist who showed up. Tanner's gut twisted. Years of carrying the guilt of their parents' death had left Cane with a haunted look and certainly wasn't good for his health. Years of carrying the anger, plus the rigors of lying for a living, had left Tanner devoid of emotion. It certainly wasn't good for his future with Frankie.

"We're both cons, you and me. Pretenders just like Mark," Tanner said, the bridge between them becoming more clear.

"What?" Cane dropped his hand from his face, palms open at his sides.

"I ran away and changed my name, because I didn't want to be anything like the egotistical punk who destroyed our family over drugs and fame."

Cane's head jerked back slightly, but he stood his ground. Tanner'd replayed that night a million ways in his mind, categorized the ways that Cane had failed, and filed him away as the villain who ruined Tanner's life. The rage had grown and wrapped its tentacles around every fleeting bit of peace or happiness Tanner could have been enjoying.

"Yet here we stand, exactly alike," Tanner said. "Turns out we've both been actors all along. You used your talent to make a living, land the woman of your dreams, and turn your life around, and I have all but destroyed mine. I can't blame that on you."

Cane's eyes softened. "When you've hit bottom, there's nowhere to go but up."

Tanner swallowed hard. Hadn't expected the conversation to cut right to the quick today. "*I* am the one who is sorry."

Beautiful sunny day. Light breeze. But there might as well have been a tornado because, one minute, Tanner was fine and the next, every ounce of energy, every venom-filled thought toward Cane, was sucked out of him, leaving a bleak void. Who would Tanner be without pain and bitterness? He had no mission now, no revenge or justice or truth to seek. No job. No love.

Who are you, Tanner? Frankie had asked him. Truthfully, he didn't know.

He stepped off the sidewalk and sagged against the vehicle.

He looked up when Cane pressed a cold bottle of water in his hand. "Do you know why I'm an actor, man?"

Tanner shook his head, guzzling the water, then wished he hadn't as his ears started to ring. Probably dehydration and sucking down a firestorm of fentanyl.

"I act because feeling your real feelings is horrible. If I couldn't pretend to be happy, I'd feel lower than a bow-legged caterpillar, as my wife would say. Am I right or am I right?"

Tanner snorted a laugh, then choked as the water went up his nose. Cane's concerned look lightened into a laugh as he thumped Tanner on the back.

"Well, that escalated quickly. Shall we hug it out?" Cane was still laughing at him.

"No." Tanner said, gruffly, crumpling the empty water bottle and shoving it into Cane's chest.

Cane suddenly looked ten years younger, that stupid lopsided grin of his widening. "Miracle of miracles. If I heard you correctly, I think you just forgave me. It only took you eighteen years, jerk."

Somehow, forgiving Danielle, bringing her killer to justice, and falling for Frankie discombobulated Tanner's emotions enough that he'd pardoned his brother in the process.

"Yeah, I forgive you for the junk in the past. Don't make it weird though, or I'll reconsider."

Cane just couldn't help himself or stop yapping. "You know what they call this? This between us." He paused dramatically, as if Tanner would actually answer his inane question. "Twinning."

Tanner groaned and slapped away Cane's hand when he attempted a fistbump. "You're still an idiot."

"But you looove me." Cane was belly laughing now, all the nerves gone.

Tanner checked his watch, which he'd forgotten to wear. "Well, look at the time. I'm late for my meeting with the DEA. The girls are waiting for you. Frankie needs you and Selah right now."

Cane tilted his head with a grin, picking up one of his wife's mannerisms. "I'm fairly sure Selah and I are not who Frankie needs right now."

"I'm not taking romantic advice from you." Tanner's

moment of weakness in letting himself be vulnerable in front of his brother was going to cost him.

"Why? I convinced the most breathtaking woman on this planet to fall in love with me. You should be jotting down some notes."

"I don't have time for this. Frankie's future is at stake." Tanner turned to the door of the Escalade and swung it open, holding on when another wave of dizziness hit.

"Seriously," Cane grabbed his arm and blocked the door. "Wherever you're going, I'm driving."

"I might have forgiven you, but I'm *never* riding with you again." If he waited a few minutes, he'd feel better. If not, maybe they had Uber up in the mountains.

Cane pulled out his phone. "Do you want me to call the ladies and have them weigh in on the decision?"

Tanner's shoulders sagged. He'd bridged the gap between himself and his brother, but apparently opened Pandora's box as well.

"C'mon, Tanner. I'm your brother. Let me help you help the woman you love."

Five minutes later, Tanner was riding shotgun in his own vehicle. As Cane turned the key, Tanner lifted another prayer. He'd survived a drug lab explosion and a bullet to the chest. Surviving Cane and his driving was touch-and-go.

"I never figured you for a stoner," Cane teased. "Look at us, brother, coming full circle. Never say never. Moving on from the past. Building bridges. Mending fences."

"Way to make it weird again." If only the drugs Tanner inhaled would have knocked him out.

Cane shouted a "yee-haw," gunning the engine. "The boys are back in town."

This was going to be a long ride.

ॐ

It had been a long day, but Frankie rolled into her suite at Rendezvous feeling, and looking, like a new woman. She and Selah had gotten fancy haircuts and dresses. Selah protested, but there was no way Frankie was setting foot or hand in a nail salon again.

The best part of the day was sharing chocolate chip smiley-face pancakes with Angel and her mom at Good Company. Well, Angel opted for a boring and healthy omelet for breakfast, but Frankie's smiley-face pancakes were to die for.

She smiled down at Angel's expectant face, her cheeks as round and ruddy as the old Campbell's soup kids. Frankie stroked her red hair and gently pulled one of the coils, letting it spring back. What would it be like to have a little girl to love? Could she be a good mom without having known hers? Frankie's breath caught at the unexpected and intense longing. Selah smiled across the table like a sphinx. She knew Frankie too well.

Janet said, "My daughter rounded up a bunch of friends she met at the hospital who are in wheelchairs, ill, or otherwise physically challenged. They are chomping at the bit to ride in a race car."

"So am I," Frankie said, meeting Janet's green eyes.

Frankie was eternally grateful. Angel's mother had to have seen Frankie and her father splashed on the front page of the *Shadybrook Squealer* by now, but still let her daughter hang out with a drug dealer's daughter. How could she disappoint them and the rest of the kids?

"Can we all go today?" Angel asked.

Selah answered for her. "You know how much Frankie loves having you on her pit crew, right?"

Angel's head bobbed up and down.

"The track is closed for the rest of the season though, so we have to wait until spring to watch you test your skills. It'll give you time to read up on racing and get pointers from Frankie."

Angel sized her up and then turned to Frankie. "Is Selah your manager?"

Frankie grinned across the table at Selah, who saluted her with her coffee mug. "Yeah, you could call her that."

"Where's Tanner?" Angel asked. "When are you getting married?"

Selah sputtered a laugh, spewing coffee onto her plate.

Angel continued the inquisition. "Are you still running the Shadybrook Shake-a-Leg with me this week, Frankie?"

Frankie's wheels spun. She'd promised to be walking in time for the race, but one hour at a time was all she could muster the energy for right now. Her physical progress had stalled and she hadn't found a new therapist yet. She certainly wasn't ready to parade down Main Street given the havoc her father wreaked in this town.

Frankie changed the subject. "How about a chocolate peanut butter milkshake before Selah and I get going?"

"Yay!" They all said together. Sometimes chocolate was as effective as Turtle Wax for buffing out the rough spots in life.

৩

A tall blonde in a black-and-white maid's uniform and thigh-high black boots stood, peering into the window of Frankie's hotel suite. Mario was out of the car and at the door before Selah and Frankie made it up the sidewalk.

"May I help you?" Mario's voice boomed like the heavy bass of a car in traffic.

The woman startled and turned. "I just got off work and noticed that bald cat staring at me. Hateful ol' puss."

Yes! Finally, someone understood. Kojak perched on the windowsill, its mouth wide, probably hissing at them.

"Do you know something about it?" Maybe it was lost and the maid would take it away, far, far away.

"Used to be mine, well, my boyfriend Buford's," the woman said as she adjusted her low-cut top and inched closer to Mario. "Always meowing for food and attention. Clawing on my La-Z-Boy. I finally got sick of it and left the mangy thing in a dumpster behind that diner in town."

"You abandoned your cat in a dumpster?" Frankie's gut twisted. "Left her all alone to fend for herself?"

That explained Kojak's aggressive attack on the catfish Momma was frying up.

"Plenty of food there." The blonde lifted her chin. "Looks like it landed on its feet. Nine lives and all."

The woman banged on the window, causing Kojak to bristle and jump off the perch. "Good riddance."

As the woman clomped down the sidewalk, long, straight ponytail swooshing behind her, Frankie realized she had the same pair of boots. No wonder the cat hated her. It must have mistaken Frankie for the woman who dumped it in the garbage and returned to torment it some more.

Selah's violet eyes were misty. "Poor little thing."

"I've seen people do a lot of evil, but abusing an animal takes a special kind of coward," Mario said, his massive hand swiping his eye as he turned to take his post beside their door.

If Frankie had any more tears left, she would have cried too for the furry monster. "Hey, let's go to the grocery and pick up some catfish."

Selah grinned. "Great idea, but *I* will go get the catfish. Tanner is waiting for you inside. You see, Kojak was reeeee-ally lucky to have found him."

"Mmm hmm." Frankie was mid eye roll when Cane burst out the door with Faith cradled in his arms.

"Sweetness." Cane's eyes locked on his wife.

Frankie finished the eye roll. "Please. It's only been a day since you've seen her."

"Feels like a lifetime," Cane said, his long legs closing the distance between him and Selah in a few steps.

That kiss though. As she watched the embrace, Frankie's heart was both thrilled for her friend and saddened she couldn't find a love like that. Selah had Cane. Tanner had Kojak.

And Frankie had, well… the project she'd been kicking around in her mind. Taking Angel around the track in the adaptive car planted a seed. Maybe that would be her passion, her new beginning, since true down-and-dirty car racing was a thing of the past. She'd find a love to call her own.

Maybe Frankie would run the idea by Tanner tonight. Never mind. He wouldn't be around to see the plan come to fruition. As soon as he broke the inevitable news that the government decided to seize all Speedway property, he'd leave. Maybe he'd give chase and hunt down her father. Maybe he'd head back to Washington and the DEA or back to Minnesota and Grandma. Whatever. Frankie had a new plan. She would survive without her fake bodyguard.

After waving goodbye to the lovebirds, who drifted off to the Charger without a backward glance, Frankie smiled her thanks as Mario opened the door for her. Once inside, she took a deep breath and let it out slowly, inhaling the faint scent of something fried and greasy.

Her moment of peace was obliterated when she heard a thud and pain stung her skin. That bald terrorist had sunk its talons into her legs and was climbing up and Frankie FELT it. Her heart pounded as the sensations accelerated up her calf and thigh. Dr. Kojak had stimulated some nerve endings more effectively than acupuncture.

"Catfish for you tonight." Frankie laughed at the ugly thing as it finished the climb and sat upright on her lap, staring her down. "Alright, double the catfish. You drive a hard bargain."

It had to get bored and stop growling eventually, right?

The cat lunged forward and dug a claw into her chest, causing both of them to shriek. So, she still had some work to do before they'd be bosom buddies.

"Frankie, is that you? I'm out here."

Kojak split and Frankie's belly quivered at the sound of Tanner's voice. No, no. She'd have none of that. She erected a force field around herself as she rolled out to the patio. He couldn't hurt her anymore.

The sight of him took her breath away, shaking the dickens out of her force field. He was half-sitting on, half-leaning against the wooden fence, one leg bent and the other outstretched. His black suit and fancy lace-up shoes were fierce but the top buttons on his dress shirt hung open to tease her.

Whoa. Those little wire-framed glasses set against his freshly-trimmed beard and hair revealed the nerdy hot secret agent man he'd been hiding all these months. Now, she couldn't get that "Secret Agent Man" song out of her head or get one word to come out of her mouth.

He turned, a smile slowly loosening his hard jaw and crinkling his eyes at the corners. "Wonder Woman," he said softly as he slid off the fence. "Thought you'd never get here to save me from my brother."

She rolled past him, she was so caught up in the scene before her: tiny white LED lights illuminated the patio and a tree in the yard, the gloriously fried scent of Chinese food wafted up from take-out boxes, a blue box wrapped with a golden cord perched on a red tablecloth, a gold candle flickered in the center of the table, and mischief flickered in Tanner's dark eyes.

"What is this?" Frankie finally found her voice, her defenses completely undone by the man standing before her with his hand outstretched. "Who are you and what have you done with my ogre bodyguard?"

"I'm about to show you, if you'll let me."

CHAPTER THIRTY-TWO

"Roses are red, dirt is brown.
Rev up the engines and hammer down."

–Unknown

As HE DRANK her in, Tanner tasted something he'd never experienced before—joy and hope. Frankie made him feel like an awkward and innocent 16-year-old with big dreams and hormones all over the map.

She'd swept up her hair in a crimson clip. Tendrils drifted down her neck and onto a matching crimson, sleeveless dress that showed off toned arms and legs.

"Diana Prince can't hold a candle to you."

Her cheeks got in on the matchy thing as she turned her head to hide a blush, then looked up at him shyly. He picked up a water glass from the table and held it to his neck, suddenly needing to cool off.

He motioned for her to take a seat at the table.

"I couldn't possibly eat. Selah and I had a huge breakfast."

He raised an eyebrow as she surveyed the table. It wasn't two minutes before she tore into the boxes of chicken lo mein and fried cheese wontons. She scooped some out and dug in, moaning with the first bite. Then, she cracked open a Mountain Dew. Selah had taken pity on him and clued him in to all Frankie's favorites. He doubted that Frankie would turn down anything labeled edible.

Grinning, he slid into the chair across from Frankie and pulled it closer. Tanner had given up trying to stop smiling around her. It felt good. His cheeks were sore, but he'd build up those muscles.

"Oh," she stopped mid-bite, "Did you want some too?"

She continued eating, without sharing.

"I fear I may lose a finger." Risking it, he swiped a wonton from her plate.

"Maybe I shouldn't have ditched Thomas the Tank Engine. He wouldn't complain about my food manners."

Tanner choked on the wonton, downing more water. "I would prefer to obliterate all memories of your dating misadventures."

"Yeah, me too," she said with a sigh, setting the fork down. "Especially Kyle."

Tanner reached across the table and wrapped his hand around hers. When she didn't pull away, he let out the breath he'd been holding. "He targeted you. You couldn't have known. He'll be in prison for a while, but I want you to consider pressing charges for sexual assault."

He could kill that guy for making her duck her chin and doubt herself.

She finally met his eyes. "It's not too late? They won't fault me for breaking his nose, among other things?"

"It's never too late to fight for yourself and for what's right." He squeezed her hand and let go.

"Let's get that freak off the streets then, permanently." She recommenced eating her lo mein, nudging the box of wontons his way. "Any word on Daddy?"

When he didn't answer, Frankie pointed her fork at him. "Nobody just vanishes. Go find him. He needs to pay for what he's done. Every employee out of a job right now at the casino and track deserves restitution."

If he knew Frankie, she'd pay the workers out of her own pockets if she could. "If he's alive, the feds will find him."

"Forgive me if I don't put a lot of stock in an agency that hasn't been able to bring him to justice for this long and who let agents like Kyle and Dani and you, for that matter, run wild under their noses." Frankie stopped. "I shouldn't have spouted off about Dani."

"You're right about her. You're right on all counts." He sat back in his chair. She sat back too, mirroring his pose and studying him. This woman would always keep him on his toes. "I'm no longer on the payroll. As much as I want Kenny Newman brought to justice, I have no interest in being anywhere but here… with you."

Hearing Newman admit he was responsible for killing Danielle and shooting Tanner had knocked the wind out of Tanner's obsession. His priority was sitting right in front of him.

If only he could pull her into his arms and make her see how he felt. Logically, he knew he needed to take things at her pace, give her time to forgive and, maybe, love him. But when he got caught up in those sparkling blue eyes, all logic evaporated.

"All of this is for you, Frankie." He waved his hand over the food and toward the lights. "All of this and more."

"Those boxes for me, too?" Frankie traced a fingertip over the small blue one, her lips parting expectantly.

Tanner licked his lips, willing his heartbeat to slow down. His speedway queen was revving it up. "Yes, but before you tear into those, something happened today that we need to discuss."

ঌ

Tanner got so serious, it had to be something about her future, something involving the Speedway or the lawsuits and criminal charges ahead. She pushed down the sick feeling in her stomach and steered the conversation another direction. "Did you and Cane have a good visit?"

"We buried a few hatchets. None in his head." Tanner smirked.

"So, you called a truce, but you aren't planning any camping trips or dress like your twin days any time soon?"

"Something like that."

She reached over and pinched his cheek. "Aww, that is twice as nice. Double the happiness."

Tanner fake gagged. "Stay away from me. You're as corny as Cane."

Frankie erupted in a belly laugh and shook until her eyes teared up. "I was picturing the two of you in a side-by-side stroller in matching onesies. I'm sorry. The twin thing never gets old, especially when the adult twins are big strapping alpha males who are way too serious. I haven't laughed like that in a while."

"I think I have some news that will keep you smiling. I had a preliminary meeting with a buddy of mine who's a DOJ lawyer."

"That doesn't sound like good news."

"Even if your father is convicted, we may have some wiggle room when it comes to forfeiture of the speedway property."

"Oh."

"Kenny leveraged the casino to launder money, so it will be seized, but your barn and personal cars aren't tainted. If the tunnels underneath the property were used in the slave trade or as part of the underground railroad, they may render the property historic," Tanner explained. "We may be able to include the pond, so you can preserve your mother's memory. If we can prove—"

"Whoa. Let me stop you there." Frankie held up a hand, then put it over her heart. "I've spent a lot of time being angry at you for deceiving me, but, when the rubber met the road, you came through for me. You saved my life. You fought to save me when the DEA tried to bring criminal charges and now you're fighting to help me save my home. I am beyond grateful."

"But…" His shoulders deflated.

She wanted to hug him and tell him it was okay if he took over and straightened out her life for her. Wouldn't that be so much easier?

"But I have another plan."

"Of course you do." He didn't seem annoyed or surprised, just confident in her.

"The thoughts of branching out on my own is daunting, but it is time to go from "that girl who races cars" to "that woman who makes a difference." Frankie enjoyed the smile her words brought to his lips. "The first order of business is bulldozing what's left of the casino. If the feds need a demolition crew, my arms still work."

He nodded for her to continue.

"Daddy poisoned our home and property, literally. I don't want anything to do with his dirty money. I would love to preserve history and my mother's memory as you said, but that pond is just a memorial to her death and Daddy's downward spiral. The government can take every piece of that property, except one."

He leaned forward when she paused. "Which one? Don't keep me in suspense."

"Can't help yourself, can you? Still bossing me around."

"Frankie," he growled. "Don't keep me waiting. What are you willing to fight for?"

"I'm keeping the track."

"That big oval patch of ground is what you want?"

"Angel was so excited about riding in the car. She said her friends wanted to join as well. I'd like to introduce a new generation to the sport."

Tanner scooted his chair up, his knees touching hers. The scent of aftershave derailed her thoughts.

"I'm uh… I'm creating a foundation that will make racing accessible, starting with kids who have special needs. We can branch out to adults."

"Where will the cars come from?"

"I set money aside from my patent. We'll begin with that and find donors to fund the wheels."

"Let me guess. You've recruited Lefty to scout out cars."

"You're catching on, Sherlock. He's thankful to have a paycheck and a job that doesn't involve Daddy." She paused a moment to refocus, then launched again. "All I need is the track and the roads leading in and out. Surely, the government wouldn't begrudge these young people a chance to develop their passion? I'll need to get the lawyer on it and tons of liability insurance and advertising and social media and…"

Her voice petered off when it hit her how much work and money this would entail. Frankie knew how to balance the books, how to drive a stick, and how to survive a catastrophic car wreck. What did she know about entertaining kids, keeping them safe, and placating parents?

"You want to hear what I think?" Tanner sat back and crossed his arms at his chest.

She'd say no, but he was going to tell her anyway. She nodded. She didn't need his approval. Why did she desire it so much?

"I think I've never been prouder of you than I am at this moment. You feared your racing career had crashed and burned, but you have risen from the ashes, and you're going to take flight again. It's brilliant."

"I can't wait to see Angel's face when I tell her." Her heart sure was soaring. "I'm going to show those kids that setbacks are just caution flags on the drive to victory lane."

"Sign me up."

"To do what?"

"Donor, cheerleader, cold-caller, whatever you need. I'll wrangle Mario to find a trustworthy social media guru. I'm a decent handyman. Did you see the roof I put on Selah's house? I mean, talent speaks for itself."

"Yes, Tanner," she rolled her eyes playfully. "Your epic displays of carpentry are legendary in Shadybrook."

"I got mad skillz." He brushed off his shoulders.

"You're such a nerd."

"It's the gift that keeps on giving," Tanner said.

"Seriously, I want to be in on this winning plan from the beginning."

Frankie tried to decode his hopeful smile. Did that mean he wanted to be a part of her life? Did *she* want him to be a part of her life? She had plenty of cheerleaders and buddies already on her team. She needed a man who would love her as passionately and deeply as she would love him, forever. If that violated her Amazon warrior code, then so be it. Deep down, she craved all that epic, soap supercouple romance. She deserved it.

~

"Frankie, are you with me?" Tanner called her name a few times, before tapping on the chair.

She had a faraway look on her face, a little teary, but determined.

She startled. "Sorry. I was building my empire in my mind while you were yapping. So, can I open my boxes or what?"

"Have at it."

She squealed and grabbed the cardboard box he'd placed on the table.

"Naturally, you would pick the biggest one first."

Sniffing the box before tearing it open, she said, "Is this Momma's chocolate treasure pie? You know I'm a scent hound when it comes to food, baby."

Her endearment hit him in the gut. Tanner had to get it under control. No normal man could fall this hard for a woman this fast. Other than his brother that is, and Cane didn't count.

She reached in and scooped a dab of whip cream on her

finger and licked it off. Her eyes widened when they met his, as if she realized he'd been enjoying the show. "Thank you."

"You deserve some pleasure after all you've been through."

After all he and the other men in her life had put her through. Shaking the guilt from his mind for a moment, Tanner pushed the small blue box toward her. She pulled the golden cord and studied it.

"Is this..." She held it up, watching it glisten under the lights.

"Your lasso, Wonder Woman. The lasso of truth. Anyone caught in it will find it impossible to lie."

She lobbed it at him.

"That's the idea. As long as you have the lasso, I will tell you everything you need to know. From here on out, Frankie, only honesty comes between us."

As Frankie opened the box, she narrowed her eyes at him, "If you think that you can saunter in here with your fancy Wonder Woman swag and sway me into forgiving and forgetting all that you—ooh, pretty! So shiny."

She lifted two golden bracelets from the box and slid them onto her wrists. He'd kind of hoped she'd let him put them on her. If she wasn't ready for him to take her in his arms, he'd have to touch her with his words and gestures.

When had it happened that Tanner's heart had healed and decided it belonged to Frankie? When he'd pulled her out of the burning lab, afraid he might lose her forever? The night they'd danced in her bedroom? No, earlier than that. It must have been the dip in the pond. Seeing her struggle and fight to walk again and conquer her fear of the water, that's when he knew. There was no other woman like Frankie Newman, no other woman for him. Never had been. Never would be.

"They're unbreakable bracelets of submission."

Her eyebrow quirked. "You know, the Amazons wore these, not only to deflect bullets, but also to remind themselves how men had chained and oppressed them in the past."

"I don't plan to take away your power, Frankie. I want to give you strength and set you free from the past."

When Frankie reached out to stroke his cheek, he closed his eyes a moment, leaning into her hand. The next thing he knew she had wrapped that lasso around his neck. The cord was loose but she held him in her grip with her bright blue eyes.

"It's truth time, buster. Start talking. First question, are you still in love with Dani?"

"You certainly go straight for the jugular." He cleared his throat when she tightened the cord. "No, Frankie. It stung that she cheated with your father, but she had already strayed. Regardless of her motives, she did shoot me in the chest. I moved on from loving her years ago. The engagement was our last-ditch attempt to salvage something that was already lost."

Danielle was his first love, but Frankie… Tanner couldn't even put it into words. He wasn't sure he wanted to. Everyone he'd ever cared about, except Cane and Selah and Grandma, were dead. Voicing his feelings tempted fate. He'd like to keep Frankie around permanently.

"Second question." She wiggled two fingers in his face. "What else are you hiding?"

If you only knew. He'd get to that secret, eventually. It

was a good one. For now, he'd clear the air on the past and take the rest one moment at a time.

"You just may hate me for this." He sighed, scrubbing his palm down his face. "When I first met you in Selah's hospital room, I thought you were the most extraordinary woman I'd ever seen."

She snorted. "When you rolled into Shadybrook and I floated the idea of a relationship, you said there could never be anything between us."

Tanner stared at his empty hands. "You lit me up from the first moment I saw you in the photo and again in the hospital. I had to put out that fire for both of our sakes. I was on a mission to bring down your father and, potentially you, if you were involved."

"I understand what you had to do, but I still feel the hurt of your rejection."

He dared to look up into her eyes, memorizing the pain etched into her face so he'd never put it there again. "The biggest lie I ever told you was a lie of omission. I allowed you to believe that I didn't want you and that other men didn't want you either."

"I don't understand."

"For a while I couldn't decide why you were single. These country boys were blind. But then your father let it slip that he took care of any potential suitors who looked your way. He put out the word on the street that anyone who dated you was a dead man. It's a small town."

"So, what you're telling me is that men in Shadybrook never came near me because they were afraid of my father? That's preposterous."

"The date who tried to kiss you years ago? Did you ever see him again?"

"Elliott?" She clutched the handrails of her chair. "He was so sweet. I thought maybe we… but he never called back."

"A few days later, he was shot and killed accidentally while hunting."

"No." She shook her head violently. "That's not true. It would have made the papers. Daddy wouldn't do something like—."

"Like murder the doctor who cared for your mother? Like order someone to murder me? Like murder endangered species for sport and mount them on his wall? Like murder Danielle and keep her photo as a trophy? Like operate an underground lab so he could murder hundreds, thousands who purchased those drugs? Like beat Russ Morgan to the ground so he could flee the country?"

"I know. I know. I get it now, but I still can't fathom why. How could he do such evil things to innocent people? How could he do that to his own daughter?" Frankie tugged the lasso around his neck and hurled it at the floor, as if she'd heard enough truth.

"Selfishness. Power. Maybe he was afraid you'd leave him as your mother did. It was his sick way of loving you, while keeping you under his thumb." Tanner scooped up the lasso and put it back in her hands. Then, he wrapped his hands around hers.

"So, the men who glanced at me and walked away—"

"Knew you were off-limits. You had no cause to ever doubt yourself." For once, Tanner was grateful to Kenny

Newman for protecting Frankie from those losers and keeping her free for Tanner.

"I don't intimidate men then?"

"Now, I didn't say that." He smirked. "A woman like you—intelligent, powerful, whip-smart funny—threatens weak men. Those qualities are alluring to a man who is secure in himself. The man who wants and loves you wouldn't let anything stand in his way of pursuing you and having you."

Frankie's lips parted as her breath caught. He was caught, too. How had all of that tumbled out of his mouth? He really needed to take control again and go back to blanking his emotions.

The brisk breeze and the soundtrack of crickets and a hoot owl in the distance seemed to intensify the impact of his words, the questions in her eyes, and the fire in his belly.

"Do you feel that?" she whispered, her eyes bright as she flipped her hands so their palms were touching, fanning the fire.

"Never felt anything like it."

CHAPTER THIRTY-THREE

I Love You to the Moon and Back and All Around the Dirt Track

FRANKIE SHIVERED UNDER Tanner's intense gaze and tried to put the brakes on her accelerating heartbeat. He shrugged off his jacket and wrapped it around her shoulders before taking his seat in front of her again. He must have seen the goosebumps and thought the breeze had caused them.

"Wow," she said nervously. "I don't know how to react to Tanner 2.0. It's so strange to see you acting human—laughing, smiling, and listening to my opinions, instead of bossing me around."

"I've heard every word you've ever said." His jaw pulsed as his dark eyes danced with hers. "Since we're truth-telling, you can admit you enjoy going toe-to-toe with me when I boss you around."

Frankie felt a tug on her wrists and realized the scoundrel had tied them together with the lasso. The corner of his mouth crooked. She bit her lip. Busted. The adorable jerk was reading her mind. As much as she liked being in control, there was something about the heat and darkness rolling off him that made her want to surrender.

"The more time I spend with you, the more I'm finding my way back to myself. The job changed me." Tanner released her wrists. "It's easier if you shut down your emotions like a robot. When you don't react, it gives you more power. Other people talk to fill in the silence. When people talk, they slip up. It made me a solid agent, but a miserable human."

"Cane's not the only one in the family with acting ability."

"Funny you mention it. He and I just had that discussion, but I am way better than him at everything." Tanner's voice was gravelly. "In fact, I'm so good you believed I was secretly a cyborg."

"I'll have to look a little deeper to confirm my theory."

Inspecting his hand, Frankie turned it over, her eyes scanning the surface and his earnest face. Using her fingertips, she slowly traced a trail on Tanner's skin from his palm to his wrist. When he inhaled sharply and his eyes shut for a moment, she got her answer. Her fingers continued the path over his white dress shirt, up his bicep and the side of his neck, lingering on his lips.

"I still suspect you're superhuman."

He kissed her fingertips and smiled. "I promise to only use my powers for good."

She wanted to kiss him. She wanted him to kiss her. Frankie wanted to freeze this moment for eternity. The moon and the stars and the twinkly-lights and the Chinese food and his delicious aftershave. Would heaven be like this? Well, this plus open roads for millions of miles, with no speed limits or brakes or wheelchairs.

Maybe he was considering the same things because he didn't speak for a few minutes.

"Tanner?"

"One last secret and it's a doozy," he suddenly looked unsure of himself.

"Ugh. Please, no more bad new—"

"I love you, Frankie Newman."

"You what?"

"You know that hole where my heart used to be?" He took her hand and placed it on his chest. "Miracle of miracles. It's full again."

Tanner's heart was beating as fast as Frankie's. Tears sprang to her eyes. This was crazy. Incredible. Wonderful. Impossible.

"But…"

"You don't have to speak. You don't have to say it back."

"I don't love you. I am not in love with you." She lifted her chin.

"Liar," Tanner said. "I see you. I know you."

"Well, hi-ho, the derry-o for you, because I'm still trying to wrap my head around forgiving you. Doggone it, I done tried to put the moves on you when we first met and you turned me down. Now, you just expect me to flip the switch and want you again?"

You and your six-pack, and your drippingly sweet love for animals and your parents and Grandma, and the way you walk into a room like the Terminator, lasering in on me and holding me captive with your eyes. Okay, if I must. She should make it hard on him, hold his feet to the flames a bit, but he was too easy to love.

"I have a lot of work left to earn your trust, but I need you to believe this one thing tonight." Tanner's face was more animated than she'd ever seen it. "I need you to trust with everything you've got that I love you. I've loved you since the beginning. I was just too stubborn to face it."

"I wasn't sure you even liked me, let alone loved me."

"I always protected you, whether you wanted me to or not. Even when the evidence looked like you might be as dirty as your father, I couldn't walk away."

"My head is spinning. It's happening so fast."

"But you love to go fast." Tracing Frankie's lips with the pad of his thumb, Tanner said, "*This*, however, will go very, very slow, until you lose your mind."

Too late. Circuits blown.

She groaned when she realized what he meant. He just *had* to be in control.

"You've got some nerve coming up in here with all this romance and heat and then putting me on ice. Well, guess what? I've survived a lifetime without kissing, sex, carnal pleasure of any kind. What's another day of deprivation? Thanks for nothing, Tanner."

He leaned in and whispered in Frankie's ear. "Some things are worth waiting for."

"I knew you'd be the death of me."

"In that case, you'll die happy, guaranteed."

ණ

Tanner teased her so much, he was about to abandon his own plans for a seductively slow build of passion. He pulled back from her chair. "I need to leave now… or I never will."

He puffed out a jagged breath, shell-shocked from confessing he was in love with her. She hadn't turned him down. Hadn't said she hated him or run away.

"What now, Tanner? What's next for us?"

Always anticipating the next thrill, the next challenge, his Frankie.

"You'll see." He winked.

That blush. That soft smile. Tanner had never truly known happiness before he saw them. This girl was it for him and the sooner he did something about it, the better.

When his phone buzzed, he looked around for it before remembering Frankie was wearing his jacket. He stood, snagging one more whiff of her perfume and one more touch of her warm skin as he lightly brushed the back of his hand against her cheek.

"Ashton," he said, as he answered the phone and watched her watching him. "You have terrible timing as usual Martin, Martinello, major pain in the neck, whatever you're calling yourself these days."

Frankie playfully reached for the phone to talk to her BFF, but Tanner held it away. No other man was ever getting that close to her again.

Mark's tone grew somber as he dropped a bomb. Tanner whistled out a breath. He could not have foreseen their magical evening ending like this.

"I understand. Thanks for the courtesy call."

As he hung up, he took a long look at her beautiful face, her forehead and mouth pinched with worry. Why did he have to be the one to keep making her sad? There was no way to cushion this blow than just to—

"Spill it," she said. "More bad news from the good guys, I suppose."

"They've recovered the Speedway helicopter in a ravine south of here. Completely burned out."

"And Daddy?" Her voice was monotone and her face blank as she reached for her water glass.

"Investigators haven't recovered his body or the pilot's."

Surviving a crash like that was unlikely, but, in his experience, only the good died young. Kenny Newman could walk through fire without getting burned.

"They'll stop the search then?" She emptied the glass, set it down, and began to pack up the trash from their meal.

"Yes. The NTSB investigation could take weeks or months, but Mark believes it was a deadly mix of fog and pilot error."

"So, that's it. It's over and we can put it behind us." She slapped her thighs and gathered her lasso and bracelets on her lap, ready to check out on Tanner. "My father got what was coming to him. All's well that ends well, right? Shakespeare would love my family and our tragicomedy. Except there's really no family now to speak of. Maybe Daddy had something to do with my mother's death. I guess I'll never know now."

Frankie's eyes teared. "Don't worry, I'm not feeling sorry for myself. Nope. He's not worth it. I will survive. I always do."

She spun the chair like a pro and threw open the door to the patio, nearly taking out Kojak as the cat hurtled toward her.

"Wait." Tanner's breath wasted.

She sped across the living room and was opening the door to her bedroom before he could catch up.

He grabbed Frankie's hand as it turned the knob, letting her go when she bristled. "Don't shut me out."

"Why? Talking solves nothing. The five stages of grief have already steamrolled me in the last few days. I don't need a pity party. Plenty of people lose their parents and don't shatter."

Tanner's throat tightened as if shrapnel from the car had lodged there. Cane had spiraled into addiction, chasing drugs and women to put himself back together again. Tanner distanced himself, moving thousands of miles away and changing his name. Yet, he chose a career that kept him from feeling anything and chose a woman who couldn't give herself completely to him because she was blanking her own feelings with drugs and other men. Whoo. They'd all make some family therapist rich.

"Tanner."

He startled when Frankie's hand, soft and warm, slipped into his. He looked into her blue eyes, hazy with tears. She could pretend her father's death didn't bother her, but she was too pure and honest to don the cloak of deceit that was his uniform.

"I'm sorry," she said, her thumb stroking his fingers. "That was the most callous thing I could ever say to you."

"Pain makes us say and do things we never imagined."

"I'm not in pain. I feel… relieved. Free."

She removed the clip from her hair. It splayed onto her face, tempting him to brush it back. Frankie was stunning, extraordinary, exquisite—the whole thesaurus. Shakespeare would have used her as a muse for romance, not that tragedy/comedy she was talking about.

"You are a goddess."

Tugging his hand, she said, "stay with me tonight."

As her gaze beckoned, he'd never desired something so badly in his life. "If I step across this threshold, I can make you mine?"

"The Amazon in me might throttle you for that remark, but… I've always been yours. You said you loved me. Show me." Frankie's words were bold but her body trembled.

Wrapped up in her, Tanner would feel no more pain or loneliness, and he'd make sure the only thing she felt was comfort and pleasure. She deserved more.

As she licked her lips, he faltered. What was he saying? Her chest rose and fell with his resolve to do this thing right.

Finally, Tanner released her hand and walked away. "I want more than one night, Frankie."

"That can be arranged."

Tanner chuckled, dragging his hand down his face to have peace from those twinkling, tempting eyes for a moment. "I want a lifetime of nights. It won't be about the pain of your father's death. It won't be me taking advantage of you in a vulnerable state. You deserve more than a friends-with-benefits arrangement like those cretins on the internet. It will be you surrendering to me from a place of strength. It will be because you are my wife and you love me as much as I love you."

How had it happened? Tanner wanted to marry this woman ASAP. One tip of her cowboy hat as she kicked up her heels and he was a goner.

Frankie sucked in a breath. "Oh. Well, goodnight then."

She closed the door behind her before he could get a clue as to whether she was angry, whether she could love him, or whether she thought the idea of being his wife was insanity. Life was so much simpler when he was playing bodyguard and had only to worry about saving her life.

He turned back to his room and took a flying feline to the chest. Kojak's engine was running when she nestled into Tanner's arms. He longed to hold Frankie, but God had a sense of humor and sent him a consolation prize. Tanner gave the cat a rubdown as he carried her onto the patio. Under a perfect full moon, he surveyed the remains of an evening that was anything but.

Tanner did something he hadn't done since he'd run out of that blazing tunnel carrying Frankie—he prayed hard—for his Wonder Woman and for the strength to be the man she needed.

Ten minutes in, he got a text from Mario who was still guarding the door. In the excitement, Tanner had forgotten to send him home.

Mario: There's an angel out here 2 see u. She says it's an urgent, time-sensitive matter.

Whaddyaknow. Tanner laughed out loud at that one and sent a fist-bump heavenward for the assist. He had a good feeling about this. Sometimes God took a thousand years to move mountains and sometimes they crumbled in a day.

CHAPTER THIRTY-FOUR

Race with Passion or Not at All

Frankie would not allow herself to fall apart. She had to keep it together for the sake of her future. She hung the do-not-disturb sign on her door and spent most of the night and the next morning plowing through paperwork to get the ball rolling on her father's estate and her foundation. The thought of making those kids smile and breathing life into a vision that was completely hers sent a thrill down her spine and beat back the gloom of her father's crimes and death.

She could cry or she could fly. Door number two, please.

She almost flew out of the chair when someone rapped on the door to the suite. Frankie peeked out the window and found a woman in a black dress, pressing the back of her hand to her forehead like some wailing mourner. They were still weeks away from Halloween. If Frankie didn't let

Momma in, somebody was bound to call the cops to report a haunting.

Frankie opened the bedroom door and came wheel-to-toe with Tanner.

"Hi," she squeaked.

A slow smile lit his mouth and languid eyes. "Hello, beauty."

"Liar." She hadn't brushed her teeth or hair, changed her clothes, touched up her makeup, or showered. If Tanner truly loved Frankie, now was the test.

"When you're in possession of the lasso, I am unable to tell a lie. Remember?" He drew her in, making her want to believe anything he was selling. They stared at each other for a long moment, ignoring the pounding on the door.

He said, "You seem like you're holding something back. Would you like to do a little truth-telling, Frankie?"

She blurted what had been weighing on her mind. "I'm sorry for snapping at you last night after you gave me such an incredible evening. I'm sorry for seducing you and shaming you when you didn't take me up on such a brazen offer. No one has ever loved me before. I don't know if I can trust it or myself."

Tanner was infuriatingly still and serious as he knelt in front of her, making her wait for his response. "Nothing to apologize for. You can say or feel whatever you need to. I can handle it. As for that seduction…"

He twirled the magnificent Wonder Woman bracelets on her wrists, keeping his eyes on hers as he interlaced their fingers. "I have never been more tempted."

"Oh. My." Goosebumps ran up and down her arms and legs. Her legs! She was getting more and more feeling back every day, but it always seemed to happen when he was around. Dr. Tanner Frankenstein was throwing all the switches and circuits to bring her back to life.

"Leaving now before you seduce me again." Tanner kissed her cheek as he rose to his feet and released her hands. He wore his standard black jeans with an unbuttoned black suit jacket and black boots.

"Where are you going looking like the Greek god of chocolate chip waffles, whipped cream, strawberries, bacon, and eggs and cheese arranged neatly on a giant plate?"

"You missed breakfast and lunch." Grinning, he patted his abs.

"You must be off on business."

He wouldn't leave now that he got the job done, would he?

The muscle in his jaw tightened. "Noticed you put out the 'don't disturb' sign, so I'm going to get out of your adorably messy hair."

"Rude and vague." Frankie rolled her eyes.

"I'll be back," Tanner said in the Terminator voice. "Trust me, Frankie. Trust me with your heart and your future."

She swallowed. He didn't ask for much.

They both jumped when it sounded like a battering ram against the front door. She'd completely forgotten about Momma.

Tanner moved toward it, but Frankie said, "Better let me. Even a trained agent can't handle her."

Tanner chuckled and put up his palms. Frankie cracked open the front door and tried to shut it again when a camera appeared, along with two of those yappy reality cooking show people. Momma grabbed the frame and inspected

Frankie. She reached down and crushed Frankie to her bosom, nearly suffocating her.

"Child, you look like you been rode hard and put away wet. I'm sorry I didn't come sooner when you're clearly suffering."

Suddenly, Momma turned and huddled up with her producers. "Poor thing ain't in no shape for visitors today. Y'all go on and leave us be a while. Shoo!"

After some discussion, Momma waved them goodbye, picked up three insulated grocery bags, and pushed her way in.

Frankie let her have it. "*One day* was all I asked to pull myself together. One day of peace. And here you bring your reality cooking show along to 'console' me?"

"I figured you'd be mad enough to hang your scoundrel father in effigy by now. Shore would make for good television." Momma cackled, then gasped. "This world and the next! Weren't you wearing that same dress yesterday?"

Frankie looked down at herself. She'd worked for so long last night, she'd fallen asleep in it.

"Child, I raised you better than that." Momma's eyes narrowed when she caught sight of Tanner.

"Living in sin in a motel room with this hulking conman. Can twins share the same brain? He and that boy of Selah's ain't got a lick of sense between them."

Momma resented Cane for taking her baby Selah from her. Poor Tanner. If he truly did foresee a future with Frankie, he had no idea the family he was getting himself into.

Tanner stepped up. "You mean, Cane Ashton, your son-in-law, Emmy-nominated actor, sports broadcaster, and the man who makes your daughter deliriously happy?"

Frankie's heart clenched. Tanner was defending his brother with a passion. Miracles do happen.

"Hmph." Momma scurried around the kitchenette, tidying dishes and scrubbing down surfaces before hefting the insulated bags onto the sparkling countertops and pulling out plastic containers. "Neither one of you girls got any business bringing a man home. Just one more thing to cook for and clean up after."

He scoffed. "I'm a big boy. If I made a woman do that for me, my mother would have tanned my hide."

"So punny, Tanner." Frankie snickered.

He winked and headed out the door. "Have a peaceful visit, ladies. See you bright and early tomorrow, Frankie."

She went to the window to watch him deftly maneuver Momma's entourage outside the door. "I need to sleep in."

"You can sleep when you're dead." Momma looked up from the containers she was popping open, a pained expression flashing on her face. "I wasn't thinking."

"*Now* you're worried about being insensitive to my grief? I can't believe you would invite your camera crew to use my pain to get sympathy viewers for your—ooh, is that pie?"

All was forgiven.

Margo poured a glass of milk and dished out a heaping slice from one of three pies. Then, she scooped out meatloaf, buttery mashed potatoes, and corn on a separate plate. "If time don't heal, pie will, Francine."

Frankie took a big ol' bite of Oreo creme. "I'm cured."

It was surprising that Momma stayed plump because she never stopped moving and fretting and cleaning. Frankie had never seen her eat any of the food she prepared. Her husband's clogged arteries and heart attack attested to the fact that he ate enough of it for both of them.

"How's Russ?"

"That man." Momma looked heavenward, sighing. "How he can be laid up and still be so hard-a-headed and hard-a-hearing, I'll never know."

"At least Russ is alive."

"Only 'cause I ain't killed him yet."

Frankie snorted, sipping milk to cover. Momma pushed the plate of meatloaf toward her and tapped it. Frankie relented and chowed down on the grown-up food, her energy and spirits lifting with each bite, until Kojak jumped up on the counter, face down in her food.

Momma gasped. "Is that the rabid varmint that attacked me at the diner?"

Frankie moved to pick up the cat and recoiled when it hissed. "Tanner adopted Kojak, all sugar and spice. He's a sucker for strong-willed females."

Momma rummaged around in the closet at the door and came back with a mop and a rag, which she shook at Kojak. The cat howled.

"That varmint's been abused. I know it's not in your wheelhouse, but let's try some love before we buff it to death, okay?"

Momma scowled at the cat, which had polished off the meatloaf. She set her cleaning supplies against the wall with a huff.

"Would you open up that catfish? Selah texted that she put it in the fridge this morning. Obviously, it's a fan favorite with Kojak."

Momma did as she was told but clutched the fish. "I ain't wasting prime catfish on that cross-eyed gummy bear."

Kojak sat on the countertop, hackles and ears raised like little horns, claws unfurled. *Love. Love. Love. Love the cat. Love the beehive. Or maybe kill them both with kindness.*

"Hand over the catfish now, Momma." Frankie growled, causing the beast to look her way. "Nice kitty."

When Frankie finally got her paws on a tiny piece of fish, she set it in front of Kojak and drew her hand back quickly. The cat snarfed it up and took a step toward her, meowing. Progress. Frankie offered another piece, which the cat greedily accepted. She set each piece of fish closer to her, until the cat had moved onto her lap. As Kojak ate, Frankie patted its velvety head. Kojak looked up suspiciously but went back to eating.

"Well, I'll be," Momma shook her coif. "Proves what I've been saying all these years. Food binds us together, whether human or beast."

Frankie grinned down at the cat, which had agreed to a truce and was purring and eating fish from her palm. "You're a much easier beast to seduce than your daddy,"

"What?"

"Nothing. Nothing." Didn't mean to say that out loud.

Thank goodness Tanner hadn't taken the catfish, er, bait that Frankie had dangled in front of him. She wasn't in any shape to spend the night with him, but falling asleep with his arms around her would have been comforting.

"How are you feeling after you almost got yourself blown to bits, twice now? I just heard about Kenny, God rest his soul, if he had one."

Frankie looked up into warm eyes as Momma stroked

Frankie's hair. She rarely saw Momma's gooey center, which, like her pies, was guarded by a crusty exterior.

"I have long-suffering and caring friends and family. I will survive."

"You always do." Momma nodded, her voice betraying a hint of pride. "So much like your momma. A fighter."

Couldn't muster a sniffle over Daddy, but the mention of her mother had Frankie's tears on a hair trigger. Frankie swallowed them back and lost it again as Margo set down a box of knickknacks and a single Polaroid in front of her on the counter.

"I especially liked Tanya's smile in that one. She was on top of the world, just having her precious baby girl."

Mommy. Frankie sipped in a teary breath and let it out slowly as she studied the woman who'd left her with more questions than answers. In the photo, her mother gazed down at a tiny infant wrapped in a red, white, and blue blanket. Kenny Newman held her free hand, a genuine, wide smile lighting his lips.

"Thought you'd like to get a picture deep down in your heart of your family happy. No sense in dwelling on all that misery."

"It helps more than you know." Frankie brushed at her eyes.

"Woo, Tanya had some crazy big hair back then," said the woman with the B-52 on her head. "But a light shone from the inside out. Always singing hymns and Bible songs to you."

"She was spiritual?"

"Prayed for you and your daddy every day. Don't the Lord love to set a saint beside a sinner!" Margo cut her eyes to heaven, likely seeking strength to deal with the gambler she'd married.

"How do I know if a man is a saint or a sinner? How do I know if he loves me when I don't know what love is? How do I find a love that lasts longer than the ink on this faded Polaroid?"

Momma leaned on the countertop, studying her and Kojak. "The man worth keeping is the one who will run through the elements with you, never letting go of your hand or your heart. He won't back down and escape to the racetrack to gamble or retreat to his work when things get tough, when the money gets tight or one of you gets sick or hurt, or when someone dies and it rips your world apart."

"That's so profound, Margo." Frankie was impressed.

"It's hogwash out of the *Good Housekeeping*, but it's advice your momma would have given you. She believed in eternal love and hope and other such nonsense. I'm here to tell you that, if that man who just walked out of here is the one you're talking about loving, run the other way. Roll the other way. Don't risk it. Men ain't worth it. You'll find out."

Aaaaand, that's the end of bonding time with Momma. Back to reality.

"Well, I'll be on my way," Momma put the mop in Frankie's hand. "Time is money in showbiz. See ya bright and early tomorrow."

"Why does everyone keep saying that?"

"You'll see. Be awake and presentable at 6 a.m., rain or shine." Momma scooped up her bags and scooted out the door.

Sounded like Frankie would be called upon to brave the elements Momma mentioned. Tanner's face flooded her senses. Tanner revealed his own scars when he baptized her in the pond's muddy waters. Tanner carried her through the rain to the warmth of his car. Tanner wrapped his jacket around her when the air grew chilly during their dinner date. Tanner tried to free her from a burning car. Tanner sprinted through smoke and fire to transport her to safety. It was Tanner who never backed down and had run through the elements with her in his arms.

It had always been and would always be Tanner.

CHAPTER THIRTY-FIVE

My Heart is On the Track

THE SUN CAME up over Shadybrook and the Blue Ridge Mountains like an explosion of burnt orange, gold, and garnet, but it couldn't compete with the fireball rolling toward Tanner. He wasn't about to step out of Frankie's path as she and Selah made tracks up the sidewalk in front of Good Company.

Frankie's ponytail bounced under her ballcap as she laughed at something Selah said. Tanner smiled to himself when the bracelets he bought her glistened in the light. They matched her Wonder Woman leggings, blue tennis shoes, and red t-shirt perfectly and yet still didn't match her beauty.

His brother elbowed him in the ribs. "I tried to warn you. Those two are a force of nature. It's useless to resist."

Tanner shot Cane an obligatory eyeroll, but he was

right for once. He'd caught Tanner was his mouth hanging open and his heart on his sleeve.

"If this is the Publishers' Clearing House crew," Frankie said as she surveyed the crowd gathered at the diner door, "lay it on me. Where's my big fat check?"

"You'll have to earn it first." Tanner took her hand and kissed her cheek.

Frankie startled and looked up into his eyes, probably surprised at his PDA. Plenty more where that came from. All in good time.

Momma threw open the door and held it for Angel and her mother. Frankie's friend Gina came out, followed by Mario, Tanner's Grandma Iris, Frankie's mechanic, Lefty, Selah's Aunt Ruby, her best friend Pearl, and a bevy of frisky church ladies who had already tried to make Tanner's acquaintance. Tanner edged closer to Frankie.

Frankie's head swiveled as she hugged her well-wishers. "What are y'all doing here? Selah and I were going to hog out and then go for a walk."

"Did you forget what day it is?" Angel tsked, rolling her wheelchair in front of Frankie's. "You promised to run the Shadybrook Shake-a-Leg with me."

Tanner, too, had forgotten about the race until Angel appeared at his door the other night with an idea to rally Frankie. When Tanner gave Selah the news, she'd come up with another idea and the plan had grown bigger and better. Today promised to change all of their lives forever.

"Oh!" Frankie's eyes lit for a moment before her face fell. "Honey, I'm not exactly a hometown hero after all that happened with Daddy. We might get rotten tomatoes thrown at us."

"Well, I have plenty tomatoes to throw right back at 'em," Margo offered. "And I know enough of the town's secrets to keep anybody from throwing stones."

Aunt Ruby and Pearl nodded solemnly at each other, muttering "Ain't that the truth?"

Selah took Frankie's other hand and squeezed. "Nobody's throwing anything. Well, Momma might throw a hip out walking, but everybody loves you, Frankie, if you haven't already figured it out. We're all here to celebrate the beginning of a new era—your future."

"But you have to wear a different t-shirt." Angel clapped her hands before picking up the t-shirt in her lap and tossing it at Frankie.

Frankie picked up the shirt, held it out, put it back down, looked around, then held it up again. "It's beautiful and I just realized that you're all wearing the same shirt. Even Tanner is wearing it! What is this?"

Her blue eyes shone, hazy with tears as they held Tanner's eyes, rendering him speechless. He'd felt kind of goofy wearing a t-shirt, sweats, and sneakers again, but, seeing her reaction, he never wanted to wear anything else.

"It's your racing foundation, Frankie," the kid answered, saving him. "Wheels to Wings. Isn't that cool? Selah worked up the design and Cane got the shirts going. Tanner came up with the name."

Tanner cleared his throat, thankful when his brother slapped him on the back. How quickly this woman caused him to go from brooding to blubbering.

Tanner managed to say, "The red, white, and blue is a nod to Frankie's love of country and Wonder Woman. The flying wheels with wings design symbolizes the freedom, power, and hope your non-profit will bring to kids and adults with physical challenges or illness of all kinds. You're giving them a new life and I have a hunch they'll give you the same."

Tanner reached over and chucked Angel lightly on the chin. She beamed bright enough to live up to her name.

Having one or two like her would be fun. Holdup. What? One thing at a time. Frankie picked that moment to give him a sly smile. Tanner sighed. Oh yeah, they were definitely having kids.

Tanner could feel someone's eyes on him. Selah had that "I-told-you-so" gleam. She earned the right to gloat. Her advice had helped him to regain Frankie's trust.

"You know what else has wings or feathers as the Emily Dickinson poem goes?" Selah turned her pointed gaze on Frankie and handed her a seven-figure check that made Frankie's eyes bug out. "Hope."

When Selah's voice caught, Cane finished for her. "Your friends and family, including some Hollywood pals, donated all of this in 24 hours for Wheels to Wings."

Tanner interjected, "Included in that are my paychecks from Kenny Newman. I never spent one dirty dime that he paid me to protect you."

"Thank you will never be enough to repay you." Tears streamed down Frankie's face as she looked around her fan club, smiling at each member.

Selah clasped her hands together and did a little happy dance. "Soooo, what do you think?"

"I think it's the dawning of a new day," Frankie looked up at Tanner, "for Wheels to Wings, for hope, and for love.

Let's get these shirts out on the road and show 'em off. Everybody start your engines."

Angel raised a whoop and a holler and everyone, even Momma, cheered and clapped.

Tanner put his mouth to Frankie's ear. "Can we revisit that love part first?"

"I'm ready." The goosebumps along her neck confirmed it.

Tanner's blundering brother ruined their moment. "So, now that Frankie is making an honest living, will you be re-joining the DEA? Or, offering yourself on Craigslist as a bodyguard for hire."

Tanner answered Cane gruffly. "I'll do anything in my power to help Frankie and those kids, but she'll make this non-profit a success on her own. So, I've thrown my hat in the ring for the sheriff's election."

Frankie said, "I love the idea of dating a man in uniform. Life just gets better and better."

Tanner winked as he slid his hand into Frankie's.

Selah and Cane gave each other a knowing look and laughed.

Selah said, "Remember when Frankie visited me at the party at Cane's beach house and Tanner came charging in looking for her?"

Cane added, "Tanner would have thrown Frankie over his shoulder and carried her back to Shadybrook if Grandma hadn't been there to intervene."

Tanner rubbed his beard, looking at his shoes. "I have no recollection of such event."

Selah punched Tanner's bicep. "Let me refresh your memory. You stood on one side of the room and Frankie stood her ground on the other: gunslingers. I said something like, 'Tanner walks into a room like Wyatt Earp.'"

Cane lifted his chin toward Frankie, "And I said, 'Wyatt Earp meet Annie Oakley.'"

"So, even back then, Cane and I had some inkling of the kind of man you really are, Tanner."

Cane leaned down and dropped a quick kiss on Selah's lips. "My wife is always right on the money."

Tanner glanced from Selah to Frankie, "For once, we can agree on something. I'll repay Selah by cleaning house in the Sheriff's Department, starting with your old bully, Deputy Cody Buchanan. He was knee deep in Kenny Newman's operation."

Selah squealed and hugged Tanner. "Thank God. Cody and his father have been a scourge on us for decades."

"Once I win the race, he won't hurt our family anymore, little sis." Tanner's grief for his parents had blinded him to the family standing right in front of him. Soon, he'd make that family a little bigger if Frankie agreed.

When the loudspeakers crackled with an announcement about the start time and course rules, Frankie said, "Speaking of races, will you be running with me, I mean, dragging along behind me?"

Tanner barked out a laugh. "I've been training for this. Not to brag, but I clocked a pretty decent time when I ran out of a burning building last week."

"So, you're carrying me then?"

"Nope, you're on your own." Tanner dropped her hand and stood behind Angel's chair. "I'm escorting this little lady."

Angel said, "Let's be fair and give her a head start."

"No way," Tanner said. "She'll have the advantage in her new set of wheels."

Tanner nodded towards Lefty as he wheeled in a handcycle they'd rented for the weekend.

"Tanner got you a stretched-out tricycle, Frankie!" Angel blurted as Frankie gave her a high-five. "You have to practice first. I hope you've been pumping iron."

Frankie ran her fingertips lovingly along the long, lean recumbent three-wheeler as Lefty handed her a pair of gloves and showed her how to power the cranks and brake levers.

She tore her eyes away from her new toy long enough to ask, "You did this for me?"

"With a little help from my friends." Tanner shrugged.

"Maybe once we raise capital for Wheels to Wings, we can invest in handcycles for Angel and the foundation."

"That's my girl, always thinking ahead," he said, helping Lefty lift Frankie into the seat. "It doesn't have an engine. Think you can handle it?"

"I speak fluent racing, no matter the vehicle." She laughed, slipping on a helmet, completely in her element. "The question is, can you handle *me*?"

CHAPTER THIRTY-SIX

See You at the Finish Line

How had Frankie never noticed before that Shadybrook was covered in loose gravel, speedbumps, and hills? She'd thought physical therapy was a challenge, but this was a new kind of sore. Why had she agreed to a 5K in front of a whole town of people who'd known her her entire life and were waiting for her to fail as her father had?

Was it raining? No, it was just sweat flying from every pore on her body and dripping from her face. How much longer? Her shoulders and arms screamed. *I'm not going to make it.* She couldn't fall back on her legs or her glutes to carry her as she had in running. Frankie looked to her left and caught a glimpse of heaven that motivated her to keep striving.

As Tanner pushed Angel's wheelchair, the little girl threw her arms in the air and yelled, "Who's gonna win, Tanner?"

"We are!" Tanner half-shouted, half-coughed, smiling like a man walking out of prison and getting his first rush of fresh air.

He was splotchy and sweaty and heaving and sucking air and really happy. The best part was that he wore the shirt emblazoned with a name he'd dreamed up for her. *God, I love him.*

Frankie glanced heavenward. *Give me strength, I love this man. Thank you for gifting me a better life than before. Thank you for the promise of adventure ahead.*

"C'mon," Tanner glanced sideways, shining that sexy, sweet, infuriating grin her way and picking up the pace, "let's cross the finish line together."

Energy blasted through her arms as she cranked it. Frankie had crossed plenty of finish lines before in first place and run around the winner's circle on two legs. Coming in last had never felt so good.

A cheer went up as they raced over the finish line. Selah and Cane, who had run together, rushed over to give them dripping hugs. Tanner got the okay from Angel's mom and lifted the girl carefully from the chair, hoisting her in the air to another round of cheers. When he set Angel back down, he turned to Frankie with a look that made the world fall away. He didn't seem to mind the constant ups and downs of having to bring his considerable height to her level and lift her up.

He slid the race medal around her neck before crushing her against him.

"That was amazing. You were amazing," she murmured against his ear, the rush of adrenaline making her light-headed. "I love you."

Tanner pulled back, dark eyes wide. "What did you say?"

"I love you, Tanner Ashton." She ran her fingers through his hair and down his beard, resting her fingertips on the perfect lips that had yet to claim hers. "But I still beat you by six feet, at least."

Tanner chuckled, setting her down into her regular wheels and bringing his lips tantalizingly close to hers again before he pulled away. She was determined not to initiate the kiss. If he desired her, he would pursue her. It stung a bit, but he'd said he didn't want to be like those other guys who'd only wanted her for sex.

His next words sent shock waves through her system. "Our marriage is going to be a healthy competition, isn't it?"

"I see it as friendly motivation." Frankie's heart went into overdrive as the full impact of what he'd said sunk in. She clutched at his t-shirt. "Whoa, hoss… What did you… Marriage?"

Frankie must have pushed herself too hard during the race because she was hallucinating. Tanner Ashton, growly half-man, half-robot bodyguard, knelt on one knee, looking up at her as if he didn't want to be anywhere else in the world but here with her.

"Yes!" she squeaked out before he could say a word.

Laughter erupted around them. Frankie gasped. She'd forgotten that her friends and family were witnessing the most momentous occasion in her life. "Pipe down, y'all. I'm having my moment here."

Tanner laughed so hard he brushed tears from his eyes. At least, she thought they were from laughter.

He said, "I was so afraid we'd never get to this moment, that you wouldn't make it out alive, you wouldn't forgive me, or wouldn't love me. But here we are, standing on a finish line that feels like a starting line."

She sighed happily.

Tanner continued. "I never put stock in happily-ever-after until I saw that photo of you, then I met you and there was this glimmer of something I couldn't put a finger on. You, Francine Newman, breathed hope and joy into a dead man walking."

Frankie's hands pressed against her mouth, holding back what would either erupt as a sob of happy tears or a squeal of YES! YES! YES! She was going to make this man happier than he'd ever dreamed of. She was very competitive like that. *Give me some lovin' and I'll double down, baby!*

"I've never talked so much in my life, that's how you've changed me." He took another swipe at his eyes.

"Just get to the question and I won't make you speak again."

"Sometimes the good stuff takes time, speedy. If you open that medal you're wearing, you'll see."

Frankie looked down at her gleaming Shadybrook Shake-A-Leg medal, fiddled with it, and found something shinier inside: a diamond and ruby ring. She inhaled sharply and breathed out, "Tanner."

"I want to live this adventure with you, Frankie. Ride the highs and lows, make you as happy as you make me, weather the storms, all the cheesy metaphors, let's do it together."

Jolted by his mention of weathering the storms, Frankie looked up and met Momma's eyes. Momma nodded, her hand over her heart, acknowledging that Tanner got the *Good Housekeeping* seal of approval. Frankie's tears began to fall. If only her mother was here to see this, to meet the man who'd literally carried her through some of her darkest days.

"I love you so much I've lost my mind. Marry me and put me out of my misery," Tanner at last asked the question she'd been waiting for. "Do me the honor of being my wife and don't make me wait."

"Now who's bossy and in a hurry? I have something to say as well." Frankie set the ring into his palm and covered his hands with hers. "Paul Newman, my namesake, once remarked that it's pointless to pump the brakes when you're upside down. You, Tanner, turned me upside down. I didn't need you or any man to save or take care of me, but I choose you."

"Does that mean…"

"Yes! I will marry you!" Frankie lifted her left hand and wiggled her ring finger. "But Kojak will under no circumstances be my flower girl."

"Hallelujah!" Selah shouted behind them.

Angel did a 360 in her chair. "If you're up and walking by then, maybe you'll dance at your wedding."

Frankie said, "Don't worry. Even if I'm not dancing, I'll can still hang from the chandeliers!"

Once Tanner slipped his ring on her finger and kissed her hand, a cheer went up. Her sore shoulders shook as she cried and laughed. Tanner grew still, his dark eyes misted over like fog rising from the pond just before sunrise. Leaning in, he cupped the back of her neck and stroked her jaw with his thumb.

"Thank you," he whispered before drowning out her response with his lips.

As her eyes drifted closed, she slid her hands over his

shoulders, pulling him closer, craving more of the sweetness and heat. Where had kissing been all her life? The man had some abs and some guns and some skills. When they finally came up for air, she decided whatever she'd done to make him thank her with a kiss, she'd do it again and again every day as long as they lived.

"First kiss, best kiss," Frankie said.

Something crazy beautiful came to life in the black depths of Tanner's eyes.

"Nah. You ain't seen nothing yet." He touched her chin and dragged his thumb over Frankie's lips, making her as hot as the cayenne in Momma's spicy chocolate pie. "I do know a thing or two about chemistry."

The End

Connect with the Author

Sign up for Connie Kuykendall's newsletter:
http://eepurl.com/bBmiRT

Join Connie on Social Media:

WEBSITES
www.CurledCrusader.com
www.ConnieKuykendall.com

FACEBOOK
www.facebook.com/CurledCrusader

GOODREADS
Type Connie Kuykendall in Search Books

PINTEREST
https://www.pinterest.com/CurledCrusader/

INSTAGRAM
https://www.Instagram.com/CurledCrusader

TWITTER
@CurledCrusader

Acknowledgments

Thank you to

God, the author of my life;

Mom, the one who has heard all the woe-is-me writing angst and tells me to keep going when the going gets tough;

Beta readers, Elizabeth McEnery, Kristen Antonucci, Tonia Shevnin, C.D. Gill;

RaeLee May Carpenter, my editor and author of The Morning After;

The talented cover designers at www.damonza.com; and

My readers—may you embrace the fabulously flawed reflection in the mirror and know that you are God's beloved.

Made in the USA
Monee, IL
24 June 2022